To my favo[r]

Merry Chris[t]

Matthew D. Bradaher

Ecclesiastes 4:9-12

To my favorite sis:

Merry Christmas!

Matthew J. Bearden

Ecclesiastes 4:9-12

Grim Hope

Matthew D. Brubaker

authorHOUSE®

AuthorHouse™
1663 Liberty Drive
Bloomington, IN 47403
www.authorhouse.com
Phone: 1-800-839-8640

First published by AuthorHouse 11/22/2009

ISBN: 978-1-4490-3653-9 (e)
ISBN: 978-1-4490-3652-2 (sc)

Library of Congress Control Number: 2009911979

Printed in the United States of America
Bloomington, Indiana

This book is printed on acid-free paper.

Acknowledgments

I would like to first of all thank God for giving me the gift and passion for writing. My prayer is that He will use this book in more powerful ways than I can possibly imagine. I would also like to thank everyone's support in encouraging me to finish this book. Honestly, without their encouragement the book would have never been finished, must less seen print. One friend has helped me more than any other in regard to this book, and for that I thank you Rachel Chater. Your honest input and hard work in helping me to edit this book proved invaluable.

Chapter I

July 25, 30 PAW (Post-Atomic War)

7:17

Gideon walked around the inside perimeter of his house, checking to see if anything was amiss outside. He was a tall, powerfully built man with dark eyes and black hair. There was nothing to cause him any concern. It was a bright, clear Sunday morning. The bright sun gleaming off the beautiful downtown skyscrapers made Gideon hopeful he was going to have a day as wonderful as the weather currently was. He then went into his spacious bedroom and locked the door behind him. His family looked up at him anxiously as he closed the blinds in the room. After walking over to the bed, he flipped the queen-sized mattress on its side and then reached down into a slit cut into the bottom it. From it he pulled out the family's new, but worn, Bible. The family all relaxed then as their father sat down. It was safe to conduct their weekly time of worship of their Creator. They all waited in eager anticipation for Gideon to begin.

Gideon looked upon his family with the pride and love that only a father can really have. He allowed his gaze to roam around the circle, basking in the joy his family felt at being able to worship their Holy Father that morning with their earthly father. First his eyes alighted upon his beautiful wife, Deborah. He loved her even more than he had when they had married nine years earlier. She had a wonderfully compassionate heart and always did her best to make Gideon and the rest of the family happy. Gideon next looked at his eldest son, David, whom was seven years old. David promised to grow up to be a strong leader like his father, yet combined with the tender heartedness of Deborah. As proof of this tender-heartedness, David was allowing Gideon's youngest child, Mary, to sit upon his lap. She was only one years old, but was a child full of laughs and smiles. Her presence in the family never ceased to make them smile. Next to them sat five year old Ruth. She was shy around strangers and tended to cling to her mother, but was full of an innate curiosity that often overrode her shyness. The last of Deborah and Gideon's four children was Levi. Levi was a very energetic three year old with a little bit of a rambunctious streak in him, but when prodded enough he listened quite well. His antics were never malicious, just something that caused Gideon and Deborah to keep a closer eye on him than the others. Gideon loved his family dearly and did his best to protect and provide for them.

As Gideon sat down in a circle with his family the usual request came up. "Father, can you tell us the story of Gideon again?" David, his eldest son asked.

"Please father!" begged Ruth and Levi. Deborah gave Gideon a sympathetic smile. Deborah was used to fielding this same request every Sunday that Gideon was at work, which was quite often.

"I will tell you the story of Gideon, but only if each of you can tell me three reasons why you love God." Gideon replied. "David, would you please go first?"

"Yes, father. I love God because His Son died on the cross for us, He always provides for us, and because He has always protected our family."

As soon as David finished speaking, an explosion shook the house. Smoke wafted into the bedroom from under the locked door. Gideon and his family could smell the explosive charge and feared that the house might be on fire. Gideon and Deborah feared they knew who had set that explosion off. Gideon rose and went to the bedroom door as Deborah corralled the bewildered children into the far corner of the room. As Gideon opened the bedroom door, twelve armed men in government uniforms rushed towards the now opened door after breaking through the front door. Their uniforms each had the letters CRZ. Every Christian feared seeing these three letters which officially stood for Combating Religious Zealots. To Christians those three small letters meant torture and death.

Gideon did not hesitate to strike out at the men as they tried to force their way into the bedroom. He was unarmed, but he had a family to protect. The men seemed to have orders to take him alive as they had no firearms on their persons. That did not mean they were unarmed, though. Each of the CRZ soldiers held a club in their hands. Gideon knew this gave him just the slimmest chance of defeating them and saving his family from certain death. He hit the first man in nose with the binding of the Bible, instantly breaking it. Another man he kicked in the groin. The third and fourth men tried rushing the door together. Gideon was struck in the stomach, but ignored the pain with the ferocity of a man whose loved ones are threatened. He threw one man out of the bedroom into the other men while being struck with a police baton by the only man still in the bedroom. Gideon fell to one knee under the repeated blows before managing to grab the baton and flipping the man over his back on to the ground. He wrenched the baton out of the man's hand and began striking his face with it. The man's face was becoming a bloody mess when a couple of the CRZ soldiers shot a taser and hit Gideon. The thousands of volts made Gideon's muscles contract and lock. He fell to the ground while a large man dressed in business clothing entered the bedroom behind the remaining CRZ soldiers. Even though Gideon was helpless to move, the CRZ soldiers were obviously keeping their space away from him.

The electricity still coursed into Gideon's prostrate body as he looked up at the man coming in. The man was large and obviously strong, but probably in his early sixties. He was still incredibly fit, although his head was balding. The man shaved the remainder of his hair, but still maintained an incredibly thick red, bushy beard. As the man came forward, anger smoldering in his intense green eyes, Gideon knew his family was dead. The man before him was no other than Supreme Commander Larkin, the undisputed leader of the Maevin government, and one of the two men that founded of the city of Maevin.

"Hold him down, face down." Supreme Commander Larkin ordered, and then changed his voice to a soft, smoothing tone as he addressed Gideon. "Gideon, Gideon, Gideon." His voice was velvety, but Gideon knew all too well what his voice could sound like if Larkin let his anger come out. "You disappoint me Gideon. You were one of my best bodyguards. You've served me faithfully for years. It was not too long ago that you saved my life. You showed so much promise. Just look at what you can do unarmed to these trained men even when they so greatly outnumber you." Larkin gestured to the four men Gideon had injured as they struggled to their feet. The man he had struck with a baton lay unconscious on the ground still. "I would have made you my full-time personal bodyguard years ago if only you had no family. I would have felt so secure knowing that everywhere I would go you would be right there with me. I have never met such a gifted warrior before. Imagine how great your life could have been, how rich you would have been. I knew you would have chosen your family over the wonderful life that was in my power to grant you." Larkin's voice changed suddenly, becoming full of menace. "Now, you will have no family. You must die as well, but you will be last for your betrayal of me to that insidious theology of Christianity. You Christians and the Muslims nearly destroyed all of Earth with your Atomic War. I will not let you religious nuts do the same thing to my city! Your family will die as you watch, but I suppose you won't sit by idly as it happens. I will need to restrain you from harming any more of these soldiers. Hand me that Bible!" Larkin barked the order to no one in particular. One of the younger CRZ soldiers grabbed the Bible and handed it to Larkin. Larkin placed the Bible on Gideon's back. He took out a long, curved knife with an eagle hilt and thrust it through the Bible; the blade penetrating deep into Gideon's back, narrowly missing his spine. Gideon screamed in pain, as his family screamed in terror.

Larkin put his face close to Gideon's and whispered so only Gideon could hear, "That should work nicely to make you behave. Now, pay attention Gideon. I will kill your family, but how long it takes is up to you. Tell me the names of all the Christians you know. Tell me who it was who converted you. Tell me how you got that cursed book that is now pinned to your back. Tell me everything Gideon and they will die quickly and painlessly. Tell me nothing and it will take hours upon hours before they die."

Gideon's eyes bored into Larkin's as he growled. "I will not tell you anything. No matter what you do to my family, they will spend all of eternity in heaven. You think you are so powerful, but life is but dust and ashes compared to the eternal glory of God. When you die, you will burn in hell and that thought makes me a very happy man. I pray that day comes soon."

"You disappoint me Gideon. I thought one that knew what I am capable of would have been wiser with his answer. Oh well, you leave me no choice." Larkin looked at Gideon's family and as he did so he kicked down with his right foot on to the handle of the knife, sending it even further into Gideon's back.

Deborah and the children shrieked again, Gideon grimaced but did not utter any sounds. The pain of the knife was nothing compared to the pain of what he was about to endure. He knew Larkin would make him watch his family get tortured and eventually killed. There was nothing he could do to stop it either. Gideon looked at them and began to weep. The CRZ soldiers came forward and put zip ties around the legs and wrists of Gideon's family. A couple of the soldiers propped Gideon up against the wall so he was forced to look at his family. Gideon gazed upon his family through the tears that were streaming out of his eyes. Soon he knew they would be together in heaven. Gideon thanked God for that and prayed that each of their deaths would come swiftly and with as little pain as possible. Even as he prayed though, images from what he had seen Larkin order others to do flashed through his mind. Some of those orders he had carried out himself before he was saved.

Larkin knelt down next to Gideon's face and whispered to him, "I plan on starting with David, your eldest son. Out of respect for you once saving my life, I give you another chance to confess to all that you know."

Gideon stayed silent. Larkin nodded to the CRZ soldiers holding David. The one held him while the other repeatedly struck him in his face, breaking several bones. The entire family wept as David's cries of agony echoed throughout the room. Gideon struggled to stand up, but was held down by a couple of CRZ soldiers. He was too weak from the knife wound to fight back. Blood was still pouring out of his wound. He knew it would take several hours for him to die of the wound if he received no medical treatment, and Larkin would ensure that he did not. Gideon would be left to die while gazing upon his family's lifeless bodies. Gideon knew Larkin's ruthlessness all too well to hope for a better alternative.

Supreme Commander Larkin had stayed next to Gideon the entire time, watching his expression and getting a significant amount of demented pleasure out of Gideon's obvious pain. He nodded again to the CRZ soldiers and then spoke to Gideon is his soothing voice. "You can stop this if you want. I merely need the information I asked for."

"How did you know I was a Christian Larkin?" Gideon asked, desperate to know how exactly the fate of watching his family be tortured had occurred.

"That was the simple part. It was your own actions that betrayed you Gideon. You Christians think you are so sly but I can smell you all a mile away. You hesitate now when you have an opportunity to kill those that are against me. You constantly were distant from the other guys in the last several months. You Christians are pathetic, weak. It is going to be my pleasure to watch the last remnant of your wretched religion perish by my hand." Larkin gestured towards Gideon's son David, whom was still crying, although no one could tell since his face was covered in blood. "Now are you going to answer my question or not?"

Gideon managed a small smile. "I originally opposed the policy that the underground church recently took, but now I am glad. The church decided that we would no longer meet in large groups and only continue inside our own family units. Everyone disbanded and no longer met together. I stayed in touch with just a few others. Most of them have already been killed by the CRZ. I know very little that would help you, but what I do know I will not share with you."

Supreme Commander Larkin responded with a much larger smile, "Ah, but you gave me the information I wanted. You religious zealots are nearly extinct. Within months, if not sooner, you will all be gone from this city. Thanks for all your help. I hope you enjoy watching your family die."

"I hope you die a death more painful than any that they will experience!" Gideon spat out with hatred filling his heart. Even Deborah was scared by Gideon's look. Supreme Commander Larkin looked into Gideon's face and backed away. He stood up and spoke with the Captain of the CRZ unit quietly. "Gideon won't tell you anything, but I want you to make his family's deaths painful and slow anyhow. Make an example of these Christian nuts. However long it takes make sure they all die, but make certain Gideon dies last. I want his head on a stick in the street." Supreme Commander Larkin said.

As Larkin left, Gideon shouted at his retreating back, "God will find a weapon with which to punish you for your crimes! I know not when, not how, but I do know that you will rue the day that you ever persecuted His people! Mark my words Larkin, mark them well!" Supreme Commander Larkin cast one look back at Gideon. Gideon could see a slight amount of fear in his eyes before he jeered.

"Gideon, if your god is so powerful he can kill me then certainly he will find a way to save your family's life. Heck, if he can do all that you claim he may even find a way to save your life." Supreme Commander Larkin then exited the home flanked by his bodyguards and went back to his office in his armored car. Larkin's words got to Gideon. He knew God was powerful enough to stop the deaths of his family, but was doing nothing to stop it.

Gideon watched in horror as the CRZ soldiers first executed his two youngest children by shooting them. Not even the CRZ soldiers whom were experienced in doing a variety of barbaric things wanted to torture a toddler. They took turns beating Gideon's remaining two children, forcing Gideon and Deborah to watch. Soon, Gideon's five year old daughter Ruth was dead. David was still somehow alive, although he had already endured one round of beatings. It was now Deborah's turn to get tortured. They ripped each of her fingernails and toenails out of her hands and feet. Deborah was branded with a white-hot piece of metal crudely shaped like a cross all over her body. Gideon screamed bloody murder at the soldiers the entire time, but they paid him no attention. His screams mingled with Deborah's as the acrid stench of burning flesh permeated the room.

Nearly two hours after Larkin had left, Gideon watched as two crosses were brought into the room. His wife and son's bodies were nailed to the wooden crosses. The soldiers continued to beat them, breaking bones throughout their body. Gideon kept crying, wondering how much longer he could keep his sanity. He continued to try to get up throughout the process, but it was all in vain. The movements only caused him to bleed more and lose more strength. After about thirty minutes of being beaten on the cross,

Gideon's wife and son were now unrecognizable, and dead. Gideon knew it was now his turn to die. He welcomed the fact that death would end his misery and pain.

A new sound broke through Gideon's consciousness. Several vehicles had come to a hurried stop outside Gideon's home. The CRZ soldiers heard it too. Two of them rushed out of the room to the front of the house to discover what was going on outside. They shouted back to the bedroom, "The Stasi are here! We are outnumbered heavily! They have to have at least thirty men with them!"

The captain of the CRZ unit barked, "Take cover positions. We hold this building; do not let them take it! If we allow them through that front door we are all dead men!"

There was a flurry of activity as the CRZ soldiers took cover positions and checked their assault rifles. They took aim towards the front door, but no one came for several minutes. Finally a smoke bomb exploded just inside the front door. The CRZ soldiers let loose a volley of bullets, but at the same time the back wall of Gideon's home exploded open. Stasi soldiers poured in through the large opening, quickly decimating the CRZ soldiers. Only a few of their men had received any injuries, one of whom had died. The Stasi soldiers went around checking bodies, making sure everyone was dead. A small group of Stasi soldiers stood in the bedroom, aghast at the scene they found there. They quickly noted the crosses though and realized that the victims had been Christians. Almost all sympathy for the deceased vanished. It was a fate all Christians deserved in the Stasi's opinion. It seemed to be the only thing the government and the Stasi agreed upon.

A young Stasi soldier bent down and began to check Gideon for a pulse. Gideon opened his eyes and the young man jumped back. A few of the Stasi soldiers laughed at him, but instantly became quiet when a man carrying just a pistol came into the bedroom. He was a tall man, with bright blue eyes and blond hair. He was in his late fifties. He was a lean, tall man with wiry strength. Gideon recognized him as Chancellor Silas, the leader of the Stasi and former best friend of Supreme Commander Larkin. They had founded the city of Maevin following the Atomic War, but their greedy grabs for more power and control over Maevin had turned them into enemies. Larkin barely won out the control of the government. Silas escaped with his life and founded the Stasi. The Stasi was dedicated to only one goal, the annihilation of Larkin's corrupt government.

"Chancellor Silas." One of the older Stasi soldiers spoke. "Supreme Commander Larkin is not here. He must have left right before we got here, if he was even here at all. He has once again eluded us."

Chancellor Silas looked at Gideon and knelt down. "I may save your life if you tell me whether or not Larkin was here."

A small amount of blood trickled out of Gideon's mouth as he labored in his speaking. "He killed my family."

Chancellor Silas looked sad, but not surprised at the news. "At least we know our information was correct. That is an important bonus. Our source for information may prove just as useful and timelier in the future. Spread out and collect any useful supplies you can find. We must be leaving this place soon or Larkin will have a chance to turn the tables on us."

The young man whom had found Gideon spoke up while gesturing towards Gideon. "Chancellor Silas, what do you want us to do about him?"

"Nothing at all. He is a Christian. He deserves what the CRZ soldiers did to him. By the look of that wound he will not be alive much longer if he receives no medical attention. It is merely one less Christian in this city. Hurry up, men, we must be going soon."

Gideon stared at the remains of his family as the Stasi moved around the house in a hurry looking for supplies. Several men commandeered the weapons and uniforms of the dead CRZ soldiers. Gideon barely noticed them as he wept over the scene in front of him. Soon, the Stasi left. The sounds of cars driving faded into the distance, leaving Gideon bleeding to death in his own bedroom, his crying eyes looking upon his family as a rage he had never experienced welled up in his soul. Gideon felt himself wanting to fall asleep into unconsciousness. Knowing that to succumb to the feeling would be certain death, he allowed himself to slip into unconsciousness with his last thoughts resting on the fact that he would soon be with his family in heaven. Within a couple of moments, his heart stopped beating and Gideon was dead, yet another victim of the civil war that embroiled all of Maevin.

Chapter II

October 24, 32 PAW

23:17

A man walked quickly, but without seeming to be in a hurry, through the streets of Maevin a couple of hours after all traces of the sun's light had disappeared. It was illegal to be out after 23:00, but this man did not seem very concerned with keeping the laws of the city. In fact he was currently breaking more than just that one law. In addition to breaking curfew, he was also carrying two Colt 1911 Model .45 caliber handguns with a belt full of ammunition on a Western style belt complete with holsters, and worse of all he was displaying the symbol of a cross on both his large, silver belt buckle and his black cowboy hat. Displaying a cross branded him as a Christian, and marked him for execution in the government's eyes. The night was very dark in the city of Maevin as the city experienced a mandated electrical blackout each night except for buildings deemed necessary for the operation of the city. This man seemed to be even darker than the night though, in both demeanor and appearance. He had a narrow, long face with dark, deep-set large eyes. His hair was jet black and fairly long. While walking he appeared to be on a mission from which none could avert him. He made his way to the end of a dank narrow alley with condemned buildings on either side. The alley dead-ended a few yards ahead, but at the last sewer hole before the dead-end the man vanished underneath the streets, carefully sliding the sewer manhole cover back in place after him.

Once underground he began to move even quicker now that he felt completely safe. The sewers were empty, long ago abandoned for newer ones. The fact that the sewers were abandoned did little to improve the smell. The man ignored it as he carefully picked which tunnel to take. It was a maze down there. One could become lost very quickly. After ten minutes of walking, making a turn every minute or so, he finally came to a gate. The gate was rusty and seemed to have not been used for decades, but he entered a combination into the keypad near the gate and it swung open easily on greased hinges. He walked through the opening, carefully closing the gate behind him. Another gate ahead was manned by a half dozen lightly armed men and women. The leader of this rag tag group stepped forward.

"Identify yourself immediately stranger or you will be killed!"

The man gruffly, but clearly, stated "My name is Rhys. You must be new not to know me. I come here often to see what Paul bids me to do." Rhys glowered at the young leader, whom immediately felt much less confident under the withering stare of Rhys.

"Ah, um, yes. Paul, uh, told me you may be coming and that I was to let you in. Sorry, I was just trying to do my job." The leader of the guard stuttered over his words as the others snickered, they could have warned their leader that it was Rhys before he had made a fool of himself, but they found it too funny to let their new leader stumble over himself in the presence of Rhys. They too felt just as intimidated by Rhys, but tried their best to not cross him. No one knew what the purpose of his meetings with Paul really was, but the rumors of his actions he claimed to commit to protect Christianity from the government and the Stasi were horrifying. Indeed, they doubted he was a Christian at all. No Christian's conscience, they reasoned, should be able to allow a man do half the things that Rhys was rumored to have done. They hoped that it was all rumors. Why he had such frequent business with their leader in the Christian Underground Church was beyond their comprehension. Despite his critics though, his actions over the course of the last three months had no doubt prospered the Christians and hurt both the government and Stasi, although many of these actions had violated laws of the Good Book, not to mention nearly every law in the city. His true motivations for helping the Christians were unknown to all, even to Paul.

Rhys said nothing as he passed the new leader of the guard, but as he strode near the rest of the guards, they all stopped their snickering, fearing that Rhys may not understand that they were not laughing at him. Rhys ignored them however, as was his wont. He soon found himself in the office of Paul, a very familiar place for him to be, although it had been a couple of weeks since he had found himself there. He looked around it taking in the usual details looking for anything out of place. There were pictures on the concrete walls of Christ's crucifixion, some of his miracles, and a multitude of religious leaders from the first century to the twenty-first century AD right before the nuclear war had happened. Paul's large oak desk was in the center of the room resting on a plain area rug. Rhys took a seat on one of the two cold, metal chairs with a minimal amount of cushioning in front of this large desk. Sitting on this chair made one look up at Paul, whom was seated on a large office, leather chair with a high back. Paul was looking at his computer as usual, papers strewn all over his desk. There was Paul's Bible sitting on the corner of the desk. It was a much worn Bible, although Rhys had very rarely seen Paul open it. Rhys then looked upon Paul himself.

Paul was an elderly man whom had a face creased deeply from a life of many laughs that came quite easily. However, underneath the easily smiling face was a steely reserve that allowed him to lead the Christians during such a tenuous time. He was gentle to all the Christians, but many knew that he was capable of calling others to fight to the death for the Underground Church's ability to stay alive. His prayers all led towards Christians once again being able to freely worship in Maevin, but that had not seemed likely to happen in his lifetime until Rhys came along.

"It has been a while Rhys." Paul said, finally looking up from his computer to pay attention to his guest.

"I have been very busy." Rhys said in his short manner.

"I would ask you with what, but you have many times demonstrated your impressive ability to elude questions and keep your life and activities beyond those that I request hidden."

"Hmm…is that a spiritual gift Paul?" said Rhys with sarcasm.

"Do not mock Christianity in that way Rhys. I know that you believe, otherwise you would not risk so much. However, I do not presume to know anymore about you than that. God is using in a way that would destroy anyone else, and it breaks my heart to continually request the things I do from you, but you are the only one who could carry out these missions. How you do so I do not know. I simply know to be grateful, although I fear the price that your soul and your salvation shall pay due to your actions."

"You forget your own salvation. I am merely the tool, you are the carpenter. I am willing to be that tool once again, although there will soon come a time I will act only under my own bidding. Until then do not feel sorry for what you bid me to do. It is necessary and has been a long time coming. So speak, what would you bid me do now?"

"I may be the carpenter it is true, but I sincerely hope that God is my architect." Paul paused in a moment of serious thought before continuing. "I have a special job for you. We have operated in the shadows for long enough and taken only marginal risks. We will accomplish little if we continue to do so. The CRZ is doubling their efforts against Christianity. I need you to shift the focus of the government from their persecution of Christians to the Muslims. Islam is weaker than Christianity currently, and the government knows it. Because of this Christianity has been forced to face the brunt of the government's program to eliminate all religious zealots. Larkin thought he had us nearly extinct months ago. It angers him that we still exist. I want you to frame a group of Muslims, or even just one Muslim for the murder of a high-ranking government official. The target I have in mind is Ji Harlow. She is the head of the…"

"The CRZ division, I know who she is. Do you really think this is the solution; what if the Muslims or the CRZ find out it was the Christians whom have been responsible for this? It will be even worse for you then."

"It would become even worse for us," Paul emphasized the word us, lumping Rhys in with all Christians in doing so. "This is exactly why I am giving the assignment to you. You have not failed me yet, and I pray that you will not this time. I do not like it either, but I do know there is still much hostility between the Muslims and Christians underneath our respective struggles to survive. The only thing keeping these hostilities at bay is both of us have a common enemy for now. If the government ever crumbles, this common enemy will cease to exist. At that point the old wars between the Muslims and the Christians will flare up again, and we must be more than a match for them otherwise we will tear this city apart with another new war. I know the backlash the government will produce against the Muslims will be fierce and terrible for them to endure, but in all honesty they will have to face it soon enough or this city will be destroyed. It is better that the government does it than for us Christians to wait until we are, God willing, in power to attempt it. With the Muslims being taken care of by the government, we can concentrate on the government and the Stasi. The Stasi have launched a renewed offensive against the government in the past several months after seeming to be nearly extinguished. How they are managing to come back so strongly I have no idea. I will soon be asking you to carry out some missions that will pit the government and the Stasi against each other. We need to weaken all the other factions in this city, using them against each other, until we are stronger. The long-term goal of us Christians is to unite together and be once again able to share the message of Jesus Christ openly.

"I know not all Christians would agree with what I ask you to do, but I deem it the only way we can possibly accomplish this. If only they knew the sacrifices a select few took for the good of many they would not be so harsh in their judgments of you. I fear the sacrifices to reach my final goal of Christianity being allowed by the government will come at an even greater price. I pray that as soon as we gain the ability to worship freely again no Christian will be forced to make the choices we face Rhys. We cannot enjoy a period of peace though if the Muslims are still alive and well. History has repeatedly shown us, particularly during the Atomic War, that Muslims and Christians cannot coexist together."

"I will carry out this mission, though I urge you to reconsider your assumption that Christians and Muslim cannot coexist." Rhys said heavily, with a weariness of the actions he was forced to take by the extreme circumstances under which he lived.

"Christians and Muslims have reconsidered that issue for centuries. Each time it caused only a momentary lull in warfare between the two religions. Our religions are too close together, yet not close enough, for us to be able to coexist. One of us must be right, the other must be wrong. This is why our wars have always been the bloodiest in history. Though, out of courtesy for all that you do for me, I will reconsider."

"Your orders will be carried out, as I deem prudent and most effective in my own time and methods." Rhys stated without emotion, already building his firm exterior of emotionless invincibility that he used for every mission.

"I would not have it any other way Rhys."

"Nor would I Paul, nor would I."

With those last words Rhys stood up and strode out of Paul's office and disappeared into the streets of Maevin once again.

October 30, 32 PAW

3:13

Around three in the morning there walked a carefree, cocky man through the streets of Maevin. He was dressed in black combat boots and had a Kevlar vest on. On his right hip and left ankle were hostlers with a 9 mm Glock at his ankle and an oversized .50 caliber Desert Eagle at his hip. On the right ankle and the left hip was a pair of long combat knives. The man also had an M41A slung over his shoulder. Multiple full magazines for both the assault rifle and handguns were visible in the pouches of his body armor vest. He was a strong man, probably in his mid-thirties. He was bald, but did not wear any hat despite the coolness of the night. His steel grey eyes took in every detail around him, never ceasing their constant movement. His pace was as swift as his eyes, despite the fact that he was carrying a female's body over his shoulders. The female's head had a bag over it, but there was no movement at all from her. The streets seemed abandoned, but the man paused often in the shadows of the buildings before brazenly strolling to the next spot of darkness. He knew that around every bend and in each shadow could lurk the Maevin Police or the CRZ. They were brutal in their tactics of enforcing laws, often breaking many laws in their enforcement of the law that they claimed had been broken.

The man eventually disappeared around an abandoned church. The church was extremely large with flying buttresses around the exterior. The stained glassed windows were mostly broken, but the ones that remained gleamed beautifully during the day. The steeply pitched roof rose high into the moonless night sky. At the top of the roof peak was a weathered stone cross that had been broken into two pieces. The bleak, dark church building was kept as a stark reminder to all of the systematic extermination of all religious zealots. Churches had been allowed for a while under the rule of Larkin and Silas, but once Larkin got an iron-clad grasp on power he set in motion his ban of all religious zealots by founding the CRZ.

The heavily armed man walked forward confidently as he moved around the corner of the church to area in the back. Once near the back of the church, he entered into an abandoned, overgrown garden. At the middle of the garden was a large well. Once at the well he cranked the old handle three times clockwise, then 8 counter-clockwise, and then

5 times clockwise again before allowing the handle to slide back to its original position. At that point, several armed men came out of hiding in the garden and approached the man. The man dropped the body of the woman and stood there casually as though he had expected such a reception.

"You obviously know the code, but we don't know you stranger." Spoke the leader of the ragtag unit of soldiers that warily surrounded the man. Their wide assortment of weapons all pointed towards his torso. They nervously eyed him for any type of movement. Indeed they seemed much more nervous than the stranger who was greatly outnumbered.

"I know many things about you Stasi, Captain Merrit, though you seem to know precious little about me. Fortunately I came prepared for that possibility." The heavily-armed man spoke in a cocky, condescending manner. He put off the impression that he thought he was invincible, and that everyone else should think so as well.

"Impressive, you know my name, but you must impress me even more if you think that I will allow you to pass any further without giving me your name. Even your excessive amount of weapons will not protect you now. We have had snipers fixed on you since the moment you came in sight of the church. You will go no further without my leave."

"Any further? What is there further ahead? You must think me ignorant that you do not venture to say the obvious, that where I currently stand is above one of the last four strongholds that the Stasi believe they can hold in force against Larkin's government. All I need to do is pass down this well and I will soon be in sight of Chancellor Silas himself."

"How do you know about Chancellor Silas stranger? I did not know of that myself until an hour ago." Said Merrit, immediately chastising himself for allowing his amazement to let that information slip.

"My friend here told me where I could find Chancellor Silas." The stranger said even more cockily than his usual manner with a kick delivered to the body of the woman at his feet as punctuation.

"And who might your friend be?" asked Captain Merrit suspiciously.

"Ji Harlow." The stranger spoke clearly, but it fell heavily on the ears of those around. The connotation of that name had spelled doom for anyone whom had opposed the government and its activities. Her main focus had been on killing religious zealots, but Ji Harlow had begun to assist the Maevin Police in the extermination of the Stasi as well. The Stasi had come to fear her as greatly as Christians and Muslims had.

Captain Merrit stumbled upon words in his mouth, but none of them could seem to grasp the situation. After a moment of hesitation, he walked forward and flashed a complicated signal down the well, forgetting to make the stranger turn around so he would not see the signal.

Immediately a response came and then an elevator came up the well. The stranger slung Ji Harlow over his shoulder again and then hopped over the stone wall of the well onto the elevator platform. Quickly, the elevator started back down and soon the stranger was faced by a couple more guarded barricades below ground. He passed quickly through these, obviously the men had already heard of the precious cargo that the stranger carried on his back. After the second barricade a team of six heavily armed men and women guided him to Chancellor Silas.

Chancellor Silas was a practical man whom was known equally for his intelligence and ruthlessness. He had blond hair and blue eyes. The hair however was beginning to thin, but his eyes were perpetually thick with passion. His body was long and thin, but no mistake could be made that this was a man not to be trifled with. None had survived being Supreme Commander Larkin's chief target for extermination as long as Chancellor Silas.

The stranger dropped the body unceremoniously next to Chancellor Silas' feet. Silas looked up and his eyes betrayed the shock he found to see the man before him dressed so openly for combat. The Maevin government permitted none but their own employees to even own weapons. "Who are you, and what do you want in return for the gift of this devil of a woman you lay at my feet?"

"I am he who gives justice out fairly, or at least that's the meaning of the name I have taken for myself. My name is

Nemesio. What I want is simple, to protect the fair people of Maevin from the atrocities committed by the government. That is your goal as well I believe. I believe our mutual goal can be attained, and to prove that I give you this devil of a woman as you so aptly put it. I could use your help to achieve my goal and I believe you need my help to achieve your goal as well. In order for us to work together though we need trust. I know I will not be able to earn your trust so easily, but consider this a step in that direction."

Chancellor Silas smiled. "Nemesio, you seem to think highly of the gift that you bring at my feet. You claim that she is Ji Harlow, but the Maevin news has already reported that she is dead. Although, they have been wrong before, they once reported my death as well. Either way, your timing is poor. Not an hour ago, the news began reporting that Ji Harlow and many others were killed when the CRZ Headquarters Building exploded. They have already arrested a small group of Muslims who carried out the explosion. None survived the blast." At this news the faces of the Stasi bodyguards openly showed shock and hope as they had not heard this piece of news yet. "The woman at my feet has a bag over her face, why don't you remove the bag from this woman's head and show us what she truly looks like. I doubt that it is Ji Harlow, and indeed if it is not then I will torture and eventually execute you for lying to me. Along the way, you will tell me all that you know and the method in which you were able to discover the location of this facility and my whereabouts."

"And if she is Ji Harlow, then what?" Nemesio asked, obviously unshaken about the prospect of being tortured if he was wrong.

"Well if it is indeed Ji Harlow, then what good is she to me? She is focusing her efforts on killing Christians currently, a group I would love to see exterminated like the vermin they are. Though if she were after the Stasi currently then she would have a rough time doing so without her headquarters and a significant number of her personnel."

"Well, you seem to like extracting information through torture, so that is one option. But I have a better idea. I recommend that you use her as a bargaining chip. Christians and Muslims alike will pay dearly for her head, not to mention the government. Think of all the information, money, and bargaining power she brings to the table."

"I suppose you want something though in exchange for this gift."

"I simply need information in order to accomplish my goal, the deaths of all five Council Members of Maevin, Supreme Commander Larkin, and the utter desolation of his government." Nemesio stated without his usual cockiness. The sincerity in his voice dared others to challenge his statement.

Silas appeared overwhelmed by this statement. The man spoke as if he could easily accomplish this task. Silas had strived to accomplish the same task for nearly twenty years now and had not even succeeded once in killing any of the five Council Members, much less any of the other goals Nemesio spoke of. He regained his composure before speaking again. "Our goals do appear to be the same; though I see you seem to be much more confident about achieving them." Chancellor Silas stated calmly, but followed by pulling a Makarov pistol and pointing it at Nemesio's head. "But, I doubt that agreement will be necessary, although it is granted provided this woman is indeed Ji Harlow." Silas motioned with his pistol for Nemesio to remove the bag from the woman's head.

Nemesio did not flinch at the gun being pointed to his head. Moving without any apparent concern at the gun pointed at him, he removed the woman's hood. Once he did so, everyone including Silas gasped in surprise. It was indeed Ji Harlow. Everyone in the city had known her as the face of the cleansing of the city as she liked to call it. She was often on the Maevin News touting her campaign. There was no doubt in the minds of the people surrounding Nemesio that he had indeed brought the woman that had brought them so much pain and death. All of the Stasi looked at Nemesio with wonder. None knew how this stranger had managed to accomplish this feat by himself when they had failed in several attempts, with many more men.

"How is this possible?" Silas asked, speaking everyone else's question for them.

"It has taken me a very long time of planning, but it is just a first step in the right direction. I plan on taken many more, but my steps will be much easier to attain if we work together."

"How did you manage this feat of capturing her?"

"A magician never gives away his secrets." Stated Nemesio with a cocky smile.

Chancellor Silas thought for a long time before speaking. "I wish to know more about you Nemesio. I agree to help you with your goal, but I need you to do a mission for me first to further cement trust between us. I will choose my best unit to help you; they will not slow you down at all."

"With all due respect, Chancellor Silas, if that was true, then that unit would be the ones in front of you with Ji Harlow at your feet, not me. Of course they will slow me down, but I perhaps will find them useful after all."

"Very well, we have a one mission agreement, after this one mission then we will reevaluate." With that the two men gripped hands, but it was more a test of the strength of their grips than a sign of friendship and trust.

November 2, 32 PAW

21:27

"Commander Franklin, you have a visitor." Kelly stated in her clear voice that sounded like it should be on a telephone, which she spent most of the day doing anyhow. She was working overtime again, but then again so was Commander Franklin.

"Who is he?" Commander Franklin asked, he had no one with an appointment for that day and Kelly normally did not trifle him with visitors unless they were extremely important, especially this late in the evening.

"He says his name is Agmund and that you would be a fool not to talk to him. I think he is a fool, for he tried carrying a sword into this building. He has allowed no man to remove it from his possession or even come near him. I thought if nothing else you would want to attend to the situation. Should I have the men bring him in?"

"Sure, Kelly, if nothing else at least this man seems to be interesting or insane. Either way I would like to talk with him." Franklin was busy; he had just been promoted to the position of Commander of the CRZ after the bombing of the old office. The unit had lost more than forty percent of the staff. His cluttered office showed he had had no time to unpack. However, he felt as though the distraction would be welcome at this moment.

Promptly after getting off his direct line with Kelly a man proudly walked into Commander Franklin's office in the middle of a group of CRZ officers. He was a few inches taller than the men around him and was dressed in a simple white tunic. The face of Agmund was fair to look at. His dark, brown hair was neatly groomed, his face was clean shaven and he had a square, heroic looking face. He also looked fairly young, but you could tell that he had seen some bloodshed by the scars on his face. The only item he seemed to carry was a large, simple broadsword. Franklin looked at the worn scabbard and guessed that the blade had seen some bloodshed as well. Despite its rough edges, it looked as well taken care of as its owner. Commander Franklin could not help but be intrigued by this Agmund character. He looked like he walked straight out of a book.

"Men you may leave me with Agmund. Although Agmund I must warn you, I will not allow you to close the distance between us." Commander Franklin stated sternly while slapping a Glock .38 on the counter of his desk. Agmund did not reply, but he did stay where he was. Commander Franklin seemed pleased enough with this and the men left with a nod from Commander Franklin.

"Now, Agmund, who are you and why did you demand a meeting with me?"

"Who I am is the protector with the sword. For far too long has the city of Maevin permitted the Stasi and the religious nuts of this city to survive. I look to restore power and honor to this fair city. The evil forces that oppose the true leader of this city need to be eradicated. You find yourself in a precarious position as you take over the CRZ after the bombing of its old headquarters and the loss of personnel. I am here to help you." Agmund spoke eloquently with pure passion in his voice.

"Everything you say is true, I will grant. But, I do not see how you are the solution to my problem?" Commander Franklin asked incredulously.

"Well there is a simple solution to that problem. I will prove to you that I am. I have a mission in mind, although I need some men to come with me. If I succeed in the mission hopefully we can work together more in the future and achieve honor and glory for this city through our partnership." Agmund said.

"What would be your first job?"

"I know the location of one of the strongholds that the Stasi is currently using. What I need is a team of experienced soldiers to help me clear that rat nest out. There will be no fee to pay me; any men that die will not be from your still hurting division, but the Maevin Police. Also, this is the only way I will give the information to you that you want so badly. I will lead the team myself; if I succeed you and I may enjoy a long, fruitful working relationship together. It is a small price to pay for such a big payoff if it is a success."

"I will make some calls. I suppose it would be pointless to ask for your phone number or address to contact you when I have your answer." Agmund made no motion to indicate he was going to speak, or that he was amused by the attempted joke, so Franklin continued. "Very well, come back in three days and I will hopefully have your answer. I will let my men know to let you pass."

Agmund gave a slight bow in respect and walked out of the brand new CRZ headquarters. Commander Franklin scratched his head and then immediately went back to his work, he could not rest. Supreme Commander Larkin was pissed due to the bombing and expecting results yesterday. Commander Franklin was determined to give him those results, even if it meant stooping as low to even consider using nut jobs like Agmund.

Chapter III

November 5, 32 PAW

19:58

Three days later Agmund came back into the office of Commander Franklin. He had a SWAT team of Maevin police waiting in the basement of the building. Doubt swirled in Commander Franklin's mind about the success of this proposed mission from a guy whom he knew absolutely nothing about. The last three days Franklin had tried every resource at his disposal to discover more about Agmund. No one had heard anything about him. This made Commander Franklin nervous. So nervous he had deemed the mission top-secret to the point that not even Larkin knew about it. Only the people undertaking the mission, Police Commissioner Battig, and Lieutenant Longstreth were informed about the mission. Supreme Commander Larkin had made it abundantly clear that Commander Franklin was only being given enough rope to hang himself with in his new position, although that was about the only amount of rope anyone working for Larkin had. If it turned out to be successful Franklin could always take credit for it later. If it was unsuccessful, as Commander Franklin feared it would be, Larkin would be none the wiser. This fear is why Commissioner Battig and Commander Franklin had chosen the SWAT team that now waited in the basement. Each of the SWAT team members was single and young, but excellent at their jobs. The only exception was their leader, Captain Mace, whom was pushing fifty years old. Commander Franklin had learned from Police Commissioner Battig that Mace had recently lost his wife to cancer and had expressed an interest to take the most dangerous jobs. The two had agreed to use the SWAT team led by Captain Mace for the job. Commander Franklin was taking a huge gamble on Agmund, and was hoping it would pay big dividends, but his doubts forced him to take all the precautions he could.

Agmund walked straight up to Commander Franklin's desk. Commander Franklin's pulsed picked up. Commander Franklin prided himself on knowing as much as possible about all that came under his jurisdiction. Agmund was an unknown, and that made him nervous. What added to the nervousness was the fact that he kept picturing how easily that sword could separate his head from his shoulders.

"I trust you have made everything ready as I requested." Agmund stated with force and confidence, controlling the conversation from the very start.

"Yes, the SWAT team is waiting in the basement for your arrival. They know they are to follow your orders." Commander Franklin stated.

"Of course you mean they are to follow my orders as they deem prudent. Surely you have not given me complete free reign and have warned them that I could be dangerous to them and this government." Commander Franklin made a motion to begin to speak, but Agmund held his hand up to stop him. To Commander Franklin's amazement, he did stay quiet, something he was not accustomed to doing in the presence of his charges. "Do not be concerned that I know you have done so, we have no past history together. You have absolutely no reason to trust me. If you had not done so then you would be a great fool. I did not come to you because you are a great fool. I came to you because you have the means and the motivation with which to help me."

"And Agmund, pray tell, what exactly is my motivation?" Commander Franklin asked, his curiosity getting the best of his usual discretion.

"You have succeeded in everything you have attempted thus far. You graduated from high school and Maevin University top of your class. Your time in the Maevin Police was exemplary. Now you find yourself in the greatest challenge of your life, turning around the CRZ when a significant portion of its personnel was killed in the explosion two weeks ago. You are highly motivated to succeed, at all costs and no matter the risks. That is your motivation, as it always has been, to succeed.   Of course you have doubts that this mission will succeed, and again it is because you are no fool."

"Very astute." Stated Commander Franklin. He was now even more concerned about Agmund. Before this meeting Agmund had just seemed like a crazy nut that perhaps had gotten fortunate enough to stumble upon a Stasi stronghold. Now that Agmund knew so much about him, Commander Franklin was forced with a much more dangerous option. Agmund was a man with powerful resources, a cunning intellect, and was perfectly sane despite his apparent oddities. Commander Franklin was considering cancelling the mission, but the potential that he could develop Agmund into an asset for the government was too tempting. The mission would go ahead as planned, but Commander Franklin was determined to keep a close eye on Agmund. He needed to know more about this man.

"Well Agmund, I will have my men guide you to the underground garage where you can brief your men and precede with your mission at your discretion."

"There is no need to have your men guide me. I know the way."

"Really?"

"Yes, it is down."

"It is more complicated than that."

"Of course it is, but the main thing is you do not trust me on my own in this building."

"But of course, otherwise you would consider me a great fool."

"Of course." Agmund said, and then smiled disarmingly, immediately breaking the tension that had built significantly in the room.

Agmund walked out of the office and then was immediately joined by four burly, armed CRZ soldiers who escorted him down to the basement. After Agmund had disappeared around a bend in the hallway, Lieutenant Longstreth came into the office responding to the text that Commander Franklin had sent during his meeting with Agmund. Lieutenant Longstreth was a petite woman with raven hair and a simple, yet attractive face. Her long limbs enabled her to hold her own against most men in the department though, not to mention her tenacious ferocity and quick temper. Commander Franklin had immediately brought her with him to CRZ when he was appointed to the position, having worked with her for many years in the Maevin Police. Most of the people in CRZ feared her, but they also respected her as well. It was the best combination to have in Command Franklin's opinion.

"Commander Franklin, how can I best serve you?"

"By succeeding, Lieutenant Longstreth, as always you can serve me best by succeeding as you always have before. I need you to observe the operation that Agmund is heading. Do not let anyone know, especially Agmund. My original fear was that he was just insane and wasting my time on a wild goose hunt. However, in my most recent conversation with him I realized that he is probably not insane at all, but far more powerful and intelligent than I could have originally imagined. He knew my past and even claimed to have the building plans memorized. Those files are extremely confidential. Follow him with extreme caution. I need to know as much as possible about this man. Report every detail to me. I am hoping that he is a genuine weapon we can use against the government's enemies, but I cannot yet trust him. Observe as much as you can, but do not let Agmund see you."

"As you wish, Commander Franklin." Lieutenant Longstreth walked out the door and made preparations to follow Agmund. She wished she knew his final location, but only Agmund possessed that information. It would be tricky to do surveillance on a team of professionals and one potentially dangerous adversary, or hopefully powerful ally, without a team to back her up and rotate the assignment of keeping an eye on the target. The difficulty of the assignment is why Commander Franklin had given the assignment to Longstreth though and she would do her best to not let him down.

Meanwhile, Agmund had arrived at the basement and briefed the SWAT team on the dangerous mission. He gave them a lot of tactical information without giving away the location. The location of the base was Agmund's ace in the hole, and he was not about to show that any sooner than he had to. The SWAT team did their best to stay professional, but it was obvious to Agmund that they did not trust him. Agmund was okay with that though, their trust was not what he needed on this assignment. As the men piled into a roughly used government utilities van that Agmund would drive to the site of the raid, a tangible mixture of fear, nervousness, and excitement filled the air around the twelve SWAT team members. The SWAT team always felt this before a mission, but with an intense curiosity they noted that Agmund did not seem to exhibit any of the feelings of nervousness they had. They only sensed a heightened sense of excitement, but no fear or nervousness.

Lieutenant Longstreth watched the utilities van as it left CRZ headquarters. It was a dark blue utilities van with no windows in the back. Most of the equipment that was normally housed in the back of the van had been removed to allow for the semi-comfortable transportation of the SWAT team. Agmund himself was driving the vehicle. He was dressed in Maevin City Utilities uniform that matched the exact hue of the exterior of the van. Captain Mace sat next to him in the front similarly dressed. Lieutenant Longstreth swung into traffic a few vehicles behind the van. Fortunately the van was very large and easy to spot and identify. Lieutenant Longstreth wondered if Agmund was as intelligent as Commander Franklin claimed. Certainly an intelligent man would be smart enough to choose a vehicle that was not so easy to spot and follow. Longstreth guessed that Agmund had not counted on anyone following him. She almost allowed herself a small smirk that she had the element of surprise, but then she reminded herself of Commander Franklin's warnings. She would operate under the assumption that Agmund had chosen that vehicle for a yet unrevealed purpose.

It did not take Lieutenant Longstreth long to find out why he had chosen that particular van. After making a right turn on a yellow light, Agmund stopped outside a business and checked the utilities meter. The unexpected stop, Longstreth knew, would serve to throw off any tails and expose them more easily. The tails would have to either stop or drive past. Either action would be noted by Agmund. If Agmund repeated this maneuver a few times any vehicle tailing him would be noticed at each stop. The light took two minutes before it turned back to green for Longstreth. By then Agmund had returned to the vehicle and was driving further to the east. That light had worked out perfectly for Lieutenant Longstreth, but she feared that she might not be so fortunate at the next stop.

Just a Longstreth was hoping that Agmund may not stop again; he made a sudden stop outside a factory a few blocks away from the last stop. He again checked the utilities meter. This time Lieutenant Longstreth had no choice but to drive past the van. At the next street she turned to the left and parked her vehicle along the road. Then she hailed a taxi cab and had it drive around the block. As she turned onto the street where Agmund had stopped, she noticed the van up ahead making a left turn. She ordered the cabbie driver to catch up to the van and persuaded him to make it fast and discreet. He looked at her strangely and hesitated, at which point she pulled out her identification and he immediately became nervous, but responded. She wondered if he was secretly a religious zealot based on his extreme reaction to her identification, but cast that thought aside in order to concentrate fully on the task ahead of her. The van was a couple of cars ahead, but thankfully the cabbie driver was keeping it in view without advertising the fact that he was following the van. Longstreth thanked her luck and started breathing more easily, until Agmund made a stop at yet another building. Longstreth ordered the cabbie to drive past the building and watched as Agmund read the meter once again. At the next intersection she barked at the cabbie to turn right. After driving a couple hundred feet she demanded him to stop the cab. He did so promptly and she got out. As soon as Longstreth shut the door he sped off down the sparse streets. This made Lieutenant Longstreth feel even more certain the man was a religious zealot, but she did not have time to do anything about it. She had a mission to accomplish. There was a Jeep parked along the street that Longstreth hopped into and attempted to hot-wire. The Jeep roared to life after Longstreth finally got the correct wires to touch, just in time for the van to come by.

She pulled into the meager traffic and followed the van, just as night settled ominously on the city of Maevin.

Agmund drove two blocks down the road and stopped outside an abandoned military base. After the Atomic War, there was no need for a military to protect against other cities or nations as Maevin had heard only rumors of other cities. The only threats came for the remaining cities of Earth came from inside the city walls. Only police were needed to enforce the laws of Maevin, which Larkin and the Council were free to do as they pleased without any higher government oversight or binding Constitution. Lieutenant Longstreth was again forced to drive past the van and parked a couple of blocks down past the base. She had the distinct feeling that this would be the last stop. An abandoned military base would be perfect for the Stasi to use as one of their headquarters. Lieutenant Longstreth watched from a distance as the SWAT team streamed out of the vehicle and quickly cut an opening in the barbed wire fence. Agmund had changed back into a pure white tunic, one that seemed starkly out of place with the tactical black uniforms of the SWAT team. It was Agmund who led the way through an opening that the team had cut in the fence. He carried his sword in his hand, the empty scabbard hanging at his hip; the SWAT team at his back carried their usual tactical gear, with their SKSII assault rifles in hand. Each of the rifles had night vision scopes, green lasers sights and sound and flash suppressors attached to them. The SWAT team also had several other goodies packed away in their bullet-proof vests, serving effectively well to prepare the team for anything they may face ahead.

Lieutenant Longstreth waited as they went cautiously around multiple buildings before using the gap in the fence to get into the base as well. She made her way to the middle of the base, keeping only brief glimpses of the SWAT team and Agmund in sight. At the dead center of the base were four identical five storied buildings. These were the old Army offices and they made a perfect, large square around a long, low one story building. Agmund paused in deep shadow and surveyed the buildings around him. He pointed out the locations of each of the sentries posted on buildings, in buildings, or in shadow around the square to the SWAT team members. There were ten in total. The twelve SWAT team members all looked through their night scopes to see the sentries. Agmund waited until they had lined up their shots and gave the order to fire. The sentries were all silently killed by the efficient shooting of the SWAT team. Captain Mace looked at Agmund in wonder. He had not seen a trace of the sentries until he looked through his night vision scope, but Agmund had managed to spot them all without any night vision gear.

"Good shooting. We must proceed with caution. We should have several minutes before they realize that their perimeter was breached, but it is possible one of the sentries managed to get a message back inside the base before he died. If that is the case, I am unsure of what to expect, but it could be anything from an ambush to a self-destruction of the base itself."

"Yes sir!" Barked the SWAT team in response, in part due to their training but also in reverence to the way Agmund spoke and acted. They had never met anyone so noble before.

Despite the fact Agmund had no body armor on or weapons other than his broadsword, he led the way to the entrance of the base. Even though he had just warned the SWAT team to proceed with caution, he seemed to be taking none at all. He moved smoothly and confidently to the middle of the four buildings to where the entrance to the long, low building stood. The SWAT team noted a couple of very strong locks on the door and began to prepare C4 shape charges designed to blow the door with a minimum of noise and damage to the surrounding structure.

"Those will not be necessary." Agmund stated to the SWAT team as he pulled two skeleton keys out from the folds of his tunic. He unlocked the door using each key for the two separate locks. None of the men questioned where he had attained the keys; there was simply too much mystery about this man to even attempt to understand him.

Agmund and the SWAT team entered the building and paused inside the door. There were no lights in the entrance to the building and the SWAT team began to put on their night vision goggles. After getting the goggles on they realized that Agmund was no longer with the group. They scanned the room and found that they were not alone in the rectangular room filled with barrels. The opposite wall was only twenty feet away, but it was the walls to their left and right that were almost a hundred feet away that concerned them. Along each of these far walls were posted five men with automatic rifles and night vision goggles trained on them. The green lasers from the rifles were moving in small circles on their torsos. Agmund was nowhere to be seen.

"Put down your weapons and then lay down on your stomachs." Demanded a deep voice from somewhere in the building, it was impossible to tell where exactly the voice had come from.

Captain Mace cursed under his breath and then followed the commands of the voice. The rest of his men dutifully followed suit. The SWAT team outnumbered the Stasi, but they had no chance of escaping the crossfire. The SWAT team leader's mind began to swirl with all the rumors he had heard of what the Stasi did to their captured governor opponents. He just thanked his lucky stars that it was not normally as bad as what they did to religious zealots.

As Captain Mace lay prostrate on the ground he heard gunfire erupt. He took a deep breath and prepared himself to feel the pain of a bullet tearing through his flesh. The pain never came though. He dared to look to the left. He saw five men frantically running toward him and looking distraught. Some raised their rifles in his general direction but then lowered it again. The SWAT team leader looked to his right then and saw the cause of the gunfire and pandemonium. Agmund had not been idle. Four bodies were on the floor next to him, some in pieces. Agmund held the fifth man in a chokehold that was formed using not his arm, but the broadsword, as he walked forward towards the approaching five Stasi. Blood seeped down the man's neck, but Captain Mace did not think he was seriously injured. The broad side of the blade was pressed harshly against his flesh, cutting off enough of the windpipe to allow him to survive, but not enough to give his muscles the oxygen needed to struggle significantly in Agmund's powerful grip.

The five men that had been on the SWAT team's left ran past them, ignoring them in their panic. Captain Mace instantly sprang into action and let loose a couple of shots with the pistol he had left concealed in an ankle holster. Two of the men dropped with the first two shots that the SWAT team leader fired, but the other three then realized their mistake and lay prone to return fire back at the SWAT team. The rest of the SWAT team recovered their weapons and a vigorous and close firefight ensued. Four of the SWAT team members were struck by gunfire, three of them fatally. One of the last three Stasi soldiers was shot and seemed to be dead, leaving only two Stasi soldiers left. Captain Mace's SWAT team suddenly stopped shooting at the same time. They had seen Agmund standing ominously over the two remaining Stasi soldiers. The man whom he had held in a chokehold lay in a pool of his own blood behind Agmund. Agmund had somehow come to that position without being noticed or without being struck by friendly fire.

The two remaining Stasi sentries finally felt the presence of Agmund behind them as the incoming bullets had ceased whizzing around their bodies. They turned and realized the imminent danger they were in and tried to bring their guns to bear on the new target. Agmund swept out his sword in an impossibly fast and fluid motion and both heads of the Stasi sentries separated from their shoulders with a single stroke.

Agmund came back towards the SWAT team. Captain Mace spoke quickly, adrenaline still pulsing through his veins. "So that is what you meant by an ambush might be awaiting us!"

"No." Agmund said. "That is their normal security measures for this facility. If they had known that we were coming none of us would still be alive."

Captain Mace became irate and shouted, "You mean to tell me that you knew that was going to happen!"

"Yes." Agmund said in an unnervingly quiet manner.

"I suffered four casualties, three of them being fatalities because you did not let us know."

"No, you suffered those casualties in a firefight that did not need to happen. I had the situation under control. Without me you would all be dead. Now, if you want any of your men to survive this mission, you will follow my lead. We need to move swiftly before they can prepare for our arrival downstairs, the gunfire will have not gone unnoticed."

Captain Mace still seethed, but now because he knew Agmund was right. Captain Mace's own actions had caused the casualties. He was unsure how exactly Agmund would have handled the five other Stasi guards, but he firmly believed that Agmund would have done so without any help.

Agmund ran quickly to the far wall where he had started his efficient killing from. The SWAT team stepped gingerly through the blood and body parts following Agmund. They were not unused to the sight of human fatalities, but they were unused to those caused by a blade and not bullets. It was a completely different and bloodier animal.

Agmund entered a service elevator after unlocking another door that was disguised to blend in with the wall. The remaining nine SWAT team members piled in with Agmund in the rear of the elevator. "Beware; they will probably be waiting for us at the bottom of this elevator shaft." Agmund stated with a distinct authority, looking pointedly at Captain Mace. Each of the SWAT team members' pulses quickened as their entire focus shifted to the door of the elevator. They layered themselves in order to all be able to fire without getting in each other's way. The first three took a prone position, the next three crouched down, and the final three stood behind the rest. Agmund stood at the back of the elevator. All eyes were riveted to the elevator door.

The tension mounted in the elevator as the elevator descended. Every second in that small space brought the SWAT team closer to an unknown situation. Each person in the elevator knew they were in a precarious situation from which there was no real retreat or cover to hide from the enemy. The doors of the elevator opened quickly without warning. Floodlights seeped into the elevator, destroying the vision of the SWAT team. Bullets whizzed into the elevator. The SWAT team members fired blindly, but soon there was none left alive but the captain of the SWAT team. Captain Mace lay at the front of the elevator bleeding from bullet wounds. Two shots had struck him in his right thigh. A third had grazed his neck. The neck wound appeared to be fatal, but was really a superficial wound. Captain Mace knew that no one else was still alive and decided to pretend to be dead. It was his only chance at survival. He lay perfectly still, gritting his teeth through the pain to avoid crying out. He heard the approaching tread of men wearing heavy combat boots. They came close but then walked away. The floodlights were powered off and the only lights left were dim, red lights that lined the hallways.

The captain after five minutes of hearing nothing dared to open his eyes. Around him each of his men was dead. With surprise, Captain Mace observed that Agmund's body was not among the carnage. Captain Mace wondered if the Stasi had already moved his body, but knew he had heard no body being dragged away. He then looked up at the top of the elevator and saw that the door leading to the top of the elevator was slightly open. Captain Mace cursed again, this time audibly, but the promptly cursed again under his breath for allowing his anger to possibly betray the fact he was still alive to anyone in listening range.

It was obvious to Mace that Agmund had led them into a trap, but for what purpose he was unsure. He was not given much time to ponder this idea when a few Stasi men came walking down one of the two hallways that formed a V-shape away from the elevator, a perfect defensive shape to fire upon the elevator. They had most likely arrived to clean up the mess and dispose of the bodies. Captain Mace's body lay near the front of the elevator. He always liked to lead his men from the front through action. It was likely that they would grab his body among the first. The captain allowed them to come within a few feet of him. Their guns were hanging lazily over their shoulders; the men approached jeering one another with obviously no concern. The captain fired three quick bursts from his SKSII and dropped each of the three men. The noise was minimal thanks to the gun's suppressor, but the captain still waited to hear for any signs that his actions had been noted. No sound came.

Satisfied, he took the bodies of two of the men and managed to lift them through the top door of the elevator to rest on top of the outside of the elevator. He took the clothing of the third one as well as the rifle and then also managed to lift him above. He was exhausted and his thigh was making moving almost unbearable, but he had no choice but to keep moving. He thought about going back up to the surface, but then decided against it. He wanted to find Agmund and reap vengeance for the deaths of his men.

Captain Mace left behind his SKSII, knowing that it would mark him as a government agent. He pocketed his suppressed fire Glock pistol and picked up the rifle and ammunition from the soldier whom he had taken the clothing of. He took one last look behind at his men and then regretfully left them behind to face their doom of an anonymous burial or more likely, cremation of his comrades in the hands of the Stasi. He found some comfort in reminding himself that it would have been far worse if any of them had been captured alive, a fate he risked with every step he took deeper into the Stasi base.

The captain walked quickly and confidently down the hallway that the three Stasi men whom he had killed had arrived from, trying to hide the pain from the gunshot wounds in his thigh from anyone he might encounter. He saw no one at all though. The hallway ran dead straight for what felt like a half mile. Doors led into rooms at an exact distance on either side. All of these doors were locked however, and appeared to have not been used for an extremely long time.

After a distance the captain reckoned would have brought him underneath one of the four office buildings, the hallway came to a T. Upon closer inspection though, the captain realized it was not actually a T. The two hallways to the left and the right were slightly curved. The SWAT team leader guessed that it was actually a large circle that came under each of the four buildings. He heard a large, joyous sounding ruckus emanating from the left hallway. Mace decided it must be where the vast majority of the base was. It seemed they were feasting and toasting to celebrate the deaths of the government SWAT team. Captain Mace wondered if Agmund was in the center of them celebrating as well. The captain shook his head that the Stasi could be joyous when the victory had cost them so many lives.

The captain snuck down the hallway to his left and managed to peer into a large set of windows that housed the underground base's cafeteria. Alcohol, dancing, and all forms of celebrating in general seemed to be the rule of the day. Nowhere among it could Captain Mace see Agmund however. The captain chose to double back on his steps and take the hallway in the opposite direction. Even if he could not find Agmund, he needed to see if there was anything he could do to make sure his men had not died in vain on this mission. There had to be some information he could collect that would make the mission less than an utter failure. After ten minutes or so, he found a double door that led into a small room with windows along the far side. Through the window was a large cavernous room with a nuclear missile in the center of it. The structure of the base instantly made sense to him. It was an abandoned nuclear shelter/nuclear silo made to survive the end of the world. It made him wonder how the Maevin government had never found out about the existence of the underground part of the facility; much less why the facility still existed that housed such a terrible weapon. During the end of the Atomic War each side had emptied their arsenal of nuclear weapons at the other. All major cities on the face of Earth had been demolished. Mace realized Maevin itself must have been founded upon an abandoned military base that once housed a nuclear weapon but that had been long forgotten about. After a couple of moments, the captain finally noted the presence of a woman tied to a chair in the control room. The captain grasped with a start that it was Commander Ji Harlow. He had heard, like everyone else, that she was dead. He shook himself from his amazement and proceeded forth into the room.

He took off her blindfold and removed the gag from her mouth. She seemed very weak, and it was obvious that she had undergone a tremendous amount of torture. Her face was bloody and bruised, several teeth were missing, and her left arm was broken. She tried to speak, but the captain hushed her and gave her some water from the bottle he had kept on him. After giving her one of the energy bars he carried with him on missions they slowly made their way back towards the elevator. The way was much slower and intimidating now that he knew his disguise would not explain him leading Ji Harlow away. Ji amazingly kept pace fairly well, and only fell a few times. She in fact seemed to be getting stronger the further they went thanks to the food and water she had received. The fact that she was now becoming hopeful that she was escaping the hell she had just endured made it possible for her to continue walking through the pain and fatigue. The two grimly and quietly reached the elevator where the rest of the SWAT team had been massacred. Captain Mace and Ji Harlow took the elevator back up to ground level along with the bodies of the SWAT team and the three Stasi soldiers on the roof of the elevator.

Captain Mace was thankful that no one had checked on the three missing Stasi soldiers. The Stasi were too busy partying to notice. As soon as the doors opened, the captain cautiously peered out of the elevator at either end of the upper floor with night vision goggles on. He noted the Stasi had foolishly not replaced their sentries even though the location of their base had been discovered. The captain took a deep breath of relief and then nodded to Ji Harlow. She stepped forward out of the elevator first. At that moment Agmund stepped out from behind a large metal barrel. Mace was unsure of who's side Agmund was on. It did not take long for him to figure out. Agmund raised his hand, and to Mace's surprise he held a pistol in that hand. He shot once and sent a bullet clean through Ji's head. Agmund stared at Ji Harlow and seemed to ignore Mace, whom roared with anger at Agmund's continued betrayal and stormed out of the elevator. He tried to spear-tackle Agmund before he could react. Captain Mace wanted to enjoy this kill up close and personal. However, Agmund managed to bring the pistol around in time to shoot Captain Mace in the stomach before he could close the gap. He fell to the ground near Agmund's feet while writhing in pain. Agmund calmly removed Mace's weapons.

"Why did you allow all my men to die?" The captain asked in a weak manner that almost sounded like an exhale.

"Why? That is simple, because I needed your team to provide a distraction while I accomplished my real mission, finding information that told me the locations of the remainder of the bases and safe houses the Stasi use. I was impressed you managed to bring Ji Harlow all the way to me. It saved me the trouble of having to find her and kill her down there. It was a shame all your men needed to die, but I found it necessary."

"You...traitor...you...claimed...to be...a protector... with a...sword." The captain managed to mutter in his dying moments.

"I am, but I did not say for whom." Agmund stated in his disturbingly calm manner, this time punctuated with a gunshot to Captain Mace's forehead. Agmund then place Mace's body in the elevator with the rest of his men.

Lieutenant Longstreth was beginning to wonder if she would ever see Agmund or the SWAT team again as she peered at what she deemed to be the only entrance or exit out of the building that Agmund and the SWAT team had entered three hours earlier. She was standing on top of one of the four identical buildings nearly half a mile away from the building Agmund and the SWAT team had entered. She heard the sound of a large object falling heavily to the concrete roof behind her. She whirled around quickly to face the source of the noise. She found herself pointing her gun at the torso of the man behind her. She looked down the sights and realized it was Agmund. He was still dressed in his tunic, although it was no longer a pure white. Dirt and blood had stained the tunic. At Agmund's feet was the dead body of Ji Harlow. The marks on the body showed she had been tortured and then shot. Lieutenant Longstreth wondered if she was shot because she had cracked and told all she knew or if because she had said nothing. Longstreth hoped it was the latter, but by looking at the body doubted that was the case.

"She was dead when I found her. The SWAT team did not survive either. I managed to escape with her body, but only barely. There are still many Stasi down there.

Fortunately, the Stasi can ill afford to trade deaths with us, and we traded 13 deaths including Ji for approximately two dozen of them. It was not the complete victory I had hoped for, but that can be changed. I need you to call Commander Franklin and have him send a team over to destroy each of these five buildings. They are the only exits and entrances to their facility below. If they are destroyed the Stasi will be trapped and die below." Agmund turned around to leave, then stopped and addressed Longstreth again. "By the way, thanks for keeping an eye on me. Now, I will leave you to finish the job. There is no need to follow me now, I know my way home."

Lieutenant Longstreth struggled to find any words. It seemed Agmund was okay with that though and walked away without waiting for a reply. Longstreth looked at the body of Ji Harlow and wondered how in the world Commander Franklin was going to respond to this situation and the utter lack of details she had to report on their mysterious acquaintance. Longstreth had nothing substantial to go upon, but she distinctly had a bad vibe about Agmund. Despite her suspicions about Agmund, she saw the wisdom in destroying the Stasi base. The base was destroyed as Agmund had requested. Commander Franklin, and Police Commissioner Battig, was none too happy that the SWAT team had died, but thought the sacrifice worth while. Commander Franklin reported the success of the mission, the actions of Agmund, and the deaths of the SWAT team, but left out the discovery of Commander Harlow's body. It was an event that perplexed both Longstreth and Franklin so they made no mention of it to anyone. As for Agmund, he kept his secret about the information he had obtained. He deemed it would be much more useful to reveal it when it fit his purposes.

Chapter IV

November 6, 32 PAW

2:59

Maevin Police Commissioner Battig sat alone in his office. He was reviewing a hand-written message from Commander Franklin that informed Commissioner Battig of Captain Mace's SWAT team status as KIA. The only details noted that the mission had resulted in the destruction of one of the four remaining Stasi bases. Commissioner Battig knew he should be elated at the news of the base's demise, but he felt a certain sense of impending dread as he read the note. He could not shake the uneasiness welling inside him that came with not knowing exactly how his men had met their fate. If the mission had ended up being so successful, why was he not debriefing his men right now? The question nagged at Commissioner Battig, and none of the possible answers were ones that he liked.

The Police Commissioner's clock chimed the hour of 3 am in his small, but efficient office. A marginal night-time staff was in the office, just the janitor, a couple of dispatchers, and a handful of officers either filling out paperwork or chatting with each other. The night curfew enacted for the past ten years had made the police's load very light at night. It of course had not been that way the first couple of years, but the Maevin City Police enforced the law to the extreme, and now they were reaping the benefits of extremely few law-breakers at night. Commissioner Battig had been at the building for nearly twenty-four hours though, and this night promised no rest for him. He had a meeting at 7 am with Supreme Commander Larkin alongside Commander Franklin. Commissioner Battig was extremely concerned about the meeting with Larkin. Larkin had made it abundantly clear that he was unhappy about what he perceived as the government's inability to keep control over the city of Maevin. He did feel a little better knowing Commander Franklin would be informing Larkin that the Stasi base had been destroyed. That should make the meeting go a little easier. Unfortunately, Battig had precious little news to report that was positive. He was scouring the files of the past month to look for any kind of news, statistics, or reports that would show Larkin how effective the Maevin Police were against the Stasi. He only had a handful of such files thus far set aside. None of those files contained news near the magnitude of that which Commander Franklin would report. Commissioner Battig feared for his job, and possibly even his life, as the CRZ, whose job was battling the religious zealots and not the Stasi, would be portrayed as more successful against the Stasi even after their headquarters had been blown up recently.

While Commissioner Battig opened yet another file he heard a slight shuffle of a foot on the carpeted floor behind him. He tried to get up quickly, but he felt something hit him hard in the back of the head, and then he felt nothing at all.

November 6, 32 PAW

5:17

Commissioner Battig came to consciousness slowly about two hours later. The area in which he found himself was enclosed, but it was dark and he was having a hard time focusing. The first thing he knew was something he felt, the stifling hot air seemed to almost suffocate him. Sweat covered his body. His eyes finally began to adjust, and he discovered he was inside a long rectangular box. After concentrating as best he could through the pounding headache he had, he determined it was the correct size and shape to be a semi-trailer, but the walls looked to be of a strange rubbery substance. His foggy mind then figured out why the walls appeared the way they did, they were coated with sound dampening materials. As his pupils further dilated he realized the reason one would go through the pains of soundproofing a semi-trailer container. There was multiple torture devices neatly organized in the trailer. Commissioner Battig struggled against the restraints of his chair, but to no avail. He was firmly duct-taped at the ankles and wrists to the chair.

"You are going to be late for your meeting." Commissioner Battig struggled to locate the source of the sound. He strained to rotate his neck to see who had spoken to him. The man, a large, physical man dressed in black combat fatigues and carrying multiple guns and knives, had positioned himself directly behind Battig. The angle made it painful for Battig to look at his kidnapper. The man had a smile on his face and in his hands he held Commissioner Battig's personal PDA. At his feet were several files from his office as well. "But do not worry; Larkin is not going to kill you for being late. You will be dead before your meeting with him is scheduled to begin. Of course that is only going to happen if you cooperate with me." The man's smile suddenly faded, and a menacing look replaced it with astonishing fluidity. "And if you do not cooperate with me, Commissioner Battig, you will be wishing you were dead come seven am."

"What do you want from me?" Battig's voice seemed to tremble in the air. Battig winced. He had hoped that his question was going to come out sounding much stronger and defiant than he currently felt. It had not.

"These files are a nice start, but your death will be pretty nice as well. Fortunately for me that is entirely within my power. Unfortunately for you, I get to decide just how painful and slow that death will be."

Commissioner Battig turned his head back to facing straight ahead, in part to be more comfortable and in part to be able to hide the fear he felt mounting inside of him. "So you do want something from me." Battig silently chastised himself, his words were not sounding very brave at all once he uttered them.

"Yes. It is simple. I need to know how you knew about the Stasi base and who led the attack."

"I had nothing to do with that mission. I don't care who you are, I can't tell you what I don't know."

The man walked to the table in front of Battig. Battig could just see the man's back, but he could hear the sound of different implements of torture being picked up and put back down. His kidnapper was seemingly trying to decide exactly what instrument he wanted to use first. "My name is Nemesio; sorry I forgot to introduce myself. It would be a shame if you never learned the name of the last person you are ever going to speak with." Nemesio then turned around, a gutting hook in his right hand. It was designed to tear the guts out of animals. Battig was pretty certain that it would work all too well on humans too. Nemesio brought his face within inches of Battig's face and once again changed his expression to one that caused shivers up and down Battig's spine. "As for not knowing anything, I am calling your bluff. It not being your mission may be something I believe. If I had to guess, and for now that is the only option you are leaving me, it was probably the new CRZ leader's mission. What is his name?" Battig made a move to reply, but Nemesio laughed and stood up. He stood tossing the gutting hook into the air and catching it. At times he was menacing, other times he would flip a switch and seem happy and carefree. The sudden changes in attitude and demeanor were beginning to fray the nerves of Battig. It was completely unpredictable, which made it impossible for Battig to know exactly how to react to Nemesio. "You do not need to answer that one Commissioner Battig. I already know the answer to that question. His name is Commander Franklin. Please, do not underestimate me. The questions I need to know are of much more importance than that. Now, let me ask my questions again. How did you know where the Stasi base was and who led the attack?"

"Like I said, and you agreed, it was not my mission." Battig was desperately trying to buy more time, but he did not fully know why. There was no way anyone would come looking for him until the meeting with Larkin began at 7 am. Battig guessed the meeting was still hours away. He was in a hopeless situation to count on being rescued. Still, the human will to survive would not die within him. As of yet, he was trying options that would allow him to survive and avoid torture without giving away the answers to the questions Nemesio wanted. Battig liked to think he would never give away those answers, but already he was beginning to doubt himself.

Nemesio glared with all his intensity into Battig's eyes. The look alone almost made Battig insane. While Nemesio stared, Battig could just imagine all the horrible things the man was capable of doing to those who made him angry, and right now Battig could see that he had made Nemesio angry.

Nemesio's voice came out as a growl. "Last chance Battig, my patience is already gone. It was your men who died down there in that base; it was your SWAT team. You would not loan them to the CRZ without knowing something."

Battig considered his options and decided to try to get away with lying. It was a risky maneuver and one he had hoped to avoid. Thus far Nemesio had seemed to have known far too much for that option to hold much hope. "It was a random tip. A simple citizen doing his duty must have somehow discovered it and felt it was his duty to call it in. I never heard a name. The man who led the SWAT team was Captain Mace." Commissioner Battig felt better about this last lie, it was near the truth.

Without warning and with a quick striking ability that rivaled a king cobra's, Nemesio lashed out with his gutting hook. He let it sink deep into the thigh of Battig and then tore it out with a twist. Battig screamed bloody murder as he looked at a chunk of his leg being held in front of his face. As if the pain was not enough of an indication, Battig looked down at his leg to reassure himself that a large chunk of flesh and muscle was missing. His leg was a bloody mess. As he looked down he saw a large piece of hot iron slowly press down on his wound. He glared up at Nemesio, whom merely smiled. Then Battig began to feel the pain increase even more. Nemesio was searing the blood vessels shut to keep Battig from bleeding to death.

Nemesio put the iron away and grabbed what appeared to be a cigar cutter, although it was much bigger and stronger. He separated the fingers of Battig and then spoke again in a casual tone. "Commissioner Battig, I know that you lied to me. It was not a random tip by no one. Also, Captain Mace did not lead the raid, at least not entirely. There was someone else, not a SWAT member that survived the attack. He is the one I want to know all about."

Battig felt the cigar cutter close around his pinky finger. Before he even realized it he was spilling his guts in a hurried, panicked voice. "The man's name is Agmund. No one knows anything about him. He carries a broadsword and no guns. He wears white. Commander Franklin knows more than I do, but even he knows nearly nothing. The man just walked in one day and demanded to meet with Commander Franklin. He convinced Commander Franklin to let him use a SWAT team and claimed to know the location of the base. How he found out is anyone's guess. Commander Franklin agreed and hopes Agmund will be an important resource for the government in the future. That is all I know, I swear!"

"Thank you Commissioner Battig. That could have been far worse for you." Nemesio stood up and put the cigar cutter down. He grabbed the files and the PDA from Commissioner Battig's office and then he walked to the door of the trailer. Battig began to hope that Nemesio had indeed changed his mind. Right before Nemesio reached the door he spun around and threw the throwing knife he had discreetly picked up off the table while he placed the cigar cutter down. The blade pierced Battig right next to his sternum and buried deep in his heart. He was dead almost before he had known what happened.

November 6, 32 PAW

6:51

Chancellor Weiderman had been waiting for half an hour outside the trailer, straining fruitlessly to gain any indication of the proceedings inside. She waited with complete patience and poise though, only two of the admirable characteristics that allowed her to become one of the top people in the Stasi organization in the view of Head Chancellor Silas. She had been assigned along with a few of the Stasi she trusted the most to observe Nemesio and report on his actions, methods, and behaviors. She had watched while Nemesio had made his way silently through the open window of Commissioner Battig's office and knocked him out. That had impressed her enough, but afterwards was what had left her in awe. Nemesio proceeded to kill every single person in the building, including the unarmed janitors and dispatchers with an obvious rage and yet effective ruthlessness. Beneath the cocky exterior of this man was a volcano of hatred, anger, pain, and aggression that was ready to erupt at any moment. More frightening than that though was his complete ability to direct this volcanic eruption of emotion. It was an overwhelming force that no one in the police station had been ready to face. They all had perished quickly and without being able to warn anyone outside the building.

After the massacre no hint of the previous emotion could be seen, just a grim satisfaction in a job well done and if possible, a little bit more swelling to his head. He had returned calmly to the office of Commissioner Battig and left a convincing suicide/homicide note that was inexplicably written deftly in the Commissioner's handwriting. She and her team had then ridden in a police sedan with Nemesio driving. No one spoke a word as they were humbled by the extreme expression of violence and emotion by Nemesio. Nemesio seemed to approve of the silence and had done nothing to alter it. It was the longest ten minute vehicle ride Chancellor Weiderman had endured. Police Commissioner Battig's limp head resting on her shoulder during the entire ride had helped little to make it a shorter ride.

Once at the trailer in an abandoned weapons factory, Nemesio had gone alone into the trailer carrying Police Commissioner Battig. During that time, Chancellor Weiderman had taken the time to compose herself, although all her colleagues were unable to do so. She waited resolutely for Nemesio to emerge, of which he finally obliged right after throwing the knife. It was still stuck in the chest of Battig. As Nemesio opened the door, Chancellor Weiderman could see the end result of the session. She burned with a deep desire to know how all had gone, but she felt shaken once again in the presence of Nemesio and could only muster a weak question. "Did you learn anything from him?"

"Of course." Nemesio said with a smile that would have been charming in any other circumstances. Nemesio seemed unaffected by the gravity of the situation and the aftermath of the destructive wake he had sown. He walked past her and got behind the driver's wheel of the police car and the rest meekly followed, leaving the corpse of Commissioner Battig to rot away in the trailer.

November 6, 32 PAW

7:12

Supreme Commander Larking glowered at his watch. It was almost as if he was accusing it of something. It told him that Commissioner Battig was twelve minutes late for the meeting. Across from Larkin's luxurious desk sat an increasingly uncomfortable Commander Franklin. The chair he sat in was plush and extremely ergonomic, so that was not the culprit. Commander Franklin's discomfort came from Larkin's increasing rage.

Larkin looked up suddenly as a chime went off in his office. Without looking at his screen to see who wanted admittance to the office, Larkin hit the button to allow them in. The innermost of three office doors opened, each door providing an extra security check before gaining entrance into the office itself. Larkin's attention immediately snapped to the door, already rehearsing in his mind the fierce words he wanted to scream at Battig. Instead of Battig though, Nasirra's young assistant, Kyle, entered the office. He was meek as usual in the presence of Larkin, but Larkin could tell he carried himself even more timidly than was normal. In his right hand was a lengthy note. Larkin angrily snatched it out of Kyle's hand. Kyle backed several paces away and waited to be dismissed. The message read, "Around three am this morning there were sixteen murders committed in the Maevin Police Headquarters. On Commissioner Battig's desk was left a murder-suicide note citing stress from the job and guilt over the extreme actions he took to protect the government of Maevin. Commissioner Battig is currently MIA. Initial reports seem to suggest he is indeed the culprit. They are still looking for him, dead or alive."

Larkin handed the note over to Commander Franklin and then dismissed Kyle with an angry wave of his hand. He leaned back in his chair and sat back deep in thought. His mind was juggling several different topics connected to this news at once. Was his government as secure as he thought? Was the Stasi to blame for this attack somehow? Did Commissioner Battig really commit suicide or was he at large in the city somewhere? Did he really even commit the murders in the first place? Who was going to replace Commissioner Battig? How effective was his government if he could not even protect his own employees? The questions all assaulted his mind, leaving him unable to concentrate on just one thought at a time.

Looking over at Commander Franklin, Larkin could see that he was tossing some of the same thoughts over in his mind with just as little effectiveness at answering those questions. Larkin finally decided on at least one course of action and leaned forward. "Commander Franklin, I know the Maevin Police is going to handle this situation officially, and they won't have it any other way. That being said, you are going to conduct a parallel investigation. I want to get to the bottom of this. All reports are to be handed over to me personally."

Commander Franklin turned it over in his mind. "You seem to think there is much more to this than meets the eye. Do you know something I do not?"

"If I did, I would tell you if you needed to know. Right now, I only have a gut feeling, but that gut feeling has kept me alive and in power many times before. Either way, I want to know more facts than what I was just given. You are going to take care of that for me."

"Yes, sir." He paused waiting for Larkin to respond, when he did not Franklin spoke up. "Did you still want to conduct our meeting?"

"No, Franklin, I don't think that would be productive today. You have much to attend to, as do I. Leave your report with me and I will take a look at it when I can concentrate on it. There is though one matter I wish to discuss with you though."

"Agmund?" Franklin asked even though he felt he already knew the answer.

"Yes, Agmund. What do you know about him?"

"My initial assessment was he was a madman. He made grand claims about things that he knew or could do. I thought he was delusional. Instead he has proved to be a very competent and dangerous man."

"Dangerous to whom, Commander?" Larkin asked leaning forward, this Agmund character was a thrilling point of interest to him. At a time when Larkin felt assaulted from every direction by his enemies, Agmund could be the weapon he could use to counter the attacks.

"That I do not know. I think that he is one of the best assets we have against the Stasi and potentially the

Christians and Muslims as well. Lieutenant Longstreth on the other hand has been somewhat less convinced on the matter, and I can tell that she thinks he may be just as dangerous to us as to the Stasi. I felt the same way initially, but his last mission for us left me with no doubts."

"Is she just jealous of the success that he has thus far enjoyed?"

"I used to think she was beyond that, but it seems as though she is indeed jealous of him. I am cautious with Agmund for now, but I will be using him greatly in the future if he continues to prove himself worthy."

"Does he really carry just a sword?"

"Yes. We still know very little about the man. I have several men working for me just trying to dig up all they know about him, but they have discovered nothing. They can't even find the man or anyone that has even heard of him. There is little we can do but give him some wet work that is not too important and see how much we can truly trust him."

"That indeed seems to be your only hand for now. I want you to keep me personally abreast of his actions."

"As you wish, Supreme Commander. Anything else, sir?"

"No, that will be all for today. I will email you what I think of the rest of your report. Until we find out more about this Battig situation, keep on your toes. I can't afford to lose another one of my best employees."

"Of course, sir. Have a good day, sir."

Larkin brewed in his office the rest of the morning, he worried that his government was beginning to slip out of his iron grip. He tried to plot his counter-attacks, but it was impossible when he did not know for sure who the real culprits were.

November 6, 32 PAW

13:39

"What do you mean you don't know what he found out!?!" Head Chancellor Silas bawled out. His face flushed a full red. Chancellor Weiderman was perturbed. Silas could not treat her this way after all she had done for him and the Stasi.

She managed to utter a soft-spoken, "After watching him tear through that police building I was in shock. He has done more in just those few minutes than we have ever dreamed of doing with no less than two dozen of our men in a year. If we can learn to wield him as a weapon, I have no doubt that we will be able to topple the government sooner than we possibly imagined, but I fear he is an uncontrollable force. We may as well try to control a tornado's path. That man will kill anyone who gets in his way, whether they are the Stasi or government. He has amazing self-control, but I don't think he will suffer anyone else to control him."

Head Chancellor Silas's expression calmed, he had not survived being the chief enemy of Supreme Commander Larkin for so long by allowing emotion to affect his decision-making ability. "I have been imagining Maevin without Supreme Commander Larkin everyday for the past thirty years, ever since the man managed to evade my last face-to-face confrontation with him. I may not be able to control a tornado's path, a tornado seemingly strikes at random, but one thing is consistent. A tornado always brings destruction when it touches down. I merely need to point him in the right direction for long enough for that destruction to happen. I don't want to control him, I want to unleash him."

At that moment Nemesio strutted into the office without knocking as though he owned the place. He sat down on a chair and put his feet up on Chancellor Silas's desk. He had a goofy grin on his face as he looked at Chancellor Silas. Chancellor Silas was less than amused, although he was a bit startled at the sudden appearance. "There is no need to unleash me, Chancellor Silas. I am about to do that myself. I am weary of all these small missions. You Stasi do not take any real risks, any real challenge. As I have already promised you, I am going to kill all five Council Members. Once that is done, it will be time for me to kill Supreme Commander Larkin, or so he fancies himself. The Supreme Commander cannot even keep his own employees alive, and soon he will not be alive as well."

"Are you insane?" Chancellor Weiderman asked. The only reply she got was a cold, unflinching stare from Nemesio.

Chancellor Silas sought to break the tension in the office. "Nemesio, I do not doubt your ability, but do you know the magnitude of the task you are taking on? I have tried to kill every one of those people before, but every time I have failed, sometimes with as many as fifty men at my disposal. What makes you think that you as one man will be able to do that?"

"The answer is obvious. They will not expect a one-man attack. Well, of course not with the first one or two. They will catch on, but then that is when the fun and challenge of it will really begin." Nemesio laughed, though neither one of the other two in the office joined in. He stopped disturbingly in mid-laugh and then leaned forward in his chair and looked into Chancellor Silas's eyes. "Now, I do need your help to do so. I want you to track the movements of all five Council Members. Leave Supreme Commander Larkin to me. I want to know everything you can manage to find out about my targets. I will be able to carry out my mission much easier if I am well informed."

Chancellor Silas looked thoughtfully at Nemesio before replying. "I already have files on these people, although they are a little out of date. I will give them to you once I get some men to bring the information in these files up to date.

But, I need to know something first from you. What did Police Commissioner Battig tell you?"

"Nothing at first, but after some persuasion, he told me that the attack was led by some lunatic who does not use guns at all, but only a sword and wears white. The man's name is Agmund. He knew where to find the base, but Battig did not know how. He is working closely with Commander Franklin."

Chancellor Silas seemed to absorb the information thoughtfully. This new player in the game was unlooked for. "Do you think this Agmund is a threat?"

"Not to me." Nemesio laughed at his own joke. "I think the man could become dangerous. Let's wait and see. There are bigger fish to fry for now. If he becomes troublesome then I will let you have first crack at him. However, if you fail then I will then have to add him to my list once he proves himself to be worthy of being executed by my hand. I doubt it will come to that though. How dangerous can a man with just a sword be?"

"I do not like this unknown factor. Are you certain that was all Battig knew about Agmund?"

"Yes. Commander Franklin may know a little more, but Battig made it sound like Commander Franklin knows very little about Agmund as well."

"Very well, Nemesio. Come back in a few days and those files should be up-to-date." The two men shook hands right before Nemesio left. Chancellor Weiderman sat deep in her thoughts. Chancellor Silas could sense she was troubled.

"See, Chancellor Weiderman, I will soon unleash Nemesio. He will accomplish small favors for me for a while. I will stall him by saying that we just need a little more time to update those files. They are already up to date, but he does not need to know that. He will prove useful on these missions before he starts his suicide mission. But that does not mean that I yet trust him. You must continue to follow this man. Now that you have seen what he is capable of you will no doubt be less affected by it than if I were to give it to someone else. Leave your team behind this time. They will be of no use to you. I merely need someone to help me point him in the right direction. I trust that task to you. Watch his back and keep him alive. If he can accomplish his self-appointed mission then we may very well be the leaders of this city within months."

"Do you really think he can accomplish that self-appointed mission?"

"No, I guess I don't. However, that does not mean he will be of some use to us. I hope at best he will be able to kill a few of the Council Members. However, there is a slim chance he will be able to somehow accomplish it all. That man does not seem to fear anything. And a man without fear is a man that has nearly unlimited potential. Maybe he will be able to complete his mission, but I dare not place complete hope in his ability to do so. We must proceed under the assumption that he will fail. I cannot place all my hopes and dreams in Nemesio otherwise the Stasi will become extinct."

"As you wish, Chancellor Silas." She gave Silas a nod of respect and then left the office. As she walked down the dark halls of an underground Stasi base she was more determined than ever not to fail the Stasi again.

Chapter V

November 20, 32 PAW

5:57

Rhys found himself in the office of Paul once again. It had been three weeks since Rhys had orchestrated the decimation of the old CRZ headquarters, and the countless lives that had been loss in that explosion. Rhys had seen little reason to visit Paul, whom no doubt would be angry since Ji Harlow had somehow escaped his bombing of the CRZ headquarters, especially while he had been able to keep himself so busy lately. However, Rhys knew that Paul was willing to forgive others. Paul just needed a little time to let his anger cool. His ability to forgive others for their mistakes and sins was not nearly as impressive as his ability to forgive himself for his own. It was a necessary characteristic in the face of so much persecution when Paul felt forced to do much he would rather not do under more appealing circumstances. However most of Paul's close associates felt that it was not as necessary a characteristic as Paul thought. Some of the other Christians thought his associates were weak and tended to side with Paul, others thought them wise and patient on God's will. After all, had not God many times before rescued His people from exile and persecution after a time of discipline? They viewed their punishment in Maevin as a time of punishment for the sins they committed during the Atomic War. If they worked on their faith in God, He would deliver them they reasoned.

Rhys sat there and waited for Paul to begin. He did not have to wait long. Paul had had three weeks to rehearse this conversation in his mind. "Rhys, how exactly did Ji Harlow fall into the hands of the Stasi?"

"I had assumed she would die in the bombing of the CRZ building. She must have been kidnapped from it moments before the building exploded by the Stasi."

"Rhys, you have taken great liberties with the missions I have given you in the past, but this time you went too far. I only wanted Ji Harlow's death. You bombed an entire building with dozens of people in it. Your actions put us all at jeopardy, and because of that Ji Harlow fell into the hands of the enemy. I know the government is our biggest threat, but the Stasi are just as dangerous to my people."

"Do you not mean God's people?" Rhys ventured, knowing that it would further infuriate Paul, but strangely he was taking some guilty pleasure in doing so.

"Yes, I do. However I consider them my people as well for as long as God leads me to shepherd His flock."

"How will you know when to step down as a leader, Paul?"

"How will you know when to stop the violence Rhys?"

The two men stared at each other, both hitting a sore spot on the other's heart. Rhys was the first to recover however, and also the first to answer. His reply was somberly and honestly spoken. "I will know it is time to step down when there are people with less blood on their hands capable of shaping the course of events of this city towards a better future."

"Then I shall use the same measurement." Paul stated fiercely, although without much forethought. "Never mind that business for now though, we are still needed for the moment. Certainly neither Supreme Commander Larkin nor Chancellor Silas have less blood on their hands, and they are the ones shifting the course of events the most at this point. You are lucky that your audacious actions were successful in the fact that the government at least appears to believe the little lie you created. Muslims everywhere in the city are being hunted with a vehemence that they have not experienced for a decade. The Muslims had grown complacent and now they are paying the price with their blood. Unfortunately the new CRZ is less efficient due to your actions and therefore the extermination is taking much longer than I originally thought."

"Whoa? Extermination? Paul, have you really given up all hope of being able to coexist peacefully with those of the Islamic faith? You seem to be looking to not just weaken them and strengthen your position, you want them all dead, regardless of if they hate Christianity or not."

"This issue has wracked my soul for a long time now. I have finally come to a decision and I feel at peace with it. Yes, the Muslims need to be exterminated. Anything less may drag us into what nearly brought humanity to extinction in the first place. As I was saying, I need the Islamic Community, the Stasi, and the government to all falter and fail. We are not yet strong enough to take on the Stasi or the Maevin government, therefore the Islamic Community must be the target of our attacks. With the Muslims out of the way, we will be better off in the future once the government and the Stasi battle each other to nothing. It will be our job to make sure that occurs Rhys. We must force the Stasi and the government to weaken each other. If either side enjoys a decisive victory we will be exterminated like the Muslims are about to be."

"How do you deem that I can best take advantage of this opportunity Paul?" Rhys stated, willing to drop the issue of extermination versus peaceful co-existence for now. Certainly Paul had the historical evidence to support him in his decision. Muslims and Christians had been battling in the name of religion for centuries. Still, Rhys's conscience did not sit at ease with what Paul was proposing. He had known that his blowing up the CRZ headquarters would allow the Muslims to better survive the renewed focus of the CRZ. That was half his goal in the first place.

"I need you to find information for me. You must ascertain what happened to Ji Harlow. I have heard that she was kidnapped and delivered to the Stasi by someone, or more likely a small team, shortly before you blew the building. I need to know who this group is and what they learned from Ji Harlow. If that does not complicate matters, the base where Ji Harlow had been kidnapped to was blown up recently. No one knows who is responsible; all we know is that on the same night an entire SWAT team from the Maevin Police Department went MIA. The next item is that Police Commissioner Battig is missing. Each one of these things individually is a big event, but together it is disconcerting. There almost seems to be a grand conductor in the background moving pieces on a chess board that is seen only by his eyes. Keep your ears open and do what you must to discover any information that would be pertinent. I fear our scheme together could be surpassed by a player that has unbeknownst to either of us entered the game."

"Is there anything else you would ask of me?" Rhys asked, promising nothing about what he would do, which was not uncommon for him to do.

"Yes, while the Muslims are in complete disarray, I want you to topple their leadership. Their leadership is mainly centered on one man, Farooq. It is to the point that if he falls, almost all of the Muslim faithful will wither away. I need you to assassinate him to make up for the CRZ's inability to function after your little explosion."

"I shall do what I can."

"And that as always is very much indeed, in fact sometimes too much."

Rhys could not mistake the obvious warning Paul had made. He might as well have said do only what I ask, not more. Rhys tipped his black cowboy hat to a very stern looking Paul and exited the office. As soon as Rhys had exited, Paul bowed his head and said a prayer that the Lord would prevail, and forgive the actions of himself and Rhys.

November 20, 32 PAW

14:03

"Agmund, I am so glad to see you. It has been far too long my friend."

"Commander Franklin, I am sorry it has been so long since I have appeared in your office."

"I would ask you for a cell phone number or a pager, but I have a feeling that is useless." Commander Franklin laughed at his own joke, though Agmund did not. It had been a long time since either man had laughed. Larkin was constantly on Franklin's back about producing results concerning the disappearance of Commissioner Battig. He had given the assignment to Lieutenant Longstreth and she had turned up absolutely nothing on the subject. He was beginning to think she would fail him for the first time. Commander Franklin finally noticed Agmund did not seem to be humored. It was a shame, Franklin thought, it had felt good to laugh after so long. He began to wonder what was so awful in Agmund's history that he could not deign himself to laugh. "Sorry, on to business. I need your help. Are you aware of the situation concerning Commissioner Battig?"

"Yes. They have not been able to find him or his corpse anywhere in the city. The news seems unsure of what to report on the situation."

"Well that is because the government is unsure of what to tell them to report to be honest with you Agmund. Supreme Commander Larkin is on my case big time about this one. You seem to be able to discover a great many things easily, I would like for you try to find out more about this situation." Commander Franklin was happy with this test he was giving Agmund. It was an assignment that was difficult, but there was no great risk involved in looking for a man presumed to be dead and getting to the bottom of the issue. It was a perfect test in Franklin's opinion, low risk with a huge potential benefit from a successful mission.

"Can you give me what information you do have, Commander Franklin?"

Franklin got nervous about giving out information. Larkin had made it quite clear that no information was to be released concerning Commissioner Battig. He had needed to get special permission for even Lieutenant Longstreth to gain access to it. He looked for some way to avoid giving out sensitive information to someone the government knew almost nothing about. "Actually I would prefer you start from scratch. This way you will have no preconceived notions." Commander Franklin looked intently at Agmund, hoping for some sign that he was disappointed that his attempt to get information from Franklin had failed.

Agmund seemed unaffected though. "That is a wise idea Commander Franklin. I will start right away if there is nothing else you want to assign me."

"No, Agmund that will be enough to put on your plate for now. Try to make your visits a little more frequently though Agmund. Your presence is greatly appreciated. It will be appreciated even more if you perform this task well for me."

"I exist to serve." Agmund said and left the room. Coming from anyone else, Commander Franklin would have laughed; coming from Agmund, though, Franklin believed him with all his heart. The man had a certain sincerity that made it nearly impossible to laugh at him, not to mention the fact that he certainly would not join in the laughter.

November 23, 32 PAW

17:31

"Here is the proof of the death of the man you requested." Rhys stated showing Paul a digital camera. The imaged showed a clean bullet hole in the forehead of Farooq. A small stream of dark red blood had trickled down his nose and around his mouth and reached his chin, where it had matted into his beard and collected until enough of the blood had pooled there to cause it to drip to the ground. Paul struggled to hold back the dinner he had ate just a few minutes earlier.

Unable to think of anything else to say, Paul stammered out "How did you kill him?"

"With one bullet." Rhys said in a matter of fact disposition, although inwardly he felt some glee that Paul finally was forced to look at the exact consequences of the orders he had given. It took little effort for Paul to recover from the initial shock though; such was his confidence that all he did was necessary for the glory of God and protection of the Christian remnant.

"Any other additional casualties?"

"Just his two bodyguards, it was unavoidable."

"Yes, I suppose that is so." Paul breathed a deep sigh of relief and praised God for this victory and the ones he felt that were sure to come. His confidence was running extremely high thanks to Rhys, enabling him to dream up scenarios that he had not hoped to cause in many long years. He even pictured himself taking over Larkin's role as leader of the government and the church simultaneously. He was awestruck as he thought of the power he could wield in both those positions, of all the good he could do. "Now that the Islamic community is on the brink of extinction, it is time for us to weaken both the Stasi and the government. I think the best way to affect this is through indirect means. Set them up against each other Rhys, feed them to each other and watch them devour each other in their violent greed."

"As you wish Paul, so it will be done." Rhys said.

He turned and exited the office, leaving the camera behind on the desk. He knew it would be long before Paul would stop basking in the glory of his victory, despite the nagging feeling of guilt that each had pushed into the very backs of their mind. The camera sitting on his desk would continue to serve as a reminder of the gritty horror of what Paul commanded Rhys to do.

As Rhys reached the streets of Maevin he felt glad that Paul had forgotten to ask him how his investigations into the Ji Harlow and Commissioner Battig situation were going. He had nothing he wanted to report to Paul on the subject. Hopefully Paul would forget all about it as he daydreamed about the future of Maevin without Muslims, Stasi, or the government.

November 25, 32 PAW

10:45

"Agmund, you have indeed made your visits more frequent. I did not expect to see you so quickly."

"Honestly, I did not expect to be here so soon again Commander Franklin, but your assignment provided me much less trouble than it did for the Maevin Police and Lieutenant Longstreth."

Commander Franklin was taken aback, drastically. The last thing he expected was a report of success so soon after his number one field agent had failed to uncover anything. "You mean to tell me that you have completed your investigation already?!"

"Yes."

Commander Franklin waited eagerly for the news, but Agmund said nothing. "Well, man, what did you discover?"

"After looking more closely at Commissioner Battig's suicide note, I discovered some inconsistencies in the handwriting. Look here," Agmund produced an unmarked folder filled to the brim with papers. He pulled out a series of photographs. They were side-by-side copies of some of the same words. "Look here at this "i." The long part of the "i" is significantly longer and the dot is closer in this photo, although the overall height matches. Several of the letters have a small variation in them. This is just one example."

"So the letter was written in a great hurry or did someone else write it?"

"Someone else wrote it."

"Well, Agmund, do you know who?"

"I am assuming the same guy that kidnapped, tortured, and then executed Battig. The guy's name is Nemesio. I do not know anything about him other than evidently he is working with the Stasi and behind the murder of Commissioner Battig. He may have been the one to put Ji Harlow in the hands of the Stasi as well, but that is purely speculation. It is far more likely the Muslims you have already executed for blowing up the CRZ building sold her to the Stasi to finance further acts of terrorism. Unfortunately we cannot interrogate those dead men to find out for certain. Regardless, Nemesio is up for execution for his murders of CRZ employees, kidnapping, torture, and murder of Commissioner Battig. This folder contains the proof. I had to do all the same things Nemesio is accused of in order to get it as well."

Franklin took a few moments to digest this information as he glanced through the contents of the folder. Information from a great many sources revealed what Nemesio had done, but nothing about the man or his future plans. "So Nemesio is an unknown force out there?"

"Yes, he is. I was able to find Battig's body. It was at a shipping yard for an abandoned weapons factory. A deserted semi trailer had been outfitted to torture people. We don't know what he said or how bad the torture had been, but we know it was him. Some of the instruments still had his DNA on them. The Maevin police are currently staking out the location to see if Nemesio returns to it."

"You have solved this mystery when no one else could. How do you do it Agmund?" Commander Franklin was completely floored, and extremely pleased that Agmund had performed so well.

"It's all in the details, and the details are what I do best Commander Franklin."

"Well, this detail about Nemesio, what do you recommend we do about him."

"Let's keep our eyes and ears open concerning him, but there is currently not enough information to act on. If we try to act on nothing we could get burnt badly. We only have a name, but that is a good start."

"Very well, I will run it by Supreme Commander Larkin, but I approve of your idea. I just know he will be none too fond of sitting and waiting for him to strike again. We have lost too many men already in the past couple of months."

"Too true, too true."

"Well, Agmund, I hope to see you again soon. I will have more steady work for you soon, but for now, enjoy a job well done."

"Yes, sir." Agmund said and then left Commander Franklin to double-check on the details that Agmund had provided before he reported it to Supreme Commander Larkin.

Chapter VI

November 25, 32 PAW

17:33

Lieutenant Longstreth's blood pumped intensely through her veins. She had just been given an assignment from Commander Franklin to annihilate a base that the Stasi held near the outskirts of the city. What made it even more stressful was that he was demanding the assault happen no later than two hundred hours, to ensure less time for leaks to get out of the CRZ. Commander Franklin had become more wary, perhaps even paranoid, since the deaths of Ji Harlow and Commissioner Battig. His wariness though did not affect the aggressiveness in which he pursued his goals of exterminating the government's enemies. The sheer amount of firepower and vehicles that Longstreth felt she needed to accomplish the task made it likely the Stasi base would have plenty of forewarning as they made their approach from across the city. This made a dangerous mission even more dangerous.

In fact, it was a mission so hazardous that Agmund opposed it, vehemently and openly to both herself and

Franklin. Longstreth viewed it as her opportunity to put herself back in the place she deserved, the go-to troubleshooter for Commander Franklin. She had worked her butt off for years to earn it, and now this upstart Agmund had stolen it with two lucky missions. There was something about him she deeply distrusted, and she did not think it was just jealousy cropping up. She thrust those thoughts about Agmund out of her head and began to plan the attack. It would require a lot of planning to coordinate all the men, firepower, and vehicles she would need. The mission would begin in approximately eight and a half hours. She had her work cut out for her.

November 28, 32 PAW
23:57

Nemesio walked swiftly, yet without losing his usual swagger, into the office of Chancellor Silas. Chancellor Silas had barely enough time to look up and recognize his unannounced visitor when Nemesio opened his mouth to speak. "I have just recently discovered some very important intelligence. The government is about to escort several of your prisoners out of the city to be executed through radiation exposure. They have found it to be the most cost effective method of execution and a constant reminder that we truly are isolated from the rest of the world. They are moving them in two hours, at two hundred hours. They will be under a minimal escort. The information is sparse, but appears legitimate. If we act quickly, we could rescue some of the key men you have lost and make them pay with casualties to their side. It will be your classic two for one switch." All the while Nemesio had been talking Chancellor Silas had sat unmoved, both emotionally and physically, except for the discreet act of paging Chancellor Weiderman. While Chancellor Silas was digesting this new information, Chancellor Weiderman walked in, thus giving Chancellor Silas more time to think.

Chancellor Weiderman acted surprised at the presence of Nemesio, "Oh, I apologize; I did not mean to interrupt. Should I leave?" Before posing the question, Weiderman purposefully shifted her gaze to Silas, wanting Silas to answer rather than Nemesio. She knew that Chancellor Silas desired her presence; otherwise he would have not sent the page until after Nemesio had left.

"No Chancellor Weiderman, there are enough seats for you; there is no reason why you should not join us." Chancellor Silas said while still racking his brain with the possibilities that this mission could run into.

"Indeed Chancellor Weiderman it would be good for you to join us for it seems impossible for me to be able to part from you for very long." Nemesio said with a smirk, knowing that he really had no choice in the matter, but to disagree would be the same as handing more authority over to Silas. Chancellor Weiderman for her part did well not to take offense to the indirect reference to her watchdog role on his previous two missions for the Stasi. She prided herself on doing a good job and helping the Stasi, it was not personal between her and Nemesio. Both people were attempting to accomplish the same goals, although in very different ways. "So, Chancellor Silas," ignoring the presence of Chancellor Weiderman, "I would normally act on this information by myself, but with the targets being in multiple vehicles they could quickly separate from me if anything goes wrong. Besides, you are the one that has the most to gain from this operation, which is why I felt compelled to give you the information and allow you to act on it in your own wisdom."

"How did you learn of this? I have heard not a trace of it from any of my sources." Chancellor Silas said stalling for time, but also desperate to know more about Nemesio.

"The answer is obvious; our sources are not the same."

"That was not much of an answer."

"It is the only one I shall give though, so it will have to suffice. Now, what do you plan to do Chancellor Silas?"

"I say the risk is low. If your information is wrong, our ambush will just be a waste of time, no more. The only real risk is if they set up an ambush for us, but I really don't think that will be an issue. Just in case we will make sure our ambush has plenty of escape routes. If you are right, the advantages will be great. As you say the two-for-one switch will be a huge benefit, especially now that

I sense we are nearing the end of our long battle with the government." Silas tried to gather more information about what Nemesio knew, but he made no indication that he knew more than what he had already shared. "We will act on this information. It is an opportunity we cannot pass up. Nemesio, are you willing to accompany Chancellor Weiderman on this mission."

"Depends, who is in charge of the mission?"

"Chancellor Weiderman is, though if something happens to her in the ambush then you

will be in command."

"After what you have seen me accomplish these last two missions you are still asking me to follow her?" Nemesio appeared irate. It was almost too much for his ego to handle to follow a woman's lead. The way he said the word her was almost like it was painful for him to just spit it out of his mouth. "My goal is to kill the Council, not to free your pathetic prisoners of war that were not competent enough to stay out of the hands of the enemy in the first place!"

"My men are still collecting the information that you need. We could use your help on this mission. I want to see how you work with a team Nemesio. We have only witnessed what you can do alone. That is the reason Chancellor Weiderman is taking the lead."

"Nemesio," Chancellor Weiderman sought to establish the peace. She had seen firsthand what Nemesio was capable of and did not want to lose such a powerful asset on this mission. "I really could use your help. If it helps, I do not view myself as in charge of you. I have seen how capable you are when working alone. You can accompany the team and act as you see fit."

"I will go, but know this Chancellor Weiderman and Chancellor Silas. On this mission your team will merely be my backup. I will kill the government forces, although I am too good for the invalids we are likely to face. My only hope is there will be someone among the prisoner escort worth killing."

"Even if there is not anyone worth killing Nemesio, it will still go a long way in solidifying our partnership." Chancellor Silas said, happy that Nemesio was going.

"Partnership? So far Chancellor Silas I have helped you. You have done nothing to help me. The information about the Council Members best be in my possession soon. I have already gained much information on Supreme Commander Larkin. Your men are impeding my work."

"Do not worry Nemesio. Soon you will have more information than you could possibly desire on your targets." Chancellor Silas said. Chancellor Weiderman gave Silas an odd look; she knew he was planning to use Nemesio as long as possible before letting him loose on the Council Members. It worried her that Nemesio may become bitter towards the Stasi. The situation had the potential to turn the Stasi's greatest weapon into its worst nightmare. Weiderman hoped that Silas knew exactly what he was doing. He was walking a tight-walk. Any wayward step could upset the balance and cause the Stasi to plummet to their doom.

November 26, 32 PAW

1:57

Once the details had been planned out, the convoy that Lieutenant Longstreth had decided to lead consisted of thirty-six men and women. Twenty-four of the CRZ men would be divided into two Armored Personnel Carriers, six would ride in an armored government-issue SUV, and the other six was half of a SWAT team in an unmarked van. Lieutenant Longstreth herself rode in the SUV and would be coordinating with the rest of the team leaders. She watched as the team packed away the equipment for the job. They were bringing as much equipment as possible in the vehicles while still allowing room for all thirty-six people going on the mission. Lieutenant Longstreth had very little knowledge of the Stasi base other than it was at an abandoned church. It made her feel more comfortable bringing so much hopefully unneeded equipment to a largely unknown mission.

This was actually one of the reasons Agmund had opposed the mission; it lacked details on what to anticipate once at the church. Longstreth had been approved because she had assured Franklin she could handle the mission. He had known her too long not to trust her judgment, and had also never known her to fail, except for finding information on Battig's disappearance.

Within a few minutes, the convoy rolled out into the city streets of Maevin. Lieutenant Longstreth estimated she had a half an hour drive ahead of her. Initially she had favored a direct route to the base, but Franklin had advised her to take a less direct route to avoid conveying to any Stasi sympathizers the true destination of the convoy. The route would take bring them past the target about a half mile west of it while travelling north before reaching the city walls. Then they would turn east along the outer wall until they were directly north of the church. Then by heading south, the convoy would approach from the north. It was likely to be the direction they least expected, government control being strongest in the center of the city. She had agreed to the route change, seeing the wisdom of his advice. After ascertaining she had agreed to this route, Commander Franklin had surveyed the convoy and then left the mission in Longstreth's hands. He had seemed very certain of success when he left.

After twelve minutes into the convoy's trip, the buildings drastically changed from posh downtown, modern buildings to more artful and beautifully designed buildings that looked clearly neglected. Indeed it was hard to tell the difference between the buildings that were abandoned and the ones that still had residences in them. As Longstreth was dwelling on the finer aspects of the vast differences in both the buildings and the lives of the people it contained, she heard a distinct pop coming from the tires of the SUV. The vehicle lurched unexpectedly as the driver tried to wrestle it to a safe stop. It took her a moment to register what had happened, but then she had no doubt. They had hit a spike strip. All of their tires were blown. She radioed quickly and desperately to the vehicles behind her, "Spike strip is set ahead! Stop now! Take up defensive positions both to the front and the rear! Expect an ambush!"

It was too late however. Each of the vehicles behind her drove over the spike strip. The two APCs were the only vehicles that were safe from the spike strip as the tracks on their vehicles were unaffected. The APCs could not continue on though as the SUV was in front of them in the narrow one-way street with the unmarked van behind them. All vehicles came to a stop and began taking up defensive positions. They waited for the ensuing ambush, but for a few minutes all was silent. No attackers made their presence known.

November 26, 32 PAW

2:39

"Nemesio, this was supposed to be a prisoner transport, this looks more like an attack convoy!" Chancellor

Weiderman whispered, although if the situation had allowed she would have certainly been shouting. Their position poised on a low rooftop directly above and next to the convoy prevented anything above a whisper though. Men on the opposite rooftop waited for the signal to commence the attack.

"Are you not up for a little challenge?" Nemesio said with a smirk, undisturbed by the sudden change of the situation. Or maybe he was just enjoying the fact that the woman in charge did not know what to do anymore.

"This is a great opportunity. I cannot go back to Chancellor Silas empty-handed." She thought to herself about how much she had failed him recently, but did not mention it to Nemesio.

"You are not prepared to face this force. I cannot guarantee any of my backup force will survive this fight if you choose to engage the enemy, including yourself."

"We will attack. The APCs will be the toughest, but after eliminating the rest of the troops we will use C4 to take them out. They are not very mobile and with the majority of the attack force eliminated, there will be few left to man the guns in the APCs."

"As you wish. Tell me when to attack. Let me take the first shot. This snake will be much less venomous without her leader."

"Now, Nemesio, now!"

Nemesio fired his M41A Carbine once, a single .223 caliber round entered the brain of the convoy's leader, Lieutenant Longstreth. Immediately, an intense firefight broke out on both sides. The few minutes of silence was broken by a single shot. The night was lit by the flares of the muzzles as each side strived to gain the upper hand. The Stasi held the advantage of the entrenched and elevated position, but the government forces held their own with more manpower, firepower, and the cover and firepower of the vehicles they had brought. It was an intense draw, but the ferocity of the firefight lessened as the remaining men and women jockeyed for positions and the advantage. However, as the people on both sides decreased, the tension increased. The balance of the small battle promised to be easily swayed by the smallest of actions.

Several minutes after the battle had commenced, Chancellor Weiderman noted that only half a dozen of her own people remained. Eight people remained outside the vehicles on the streets, but how many more were hidden in the vehicles was unknown to Chancellor Weiderman.

"Nemesio…" Began Chancellor Weiderman, turning to address the man whom she had thought had remained near her. He was nowhere to be found on the rooftop. She turned her attention back to the scene below her and saw the man she had tried to address. He was fast approaching the rear of the APCs, but the government forces did not see him approaching. She redoubled the amount of lead she was sending down at the streets when a bullet struck her in the shoulder, knocking her to the ground. She listened as multiple rounds continued to strike the side of the building she was on while others streaked past her into the night. She struggled to regain her grip on her rifle and commence shooting again when the entire building she was on shook and the night was illuminated with a great intensity of light and heat. She rolled to the edge of the building and was rewarded with a view of success, the APCs were torn apart and the steel was melting under a great blaze. The remaining government forces had rallied around these two vehicles, and were killed in the blast that Nemesio had caused. Chancellor Weiderman radioed for the rest of her forces to rally to her. Nemesio was the first one to reach her. Only three others arrived, half of what she hoped had remained. Everyone but Nemesio was injured in some way. They helped each other off of the building, carrying what they could of the weapons they had brought. Nemesio helped them into one of the vehicles they had brought and then walked off into the night by himself. Chancellor Weiderman felt in awe of him once again. She was equally terrified and intrigued by Nemesio. She prepared herself to give her report to Chancellor Silas. He was not likely to be happy, but she planned on telling him the full truth, regardless of the consequences. Anything less Weiderman considered a betrayal of the Stasi and Silas's trust.

November 26, 32 PAW

9:18

"Commander Franklin, I understand you wished to speak with me." Agmund said as he casually scanned the room. Half unpacked boxes that had been sitting in there for weeks suggested just how busy Commander Franklin had been since he assumed the leadership of the CRZ.

Commander Franklin blurted out what was on his mind, his emotional anxiety clearly showing. "Lieutenant Longstreth and the rest of the team I had sent with her were slain. You were correct in your suspicions of both my source and the wisdom of sending out the attack convoy. They were ambushed heavily, we are assuming by Stasi forces. I can ill afford to keep losing so many men, and I can only think of one person that may be just as capable, if not more capable than Lieutenant Longstreth." Franklin paused for a second, thinking of how dear she had been to his heart. That was an area that she would never be replaced in. "Agmund, that person is you. I need you to replace Lieutenant Longstreth, but not only that. I am personally charging you with the task of discovering who was responsible for her death and bringing him or her alive to me!"

"Do you have information that could help me?"

"I know very little other than she was killed with a .223 caliber hollow point round fired from an assault rifle. It was the very first bullet fired in the battle last night. It was likely to have been fired from a professional and specifically for her. Is there anything else I can do to help you bring this dog to lay at my feet?"

"I will be able do my job most effectively Commander Franklin if you allow me to operate much as I always have, outside the system alone instead of the way Lieutenant Longstreth operated. However, utilizing the resources of your department and occasionally extra personnel and equipment, I will be able to accomplish much more than ever before."

"That is for the best. I know that you are not Lieutenant Longstreth, and I am not asking you to be her. However, I am asking you to take a much increased load upon yourself to compensate for this tragic turn of events."

"That I will strive to do to the best of my ability."

"Good. First I want you to find and bring the informant to me that gave me the information that led to the failure of the mission. The name of the informant is Jasper. He is a Christian man who I once allowed to go free for giving me the names and locations of a dozen other Christians. He occasionally comes back to me and gives me information in exchange for money. He frequents gambling parlors. His favorite is known to be The Lucky Horseshoe. This is a picture of him. Hopefully he will know something that may help our investigation." Commander Franklin handed a picture of a redhead, freckled man who appeared to be much younger than he actually was.

"I will look for him and bring him to you."

"That would be a good start."

November 26, 32 PAW

10:11

Chancellor Silas let out a string of curse words before beginning to yell directly at Chancellor Weiderman. "Why the hell did you go forward with the ambush when you knew you were not prepared for such an attack force?! You know we are out gunned, out manned, and out funded by the government forces. We cannot afford to trade blows with them! You are lucky that Nemesio was there to save you! Maybe I should have sent him to make sure you did not hurt our cause instead of the other way around!"

Chancellor Weiderman flushed with embarrassment and anger. She was embarrassed because she knew he was right. Nemesio had acted in a way that was much wiser than she had and that would have ultimately helped the cause of the Stasi better. The anger came from the fact that she expected better of herself. She vowed to serve the Stasi better. They had raised her after her family was killed by the government and she deserved to give her best back to them. While all this ran through her mind, Chancellor

Silas was waiting for a response. Chancellor Weiderman was struggling to come up with a response, when a knock on the door rescued her from having to come up with an answer. She looked and saw Nemesio again and felt just a twinge of envy of him, but then pushed it aside. She knew she could not afford such feelings. He confidently strode in, and took a seat next to Chancellor Weiderman on a comfortable leather chair that was identical to the one that she was on. He always seemed to have such impeccable timing and was never stressed. Nothing seemed to bother him. Again, Chancellor Weiderman had to consciously push that slight feeling of envy away.

"Good, Nemesio you are here. I had an assignment I was going to give to Chancellor Weiderman, but I believe I can trust you with this task more." Chancellor Weiderman's heart was crushed at this statement. How could Chancellor Silas just discard her so easily after all they had been through together? "One of my top men, Chancellor Jardoni has recently been discovered to be a source of information to the government. Luckily, he has not been one of my best leaders so he has had precious little information to give. The problem is, some of the men are very attached to him and I fear that they may leave our cause or even outright oppose it if it is discovered that I am the one who ordered his death. You must cause it without it being able to come back to the Stasi. It is a most delicate undertaking. I trust you will be able to accomplish it though."

"No offense, Chancellor Silas. But I came here to talk to you about something much more important. I vowed to kill the Council members and Supreme Commander Larkin. I do not care about this Chancellor Jardoni."

"Nemesio, I have the information you need and more is constantly being gathered. Your vow is my top mission as well, but I need you to do this favor for me first. Once this is done I will release you onto your quest. Can you agree to that?"

Chancellor Weiderman, although still quite crushed by Silas's sudden distrust of her abilities, cringed at Silas's response. She feared how Nemesio would respond. He had already made it abundantly clear he was tired of waiting.

"Of course I can. It will be a nice warm-up before the real fun begins." Nemesio said. He seemed quite happy now that he knew he would soon be able to start his quest as Chancellor Silas put it. Nemesio stayed in the room as Chancellor Silas switched his attention back to Chancellor Weiderman.

"As for you, Chancellor Weiderman," Chancellor Silas' entire demeanor and expression changed to that of one that was almost openly hostile. "You will lead the defenses of our church base. It seems as though that may have been the intended target of the attack that occurred last night. You need to be ready to stop another attack. We can ill afford to lose anymore bases, we have only three left. Between that and the diminishing number of safe houses, the number of safe places I can stay is fast disappearing. I fear if they manage to tighten the noose any tighter I may be caught in it. Once I am gone, the entire Stasi organization will likely fall. Even though you lost so many men in the ambush last night, I am certain you can manage to repel an attack that you are expecting and have time to prepare for. Even you should be up to that task for I once remember a time when I had so much hope for you."

"I will not disappoint you again, Chancellor Silas." She genuinely wanted to follow through on this second chance. Weiderman resolved that nothing was going to stop her from doing the best job she could this time.

Chapter VII

November 28, 32 PAW

21:14

Agmund walked through the door of The Lucky Horseshoe. Gambling was legal in Maevin. Some even tried it as a career, but few did so out of choice and with any success. Often the gambling was rigged and there were many citizens of Maevin that could not escape the perpetual poverty of gambling. Those that ran the gambling houses got rich, and some of the employees enjoyed a fair salary, although the working conditions were poor. Gambling houses often employed prostitutes as well, which was perfectly legal as well as long as an expensive permit was acquired through the government. Many gambling/prostitution houses operated without this permit and ran the constant danger of being shut down. The Lucky Horseshoe was one of the more successful non-licensed gambling houses that had been lucky enough not to get shut down yet.

Once inside The Lucky Horseshoe, Agmund attracted a lot of attention. He was dressed in his usual all white cloak and boldly displayed his sword at his hip. Immediately a few of the security bouncers confronted him. "What makes you think you can come in here with that archaic weapon?" snarled the largest of them, crossing his arms to make his large arms look even more threatening while the dim lights played off of his bald head. Tucked into his waistband was a prominently displayed handgun.

"My issue is not with you, I merely require one of your patrons to come with me."

"You said two things wrong there, buddy. Issues with my patrons are my issue and you are not capable of requiring anything of me. Now leave before myself and my friends throw you out of here." The bouncer's voice was full of bravado as he and his friends crowded closer to Agmund, although their eyes were definitely keeping track of his keen sword.

"I do not wish to shed any of your or your friends' blood. Let me be about my business and you will be a happier man for it." Agmund stated quietly.

"I cannot allow that as long as you carry your sword." The ringleader growled.

"I cannot depart from this sword. I can promise you however that it will not be drawn in this place."

"You are right. It won't be!" Roared the leader.

With that the ringleader threw a right cross that connected directly on the point of Agmund's chin. The force snapped Agmund's head back and caused him to stagger a few steps back. However, Agmund remained on his feet. The ringleader of the bouncers was astonished; he had knocked out men twice the size of Agmund before with that same punch. Taking advantage of the surprise of the lead bouncer, Agmund instantly advanced fighting bare-handed. He punched the ringleader in the throat, followed with a left to the diaphragm, and then while the leader was bent over double he grabbed the back of the leader's head with both hands and brought his knee up powerfully, connecting with the bouncer's nose. The knee broke the nose and caused the ringleader's vision to blur. He blindly struck out, but Agmund had already advanced to the other two bouncers. A quick kick to the temple dropped the first one. The other one was smaller, but younger than the other two and he managed to deflect the first couple of swings Agmund had thrown. However, a quick kick to the side of the knee tore the ligaments and crippled him. The man fell to the ground and a swift elbow behind his left ear knocked the man unconscious.

The next instant however found Agmund in a precarious situation. The ring leader of the bouncers had finally shaken the tears and blood out of his eyes. His massive arms wrapped around the torso of Agmund from behind and lifted him bodily into the air. Agmund found himself in the air with no chance at getting any leverage. The entire time he was in the air the bouncer's arms stayed constricted around his chest, not allowing Agmund to breathe. He knew he needed to extract himself from the perilous position, but there was nothing near for him to grab. He tried slamming the back of his head into the already broken nose of the bouncer, but the bouncer had been prepared against that tired trick. Agmund swung his heel back towards the groin of the bouncer, but it found empty air as well. The bouncer had not foolishly lifted Agmund high enough to allow that move to work either. The bouncer was far too experienced for either cheap trick to work. Agmund's vision started to cloud over. In a desperate push to stay conscious and extradite himself from the arms of his foe, Agmund grabbed the forearms of his adversary and pushed himself up. Then he swung his heel back and connected with the man's groin. The bouncer just gritted his teeth and smiled. He was wearing a cup; experience had taught him this expediency. Agmund continued pushing himself up and then swung his heel back again, this time connecting with the man's stomach. This enabled him to twist himself out of the bouncer's now loosened grip. The bouncer tried recovering, and Agmund himself desperately needed a deep breath. He took the breath however as he swung his knee again up into the nose of the bouncer. The bouncer could not be given a chance to draw his gun out. He then drove the point of his elbow directly onto the third vertebrae of the man's neck, breaking it. The man fell with a thud to the ground dead.

Everyone in the gambling house paused for a few tense moments as Agmund surveyed the room for additional threats and to see if he could ascertain the position of the man he sought. The rest of the bouncers stayed away from Agmund, although Agmund knew the police would be called quickly. He hoped that Commander Franklin would intercede on his behalf and not allow the dispatcher to send anyone. It would not be long for him to be freed of any charges by Commander Franklin if he was arrested, but he did not want to have to attempt his mission at another time.

As he finished his survey of the room, Agmund noted the target at the bar trying to talk to one of the beautiful bartenders. He seemed largely unconcerned with the events that had just unfolded as he was oblivious to whom Agmund was and that the events had unfolded because Agmund was sent to retrieve himself.

Taking advantage of his target's complete lack of caution, Agmund closed the thirty feet between himself and his target and threw his arm around the man's neck from behind and began to choke him before Jasper even could turn around. Jasper planted his feet in an attempt to throw his assailant over his back to where he could strike at him, but Agmund was too quick for that. He kicked the back of the man's knee and tightened his grip on the man's throat to further weaken him. Jasper then threw elbow after elbow into Agmund's stomach. Agmund nearly let go with each blow, but he managed to hang on. Jasper was out cold after 15 seconds. Agmund looked around to make sure no one would try to stop him and then hoisted Jasper's considerable heft over his shoulder and walked out of the door with him. No one dared to move to stop him. Once outside Agmund listened and was grateful that he heard no sirens in the distance. Commander Franklin had served his purposes well once again.

November 28, 32 PAW
23:46

Deep in the convoluted basement of the CRZ building, tucked away among all the essential equipment and rooms for running and maintaining such a large building was the room into which Agmund carried Jasper. Jasper was still unconscious, but Agmund knew that could not last for much longer, particularly not for someone with the physique of Jasper. Jasper was a man that stood approximately six feet three inches tall and had a solid frame of 250 pounds with very little fat on him. He was fairly young, being most likely in his mid to upper twenties. His black hair was already starting to recede, but was still thick in most places. He was typically an active man with a face that never stopped shifting expression and taking in everything around him, but that was of course not the case as Agmund carried him into the room to which he had been told he could find Commander Franklin. Agmund had memorized the architectural layout of the building, but the room he found himself going into was nowhere on that map. He had a deep suspicion that he knew what the purpose of the room was.

As he opened the door that seemed to lead to yet another maintenance closet Agmund's suspicions were confirmed. The room was set up with dentist chair retro-fitted with numerous straps. A cupboard next to the chair was open and held all kinds of instruments of torture in it. A water tank was at the other end; a large hose could quickly fill the tank, or be used to hose down anything in the room into the sizeable drain in the middle of the room. At the middle of the room was an open space where the floor was stained with blood. The walls and ceilings obviously had been sprayed to be soundproof as well. Some bloodstains were even visible on these surfaces.

Commander Franklin was standing at the cupboard, picking up and examining different instruments. Agmund viewed torture as dishonorable, but he was not about to tell his new boss what to do. He hoped that the torture would not be necessary, that it was all for show, but the blood stains all around him told an entirely different story.

Agmund finished scanning the room for all the information he could garner. With that done he allowed the door to slip out of his grasp and quietly shut. Commander Franklin turned around at the sound from his work of organizing and inspecting the various tools he had available to him. He seemed quite pleased. "Ah, you have arrived just on time. You have gotten yourself off to a very good start. He did not prove too difficult to subdue did he?"

"No, he did not prove too difficult. I had the element of surprise on him." Agmund mentioned nothing of the bouncers, nor his still hurting side, but not out of any desire other than he wished to give Commander Franklin as little information as was necessary to keep him satisfied.

"He may not have been any problems, but I hear one of the bouncers gave you a run for your money." Commander Franklin said with a smirk.

"That he did. I even considered breaking my promise to not draw my sword in that place, but that would have been ignoble." Agmund chastised himself for thinking that in his first mission for Commander Franklin following Lieutenant Longstreth's death that he had not kept a close eye on his every move. Not only that, but whoever had reported on his actions had done so without Agmund's knowledge that he was being watched. However, Agmund could not be at blame. Commander Franklin had planted someone in The Lucky Horseshoe where he knew Agmund would go. Everyone had watched Agmund tear the place apart. It had been incredibly easy for Commander Franklin's informant to observe Agmund's every move with Agmund not knowing it. He had not exactly taken great pains to be discreet during the mission to extract Jasper.

"Shall we begin?" Asked Commander Franklin.

"As you wish, sir." Agmund said. He neither wanted to show too much approval or disapproval for what was about to occur.

Agmund strapped Jasper down into the chair. Commander Franklin splashed Jasper's face with water, but that did not succeed in waking him up. Franklin shrugged and then broke open a stick and passed it under Jasper's nose to bring him to consciousness. Agmund could almost taste the bitterness of the chemical from his position ten feet away.

"Ah, Jasper my good friend. You are awake now. Now we can talk." It had obviously taken a while for Jasper to ascertain who was even speaking to him, and as he realized who it was, Agmund and Franklin could see the fear grow on his face. The environment in which he discovered himself in did little to ease his trepidation. "I am sorry for the rough manner in which my associate brought you here, but it was necessary as you seem to have been avoiding me for a little while now. Now, I ask myself, why that would be? Can you answer that question for me?" Commander Franklin paused, but the terrified face of Jasper made no inclination towards speech. Commander Franklin grabbed a handful of metal splinters and a lighter from the cupboard near him before continuing in his condescending manner. "Well, I can venture a guess Jasper. I hypothesize that you feel guilty for feeding me wrong information, information that led to the death of so many of my agents, not the least of whom was Lieutenant Longstreth. So, because of this you have decided to avoid me because it is just tearing you apart." As Commander Franklin uttered this last phrase he shoved a metal splinter under the middle right fingernail of Jasper. He then applied the burning lighter to the end of the metal splinter. It began to heat quickly, the metal being an alloy that heated rapidly but was slow to lose its heat. Jasper's screams pierced the stank, still air of the basement room as the metal splinter first cut deep into his finger and then heated and burned the inside of it.

"Did you not think that I would find you though? I know you too well. We have worked together too long Jasper. This is the end of the line for our relationship however. You betray my trust once, and it is done. Unfortunately so is your life." Commander Franklin said harshly. He turned the lighter off and instantly switched his tone of voice to one a consoling mother might use. "But, it's okay. All I need to know is who supplied you with the information. Who played you like a puppet to betray me? Where can I find this person or group? If you tell me this, your death will be quick and painless. Do you see this syringe I have here?" Commander Franklin held up a syringe filled with a yellow liquid. "This magical liquid will end your life free of pain. It will be over before the needle is even pulled out. However, if you give me no information I will be forced into dealing you much bodily pain. Just give me the information I need."

Jasper hesitated. Commander Franklin was confused, and angry. He had always been able to prey upon Jasper's fears and manipulate him any way he wanted. What had changed? Was it possible that he had something greater to fear outside of the room he was in, although it was out of sight and not likely to ever be able to ever affect him again?

"Jasper, Jasper, Jasper, you disappoint me." Continued Commander Franklin, still taking the comforter role. "You have never been a hero. Do not start now at the end of your life. Remember, the power to choose between a painless death and one full of agony is up to you."

"I…I…know very little." Jasper said hesitantly, as if the words were caught in his throat.

"That is okay, I am a powerful man with powerful resources. I can do a lot with very little. Just tell me what you know and it will all be over soon."

"What I do know is that the information was not false, but it was purposefully leaked to you. There is a Stasi base at the location that I gave to you. They never intended for you to reach it however. At the same time information was leaked to the Stasi to waylay you on your route, telling them that it was merely a Stasi prisoner transport. Their goal was for the two groups to destroy each other to almost nothing, and it worked. Both sides suffered a high amount of casualties as planned."

"Who is they, Jasper?" Commander Franklin asked desperately. He needed to know who to punish for his own personal suffering.

"They is the Christians."

Commander Franklin was surprised. He had thought the battle with the Christians was almost over, which is why most of his recent efforts consisted of eliminating the Stasi. "The Christians are almost extinct. How are they capable of doing this? What hope do they have? The only hope that they have is the hope that they share with you, that their deaths will be quick and painless."

"Rumor in the Christian community has it that there is a new man who may or may not be a Christian who is helping us out. He is the one who is giving Christians hope. Some even claim the man is an avenging angel of God. He is God's arm stretching out to punish those that oppress Christians." Jasper spoke of the man as reverently as though he really were an angel. Commander Franklin looked both surprised, but disbelieving at this information. He had no belief in the Christians' God. But, he was also surprised to find Jasper believing it. Jasper had never really expressed a genuine reverence for anything Christian before. Indeed, just the fact that he implied himself as part of the Christian groups denoted how much had changed in recent months.

"Do you know anything else about this man?" Commander Franklin asked. Agmund leaned forward subconsciously intent on hearing the answer clearly.

"No, I do not. I do not know of anyone who knows anything about him. I just thought he was a myth. Now I am not so sure. I found out later what I had told you about it being a set-up to both sides."

"Thank you Jasper. Now, I know you are a coward, but you have repeatedly proved to be a useful coward. You appear to be a very strong man, too bad the tenacity of your spirit does not match the tenacity of your tendons. You also as I understand take weekly classes down at the dojo. Although I promised you death, I feel compelled to give you a chance to fight for your life, literally. If you defeat me in hand-to-hand combat you will go free out of this building with only that cut under your fingernail to show for your failure of me. If you lose, I will give you this yellow liquid to end your misery."

Commander Franklin nodded to Agmund, the only attention he had paid Agmund since Jasper came to consciousness. Agmund responded to the nod by undoing the straps holding Jasper tightly to the chair. Jasper got up stiffly and stretched to loosen up the limbs that he had not been able to use. Commander Franklin stripped this shirt off to avoid getting any blood on it. Agmund was quite impressed by the physique of Commander Franklin. His baggy shirt that he wore at work gave little the impression that such a ripped man was beneath the exterior of projected professionalism. Franklin stood there patiently giving his opponent time to stretch.

"Are you ready now Jasper?" Commander Franklin asked.

"Sure." Jasper said nervously, already betraying his lack of confidence.

"Very well, let's begin."

The two quickly closed the distance between them, Commander Franklin out of confidence, Jasper out of nervous energy. Quickly after the two fists touched, Commander Franklin struck out with his right leg and kicked Jasper in the ear. The quickness and power of the blow surprised both Agmund and Jasper. Commander Franklin watched with a smile as Jasper fell to one knee and then struggled to get himself balanced again on both his feet. Commander Franklin then faked the same kick and then landed a hard right uppercut onto the pointed jaw of Jasper. Jasper staggered back a few feet, but this time recovered more quickly and threw a quick spinning kick aimed at the head of Commander Franklin. Commander Franklin was surprised at the quickness and had only managed to barely duck the kick when a second spin sent the same leg much lower this time towards Franklin's midsection. Commander Franklin deftly caught the leg and threw Jasper hard onto the concrete floor. Again Commander Franklin did not press his advantage, but Agmund suspected it was not out of a sense of honor as much as prolonged revenge.

"When I said you could fight for your life, I imagined you may actually fight. This pathetic display is not fighting!

How do you expect me to enjoy avenging Longstreth's death if you let me win so easily?" Commander Franklin gloated, but a simmering rage still boiled.

Jasper got up off the ground and charged in a blind rage at Commander Franklin. Commander Franklin blocked each of the blows that were furiously thrown. Emotion was a poor substitute for mental readiness to fight. Commander Franklin threw a hard left hook behind the right ear of Jasper. Then he followed up with the heel of his right hand to the nose of Jasper. Jasper crumpled to the ground and then Commander Franklin hovered over the body of Jasper and repeatedly slammed both fists alternately into the already bloody face of Jasper.

Jasper fell unconscious quickly under the steady stream of blows to the face. Commander Franklin got up and wiped off the blood that covered his fists and upper body with a towel. Then he took the syringe with the yellow liquid and injected into the jugular vein of Jasper.

"Good old Jasper is going to be in for a bitter surprise when he wakes up. The poison in here will make him bleed out of every orifice of his body for hours and cause him the worse migraine imaginable until eventually he bleeds to death."

"Then why did you fight him? He is obviously going to be punished enough." Agmund wondered out loud.

"I am not going to be around to enjoy it. Besides, this pathetic scum whom even gives Christians a bad name deserves a death worse than the one I just resigned him to. I also relished what I thought would be a challenge of my hand-to-hand skills, but it was none at all in the end. It was a terrible disappointment."

"Well, your skills seemed to be quite sharp indeed. The man knew what he was doing at least in theory, though I doubt the coward had fought much in reality."

"You are very astute in your observation and conclusions Agmund. Now, let's see how acute your observations and conclusions are in regard to something else. I will use every resource I can to find out who is behind this Christian ploy. My biggest resource I am depending on is you. Let us work together to bring down this new threat. My revenge is not yet complete. The next biggest issue is the fact that there is still a Stasi base that Lieutenant Longstreth failed to destroy. I want you to lead that attack. You best do so before they set up defenses or abandon the base."

"We have our work cut out for us; Jasper gave us precious little information, on both the man helping out the Christians and the base."

"Well, then let us waste no time. Leave him here. I will send someone to clean up his body later in the day, once he's dead."

November 29, 32 PAW

2:38

Paul had ordered Rhys to follow up on a report of a missing Christian who was reputedly a government informant. Rhys's assignment had led him to many different people and dead ends, but in the end he was able to track Jasper's last known position to the CRZ headquarters. Once Rhys informed Paul of what he had learned Paul had managed to obtain a maintenance uniform and clearance card for Rhys. Rhys assumed Paul was able to do so from a Christian that he knew who worked at the building as a maintenance man. Since so many CRZ personnel were killed in the explosion Rhys had set off, an extensive background check of maintenance employees would have not been very effectively carried out. Rhys donned the uniform, but still kept a gun under his clothes. The clearance card would give him access to a maintenance door that led directly into the basement floor. It was a level that was supposedly full of facility equipment and storage, but rumors of something much more menacing brought Rhys down to this level. Rhys seemed to know exactly where he was going once inside the basement. He soon came to a door that appeared in every regard identical to all the ones he had seen thus far, but his hair stood on end as he stood before the door. As he pressed his ear to the door he thought he heard faint screaming, but disregarded it as his imagination. He quietly but quickly picked the lock open and then slowly opened the door.

The first sense that assaulted Rhys was the smell of old bleach and new blood in the damp air. Then his eyes saw into the darkness inside and it showed him the dim outline of a small room outfitted for one single purpose, that of torture. He concentrated on seeing the finer details of the room from the doorway, not wanting to venture inside the room unless he needed to. A scream of pain pierced the quiet. Rhys located the source of the sound as coming from a lump on the ground that he had missed in scanning the room earlier. Rhys knew what he was about to see would not be pretty, but was something he had to see. He brought the door close to closing, but left it open just an inch in case it would lock him in from behind, which he was certain it would. Those that used the room would not want any of the victims to leave once they entered it. Rhys walked to the corner and knelt down beside a prostrate figure. He rolled the man's face over so he could see it. The face was terribly beaten, but that is not what shocked Rhys the most. Coming from the mouth, nose, ears, and eyes were steady streams of blood. The face of the man stayed contorted in an expression full of anguishing pain. Then Rhys recognized that it was the man he was seeking, Jasper.

As he continued looking spellbound at Jasper, he could tell Jasper could not sense his presence. Jasper was in far too much pain for that. The physical anguish that Jasper was going through was so incredible that it forced him into his own little world of pain, his brain not being able to process anything else. Rhys shook his head and began taking video of the room and the victim on the floor. After a couple of minutes Rhys was satisfied with what he had captured. He believed the government of Maevin was soon to be overthrown, and he wanted to be assured that no one could ever forget the atrocities that had been committed by that perverted government. This proof was nearly irrefutable and would serve the next government well in exposing and informing the citizens of Maevin the barbarism of its former government. Before leaving the room, Rhys bent down and broke the neck of Jasper, putting him out of his pain. Shaking his head that this merciful action may have put the secrecy of his mission into jeopardy, he left the room, and soon the basement. He managed to leave the building without being detected. He felt very thankful that Paul had been able to assist him. It was not often that Rhys was rewarded for the things he did for Paul.

Chapter VIII

November 30, 32 PAW

22:10

Commander Matthew was no commander at all in the martial sense of the word. He was a very powerful man never the less. He was one of six Council members who advised Supreme Commander Larkin. Commander Matthew's particular specialty was finances. Ever since he had graduated from Maevin's only University at the tender age of seventeen with a triple degree of Finances, Marketing, and Accounting he had delved into the world of banking and soon found himself being recruited by Supreme Commander Larkin. As a Council member he enjoyed a lavish lifestyle, but ran the constant risk of upsetting Supreme Commander Larkin. Indeed, the previous Council Member in charge of Finances had needed to be replaced because he had upset Supreme Commander Larkin, and paid with his life to appease Larkin's rage.

Commander Matthew had served faithfully for several years, but was still the youngest member of the Council at age 31. He enjoyed the lifestyle and lived with no fear.

He had done so since he had accepted the open position on the Council, knowing that to make decisions based on self-preservation would indeed make him more likely to die. He approached his job logically and it consumed his life. He had no family, and indeed no plans to ever have one. Girlfriends he had plenty of, as he was a tall, thin man that while he looked slightly nerdy was attractive, though all of his girlfriends were more attracted to his deep pockets than him himself.

He was leaving from a very expensive, upscale restaurant in the center of the city with one of these girlfriends, this one a curvy, voluptuous Asian named Airi. Once outside the restaurant they decided to head to her apartment for the night which Commander Matthew paid for. It was only a few blocks away so they strolled along walking off part of their dinners and chatting pleasantly.

The streets were quite busy that evening, everyone trying to make it to their destination before the city-wide curfew came into effect. Commander Matthew and Airi soon reached the apartment complex and rode the elevator to the top floor. Commander Matthew began lustfully kissing Airi as no one else was in the elevator. Airi let him, knowing he would not take no for an answer. She did not love him, but she did love the lifestyle he enabled her to have. In her opinion, giving him what he wanted on occasion was more than worth it to enjoy the life she led.

Once they reached the top floor, Commander Matthew still did not stop kissing her even as the door opened. He had his back to the now open elevator. Airi looked over his shoulder at the open door and saw a man dressed in black tactical gear with a knife held in his right arm. She tried screaming, but could not as Commander Matthew's lips were smothering hers. He noticed her change in behavior, but by then it was too late. The stranger had already thrust the knife blade deep into the base of Commander Matthew's neck angling up towards the brain. He was dead before he hit the floor of the elevator. Now, Airi was free to scream, but she was too shocked to do so. She moved away in fear of the stranger until her back was firmly pressed against the rear of the elevator. The stranger stood silently in the elevator doorway looking down upon Airi.

"Are, are you going to kill me?" asked Airi meekly, finally finding her voice.

"It depends on whether or not you are going to tell everyone the truth about what happened here." The stranger said.

"I won't tell a soul, I swear if you just let me live!"

"You won't tell a soul if I kill you as well, but that is not what I want. I want you to tell everyone the truth, not what the government is going to tell you to say. I want you to tell them that Nemesio, an agent of the Stasi, killed Commander Matthew. Not only that, but he is going to kill the rest of the Council members as well. Once that is done, he will kill Supreme Commander Larkin and there is nothing anyone can do to stop him. The government will fall, it must fall. If you do not tell the media that the killer said this to you, I will kill you as well, Airi." Nemesio threw the girl's name in to frighten her even more.

Nemesio stared into the frightened girl's eyes; in them he could see her complete fear of him. He almost felt sorry for the girl for a second, but knew he needed her to be that scared of him. He took a step back and the elevator quietly closed shut and headed back down towards the lobby with Airi still in the elevator staring wide-eyed at the corpse of Commander Matthew.

December 2, 32 PAW

4:53

Nemesio had pored over the file on Chancellor Jardoni multiple times. The man was a hardcore military man who was extremely regimented in his schedule. He woke up every morning at 5 am. From 6 to 8 am he exercised. Then from 8 to noon he was in his office attending to the tasks Head Chancellor Silas wanted him to accomplish for the Stasi. At noon he ate with his men. The rest of the afternoon was spent interacting with his charges in meetings. During the evening he again tended to more office work. It surprised Nemesio that such a regimented man would be a traitor as well. It was typically the undisciplined ones that were traitors.

As Nemesio planned the assassination, it irked him that he had to do so discreetly. There were so many more easy and effective ways to kill Chancellor Jardoni that would not allow him to accomplish Chancellor Silas's goal of keeping the true nature of the hit discreet. Nemesio had debated the pros and cons of how exactly to proceed with the mission. In the end however, Nemesio knew he had to go with Chancellor Silas' wishes if he was to accomplish his overarching goal of toppling the government of Maevin. He could kill the members of the Council without the information Silas possessed, but it would take much longer. The longer his quest took the more risk he ran of being discovered and killed before Larkin died.

Nemesio strode confidently through the city streets a few minutes before five am. He was in the center of the city, Chancellor Jardoni being one of the few Stasi that allowed himself to enjoy the comforts that the center of the city afforded, despite the increased risk of being discovered as a member of the Stasi in the stronghold of the government. Nemesio had no set plan; he was just going to follow his mark until an opportunity presented itself. The strict schedule of Chancellor Jardoni would make it easy to follow him as Nemesio could do so with minimal visual contact.

December 2, 32 PAW

23:00

Chancellor Jardoni was leaving his office at exactly twenty-three hundred hours as he always did. In part he did it just to break the curfew, but it also gave him an hour to unwind at home and then he could get his five hours of sleep, which was all that he allowed himself. As always he walked alone, but had his custom 9 mm handgun in the engraved holster of his right hip. He walked quickly, but in a very quiet manner. There was no particular reason he was either in a hurry or being quiet, it was just a permanent habit.

As he was walking, he heard a slight shuffle of feet behind him and his hand went to his pistol as he attempted to turn around. However, strong hands from behind prevented him from doing so. One hand removed the handgun while the other hand pressed a cloth to the nose and mouth of Chancellor Jardoni. Chancellor Jardoni managed to resist the urge to breathe and tried head butting his adversary. He felt the attacker's arms, but he could not seem to land any blows. He desperately attempted to drive his elbows into the attacker's body, but to no avail. He still could not find a body to go with the arms around him. He felt the lack of oxygen beginning to cause him to lose consciousness. It was then that he made the mistake of taking a deep breath in. The rag smelled like alcohol, which denoted that the liquid of choice being used to put him under was chloroform. He knew he had only a few seconds before he fainted. In his desperation he struck at the arms of the assailant, which accomplished nothing. He sunk to the cold concrete unconscious.

No one was around to see it, and even if anyone had, they would be lawbreakers as the curfew had gone into effect over an hour again. It would not have been likely that they would have done anything to help. Maevin's finest were too busy patrolling other areas to bother with the center of the city. They thought they had it under control, a fact which had served Chancellor Jardoni well until now.

December 3, 32 PAW

1:16

Chancellor Jardoni groggily came to consciousness. He took a deep breath in; he was panicked and worried about his situation. After the initial panic, his training kicked in and he began to determine where he was at. His eyes opened up and he was shocked to find that he was standing on a chair in the bedroom of his own apartment. He then felt a slight weight on his shoulders. Looking down he noticed it was a rope looped around his neck. Tracing the rope he saw that the other end was tied to the ceiling joists. There was not much slack in the rope. The chair he was on was definitely higher than the amount of slack that was in the rope. However, it was not a far enough fall to break the neck. If that chair was moved he would choke to death. There was no doubt to the purpose of his assailant, to murder him but to make it appear as a suicide. The question that remained was who, and why.

Chancellor Jardoni waited for nearly an hour on the chair, feeling hungry, thirsty, and desperate. He had tried every way of freeing himself, but to no avail. His hands and legs were bound tightly, but with a soft cloth in order to not leave any markings that would betray the masquerade of a suicide. Chancellor Jardoni was considering ending it himself and trying to kick the chair out from underneath him when finally a stranger in black military garb with a bald head swaggered in from the kitchen as he finished eating a cold meat sandwich.

"The end is near. The Stasi are failing, and soon I fear I will be discovered. I would rather end my life myself than be tortured and finally be killed by the government of Maevin once they have torn every piece of knowledge about the Stasi from me, which is a considerable amount. Thus I have chosen my end. May it not be as I fear and that the city of Maevin may eventually be freed from the tyranny of its government. Signed by… you, Chancellor Jardoni." Nemesio read on a piece of paper he held in his hands. "Look, it is even in your own handwriting." Nemesio shoved the paper closer to the face of Chancellor Jardoni. The paper indeed held his handwriting, uncannily accurate. "But, we both know that you did not write this note, nor indeed that it holds the truth. For the truth of the matter is that you are being killed for being a traitor to the cause of the Stasi. The government of Maevin does not have to torture you to gain information. They merely need to pay you."

Chancellor Jardoni had at first been unnerved by this stranger, but now he laughed. The laughter seemed to surprise Nemesio. "I do not know where you got your information or your orders from soldier, but you are dead wrong."

"Well, then let the dead man correct the man who is dead wrong."

"Sure, what have I to lose? You were closer with the suicide note than you are with your so called truth. The truth is I would rather die than betray the secrets of the Stasi. The government of Maevin must fall. They have far too long oppressed the people. They killed my family a long time ago. I have worked ceaselessly and faithfully to avenge their deaths ever since. That is but one small example of the horrors committed by this government."

The stranger seemed to no longer be paying attention. He had been extremely attentive until the comment about Chancellor Jardoni's family being killed. Then a sudden change was enacted upon the man and he appeared as though his mind was far from the present situation in the room. There was an eerily quiet moment until Nemesio's mind wondered back into the room. Once it did, he spoke as though nothing had occurred. "I can tell you say the truth, Chancellor Jardoni, you are no traitor. Chancellor Silas ordered your death. Do you know why he would have done so?"

"The old man finally found the guts to off me? It is a pity he did not do so himself in open combat. Instead he stays in his shadowy deceit and allows his pawns to do the dirty work for him. Of course I know why, I am the only man that can threaten his position as the unchallenged leader of the Stasi. I treat my men much better than he and they do not die needlessly. Chancellor Silas cannot boast of that. It is no wonder the Stasi are crumpling. He has spent the last twenty years quietly killing anyone who became strong enough in the organization to threaten his own leadership. He fears someone taking over control like what happened with Larkin. It has made the Stasi weak, in the end it will be his undoing and he will be the leader of nothing."

"No, he has a different end in store for him; of that alone I am sure." Nemesio said with utter confidence. Once he had done so he grabbed the right leg of Chancellor Jardoni and swung it into the chair knocking it over. Chancellor Jardoni attempted to talk, but no words could escape as he was strangled to death by the rope. Nemesio stood in front of him the entire time, looking him unblinkingly in the eyes until he died. Once that was done he removed the cloth bindings and then exited the apartment leaving the suicide note lying on the ground.

December 6, 32 PAW

0:03

"This is the spot." Agmund stated with authority to the team of professionals that Commander Franklin had assembled for him. A couple of them Agmund felt sure were mercenaries. Commander Franklin was taking no risks with this assignment beyond the biggest one, that of actually attacking the base that both of them knew would be heavily fortified or sabotaged. The Stasi may have decided to leave that base and they would all be walking into a death trap that the Stasi left behind for the government, but both Agmund and Commander Franklin agreed this was unlikely. The number of hiding spots was vanishing for the Stasi, but so was the Maevin's government's ability to drive them out of their hiding spots as more men were lost each day in the civil war. Indeed, their jobs were getting harder on other fronts as well due to ordinary citizens becoming more unruly. Each side had been mutually weakened by their greedy and vain attempts at strengthening each other through weakening the other. The balance in power had changed little. Agmund spoke to his men again, a last chance to talk to the men before the mission started in earnest. "Now make no mistake about it men, the enemy has had a little over a week to fortify this position and to prepare for this attack. I anticipate the worst, and even that will probably be far exceeded. What we know about this base is that it is based on an old Catholic cathedral. There are several wells on this property. The one in the center of the property is a ruse. At the bottom of this well is a series of tunnels. This is where the Stasi are hiding out. We will be bottle-necked in two areas, the top of the well and the bottom of the well. As far as the top of the well is concerned, this bottle-neck should not be an issue. We will be able to take out all defenses above ground before advancing to the well, but we will not have that luxury at the bottom of the well. There is no other route to take that would enable us to avoid the gauntlet of bullets we are likely to face at the bottom. Unfortunately we cannot just blow the well shut. Commander Franklin has demanded we infiltrate the base, capture prisoners, and attempt to ascertain any information of value in the base. The fighting will be fierce, many of us will die. However, I promise in the end the reward will be worth it. We are winning this war. Soon the city will solely be in our control, if we succeed in this mission."

The men looked grimly around at each other, all looking for a sign of weakness in the others that were going on the mission. Any weakness in any of the others would increase the risk of death for all. However, they were all men well accustomed to dealing out death and had experienced far too many close encounters with death themselves that long ago they had accepted their lives would be cut short in the service of the city of Maevin, or in the case of a few of them, the search for money and fame.

Agmund himself had been looking around at the other men as well. He saw too that there was no weakness in these hardened men. When the lead began to fly, none of them would flinch at the chances of getting hit or by the fact that each time they pulled the trigger a fellow human being may perish. Agmund felt satisfied with the men he was given. However, they were not necessarily satisfied with him. Furian, the youngest of the few mercenaries in the group spoke his dissent first. "And what are you going to do with your sword while we are at the front of the attack facing each of these ambushes? Are you going to cower behind us in your white dress or are you going to supervise us only to come at the end and claim the victory for yourself?"

Agmund was not surprised or offended at this young man's words, but spoke earnestly in reply, "I promise you this, I will be responsible for the spilling of more blood tonight than all of you together. You make fun of my white clothing, but it will soon be dripping in red. You best hope that it is not your own blood that stains my tunic."

Such was the sincerity and gravity with which Agmund spoke that no one else dared to challenge him. After an uncomfortable silence, each of the men began final checks on their weapons and took inventory of their ammunition.

Agmund had given a rough idea of the layout and game plan already, but what defenses were in store for the group was beyond even Agmund's knowledge. Therefore the plans were not very elaborate. Agmund would be available to direct the change in plans as needed throughout the mission. During the final couple of minutes of the equipment check, Agmund sat quietly by himself. At the end of the couple of minutes he suddenly stood up with a resolute expression. He climbed in one of the many civilian vehicles they were using to transport themselves discreetly to the location of the assault. The Stasi would already be on the lookout for them, there was no chance of catching them completely off guard, but Agmund's plan of approaching from several different directions at once may cause them to be paralyzed for a moment and give them the slight advantage.

Agmund's vehicle arrived at the front of the church. He asked for the time. One of the men on loan from the SWAT department of the Maevin Police, Dennis, responded that it was 0:28. Agmund nodded his satisfaction, it was the exact time that he had wanted to arrive. Everyone else was scheduled to arrive at precisely 0:29. Agmund got out of the car and promptly rushed towards the front door of the old cathedral. While Agmund ran up the front stairs of the cathedral, bullets began raining down on him from the belfry of the cathedral and from its many broken stained-glass windows. As Agmund had drawn the majority of the fire, Dennis was free to fire an RPG into the front doors of the cathedral. The doors splintered away and seemed to almost dissipate into thin air. Agmund ran boldly through the flames left by the explosion. The rest of the men began to find cover outside and return fire upon the positions they had seen just a few moments before firing upon Agmund.

Meanwhile the other teams arrived right on schedule, and began to slowly advance their way into the center of the property where the well was located. The fighting was fierce and there were many casualties and deaths on both sides. The entrenched position inside the cathedral was paying huge dividends against the overwhelming numbers and firepower of the Maevin government forces. However, it was a closer and deadlier battle than either side wanted.

Once inside the cathedral, Agmund wasted absolutely no time in beginning to remove the defenses that were laid by the Stasi. There were several machine gun nests inside the church, but all of these were designed to kill attackers outside the cathedral and prevent them from reaching the well. The Stasi had not protected the building from an interior attack because the church itself had only a strategic value for covering the courtyards surrounding it. For this reason, there were few designed defenses to stop Agmund once he reached the inside of building. Inside the church he ran quickly through the building. The men he encountered all had their attention to the outside of the cathedral. Few saw his blade coming before they felt its sting. Despite his quick pace, the cathedral was very large, so it took him several minutes to make his way through it. However, by the time he had cleared out the cathedral almost single-handedly, the courtyards outside had been won by the government forces. They were ready to advance down into the well. Agmund gathered his forces and prepared for the second stage of the assault.

"How have they made it so far?!" demanded Chancellor Weiderman. She was desperate. Many of her best shooters had perished in the fighting above her. They had been placed there by her because their truer aims in the open were more critical than the sheer firepower of the battles that would take place in the tunnel. Besides, she had been perfectly confident that none of the attackers would even reach the well. Her confidence was now shaken and she looked at the men around her. They were mostly inexperienced or had proven in previous missions to be far from adept at their jobs. She could see the fear in their eyes, a look that was quite similar to the one she now had.

At the bottom of the well, there were four tunnels. These tunnels divided at a 90 degree angle from this central point. She frantically ordered all of the men to disperse themselves evenly in the four tunnels. Then they all nervously waited for the firestorm to come.

It did not take long to come, there were several flashes at the bottom of the well. Chancellor Weiderman, and the rest of her defenders, had been intently staring at the bottom of the well when the flash bang grenades had blown. Their eyes were momentarily blinded. Chancellor Weiderman's eyes began to clear and she believed she saw a man in red running down the opposite hallway with a sword in hand. She shook her head, such a sight was impossible. Then her eyes became more in focus and she saw many men sliding down the ropes to the bottom of the well. At the bottom of the well, they all lay prone and began firing, each crawling forward to make further room for others to descend. When one of the men was hit, another seemed to replace him. There was seemingly no end to the attackers. Even worse, the bodies of the dead began to pile up and were used as a makeshift cover. Ironically it was now the attackers who were entrenched in. Some of the shots from the defenders began to sail too high and came dangerously near to the defenders in the opposite hallway. The defenders began to direct their fire more carefully. However, their shots were now much less effective. Chancellor Weiderman had relied merely on the fact that these men would need to cover the hallways with bullets. Now that they needed to aim their shots accurately she knew her chances of success were diminishing. Her brash order to take up positions in all four hallways was beginning to haunt her.

A few minutes after the first attackers at the bottom of the well had arrived reinforcements for both sides had extinguished. The number of casualties was extremely high for Agmund's forces and Chancellor Weiderman's forces. As the numbers of participants continued to decrease, the tension conversely increased as the balance of the battle hung on the few remaining lives left.

It was then that Chancellor Weiderman finally noted that no one of the far side of the hallway from her had returned fire for a couple of minutes. She brought out her binoculars to see if she could ascertain if they had abandoned their posts or been killed. Peering through the smoke and muzzle flashes she managed to see over the pile of bodies in the middle of the hallway to see a pile further on the other side. However, this pile of bodies had not been killed by guns, their deaths had been much more personal and gruesome to behold. The bodies in many cases were missing appendages and/or their heads. She began to doubt that the man in red holding a sword had been a mistake her vision had made following the flash grenades.

While she peered through the binoculars with a singular intensity she heard the scream of one of the females behind her. Whirling around, but still careful to keep her head and body low she noted with horror that all those around her but one person was dead. She let out a scream as she realized it was not one of her own soldiers that was the only person still alive, but a man dressed in white and covered in blood. He was already bringing a large sword down on a descending arc aiming for her skull. It was the last sight that Chancellor Weiderman beheld.

Agmund took a deep breath. He was a man that was in terrific shape, but this assault had been of such intensity that he found himself wanting of breath. He had also not escaped wholly uninjured. Several bullets had passed through his clothing, and not all the blood on his originally white clothing had come from the enemies he had slain. A few bullets had grazed him, but all had passed through the muscle of his body without any serious damage being dealt. He walked back towards the bottom of the well. His men were already dispersing themselves into small groups; each team taking a different hallway and making sure no one had survived while also searching for any intelligence that would be helpful. Agmund knew there would be little to nothing of any true value. The Stasi would not have risked any great intelligence being kept in the only base they knew was likely to be attacked. Any intelligence they found would likely be fictitious. Commander Franklin still demanded results though other than just demolishing the base, so Agmund was forced to check.

Agmund allowed himself to feel content that this mission had worked out so well for the government. He knew Commander Franklin had hoped for a successful mission, but did not actually expect one. He was in too desperate of a position and far too emotional to not commit himself wholly to the endeavor, no matter how illogical and dangerous the mission was. Fortunately for Commander Franklin, the planning and personal exploits of Agmund had carried the day. The success of the mission combined with the amount of men left alive would seal the fact that Commander Franklin was a slave to Agmund's service and advice. Agmund smiled as he knew that his plans were fast coming to fruition.

December 6, 32 PAW
6:19

Nemesio walked into one of Chancellor Silas's many offices. He rotated them often to keep one step ahead of the government forces who wanted his head. Larkin had always attempted to end the Stasi threat directly by killing Silas. Lately Larkin had become even more desperate to kill Silas, and Silas was thoroughly enjoying that fact. Chancellor Silas was currently hard at work looking over reports. Nemesio noted in one corner of the desk was a stack of files that had the names of the Council members on the exterior.

"Nemesio, I have greatly desired to speak with you. I thought the arrangement was for you to kill Chancellor Jardoni then I would give you the information you need to kill the Council Members. Did I misunderstand our arrangement?" Chancellor Silas asked in a manner that made it clear to Nemesio that he was not happy, nor did he think he misunderstood the arrangement.

"No Chancellor Silas you did not misunderstand anything. You wanted me to do you a personal favor in exchange for what I had already been promised. I killed Commander Matthew first to send you a clear message. That message is you need me more than I need you. My quest is something I can manage on my own. Your little information would merely make my job easier and quicker. I killed Chancellor Jardoni for you because I understood the value of the man's death."

"Was that your message, huh? Let me tell you my message. Your life is in my hands. If I want you dead it will happen at anytime I desire." Silas was extremely perturbed at Nemesio's lack of obedience. He resorted to threatening his life as he typically did with some of his other associates, though Nemesio was nothing like his other associates.

"Really? I thought the only reason you were letting me go ahead with my quest to kill the Council Members and Larkin is because you can't see any other way to attempt it. You would have been content if I had killed just one or two Council Members. In your eyes I am already a dead man, you just will not risk killing me because you are hoping against hope that I will somehow pull it off. Now that I have killed one Council Member so easily you will not dare to kill me. Even now, you doubt you can actually carry through on your threat."

The two men stared at each other intently. Silas finally broke the silence. "Never mind that issue. I am grateful that both men are dead, it matters not what order. Take your files, but answer me this first. Why did you keep that woman alive? She is telling everyone exactly who you are and what you are planning. I don't even know how she discovered either of those things, but if you had killed her in the first place the problem would have been solved."

"I told her to say all that."

"WHAT?! Why would you so freely give up the element of surprise?"

"Because I need the citizens of this city to know that the Maevin Government can be opposed. They need to know one person can make a difference in this wretched city. They need to know that the government is powerless to stop me."

"You just made your mission infinitely harder."

"I know. I relish the challenge! Think of it, all the cards stacked against me, and yet I will succeed!" Nemesio glowed with pleasure as he spoke. He let out a hearty laugh, but it was cut short by a messenger that came into the room. He whispered into Chancellor Silas' ear. Silas looked as though he had been punched in the stomach and then began to cry. Silas looked up at Nemesio through his tear-filled eyes and said, "This messenger just brought me news that the church base has been overrun. There are no survivors. Chancellor Weiderman failed in her mission and paid with her life. She was almost like my own daughter. I had watched her grow up for so long. To think, the last things I said to her were so harsh…"

"I am sorry to hear that Chancellor Silas." Nemesio said, but he seemed incapable of fully letting himself become emotional over the news. Chancellor Silas did not have that problem. It was a full minute before he spoke again.

"Nemesio, I need you to punish our enemies. Take these files." He handed over the files of the Council Members to Nemesio. "Kill them all, Nemesio, before we Stasi join Weiderman in death!"

"Consider it done." Nemesio said and then left the room, happy to have both the information he wanted and to get out of the room with a very emotional Chancellor Silas.

Chapter IX

December 8, 32 PAW

8:58

Commander Franklin typed away on his keyboard for a lengthy time before finally leaning back in his chair. He turned his attention to his visitor for the first time since the man had entered several minutes earlier. "Agmund, you continue to impress me. You have not only succeeded when I least expected it, but you have done so with many more men left alive than I could have possibly had hoped for. Your actions have continued to serve the government well in a time that we find ourselves most desperately needing it. The Stasi have their backs against the wall. It is time for us to press our advantage."

"What do you have in mind, Commander Franklin?"

"The Stasi have two bases left, we need to find out where those bases are. I have many men working on that. It is only a matter of time. There are only so many places to hide in this city. However, until those bases are found I could use your help on a special assignment. We have a picture of a man who managed to dress up as one of our maintenance men and came into the sublevel basements where we tortured the prisoner, Jasper. It appears as though he made it into the room as well. The man I sent to discard of Jasper's body discovered his neck had been broken. This is the photo of him entering the facility. My employees do not know this, but their security cards are encrypted so we know which one was used. We also take photos of the person every time they enter the building. It was a security protocol I personally insisted upon. It has paid off. This man," Commander Franklin showed Agmund a photo of a man with a long, narrow face, a lengthy goatee, long black hair, and deep-set dark eyes, "came into our facilities the other night using the security card of this man." Commander Franklin showed Agmund another photo. This time it was of a man in his mid-forties with a large belly and a close-trimmed salt-and-pepper beard. He had a large bald spot on his head where there was no longer his black, now graying hair. "He is one of my employees and I will take care of him through other means once I find him. He has not come to work since that night over a week ago. It will only be a matter of time before I find him though. The first is a complete stranger to me however. I have had other men try to find information about him, but to no avail. I want you to find out about this man and then let us bring him to the room he seemed so desperate to enter in the first place. There we will find out if he told anyone else about it." Commander Franklin seemed concerned about the situation, but confident that it would be quickly handled. Agmund however seemed very frustrated.

"With all due respect, would not my talents be best used in leading the attacks on the safe houses instead of just chasing down one man who may have video or film of this facility, but that the government can easily refute as not their facility? The government has a stranglehold on all internet and news media. This should be an easy fix."

"There are many Stasi run underground stations that run media as well, not to mention the always dangerous rumor mill that only needs to be run by word-of-mouth. The underground stations are run out of the safe houses that we still have not taken down. You would be amazed at how little equipment is needed to broadcast a radio station or print a newspaper. Normally, we would just handle it through our media, but there are two reasons I do not want to do that. First of all, that man brazenly strolled in here. He could be a potentially dangerous threat that needs to be eliminated before he can cause more harm. Secondly, the people of Maevin are not as easily trusting of the government run media as they once were. The boldness of the recent attacks by our enemies has caused normal citizens to believe that our government is not good enough. They are demanding better. I read a report just this morning about a near riot in downtown Maevin. It was meant to be a protest of the inequality of housing and services between downtown and the outskirts of this wonderful city. It nearly got out of hand. We cannot allow this man to add more fuel to the fire. This man is an unknown factor. This means his potential as a nuisance and danger to Maevin is nearly unlimited. This is why you get the assignment. I would rather you be above the assignment than to lose more men than I already have. My men should be able to handle any safe house assaults without your help for the time being."

"As you wish. I will do my best to find him, although that may prove difficult considering how little information we have to go on."

"That is yet another good reason why you have the assignment my friend."

With that Agmund left, although he did not seem very happy with his new assignment. Commander Franklin briefly pondered this attitude, but decided it may just be that Agmund prefers to engage in open warfare, not being a sleuth. Never the less, it intrigued Commander Franklin to see just how dangerous this black-haired stranger may be. He could be the first person to give Agmund a challenge.

December 13, 32 PAW

3:17

Special Weapons and Tactics Captain Valerius dispersed his team of twelve around the safe house. Behind the SWAT team were four other teams that were the backup for Captain Valerius' team in addition to providing a containment zone from which theoretically no one evading Captain Valerius' team would be able to escape from. The innocent looking house in front of Captain Valerius was only a simple, two-story home that looked like it held an elderly couple, but intelligence had traced the traitor Silas to this location. It was unusual for him not to be in a heavily guarded base, but Captain Valerius felt sure that the recent takeover of one of his bases had caused him to abandon his trust in strength and subterfuge and place it entirely in stealth instead.

Captain Valerius was the man hand-chosen by Commander Franklin to lead this assignment once the attempts to find Agmund met with no success. Commander Franklin would have preferred Agmund to at least be present for the attack against this safe house, especially if Silas were indeed in there, but the information needed to be acted upon rapidly. It was common knowledge among the government that Silas moved sometimes as many as five times a day, at all hours of the day. It was how he had managed to stay ahead of the government for so long. Commander Franklin gave the green light to go ahead within a half hour of receiving the intelligence from one of the many CRZ soldiers he had dedicated to the purpose of tracking down the final Stasi.

Captain Valerius had been a SWAT Team Captain for over a dozen years. During this time he had never failed a mission before, a fact he took great pride in. In fact, some thought he took too much pride in this fact and had allowed himself to fall in love with his own legend that he was unbeatable. His professional record was not the only thing that commended this illustrious reputation of invincibility. He was a massive man that stood 6 foot 5 inches tall with large muscles to fill out that formidable frame, especially for a man of forty-seven years old. He was a man of few words, and left his actions to inspire his men.

Captain Valerius had possibly the biggest mission of his life ahead of him. If Silas was indeed inside, it would be the perfect addition to his impressive resume. Captain Valerius hoped desperately that the intelligence he had received was accurate; the government had so often been disappointed before. The men around Captain Valerius were filled with nervous energy, yet somber with the knowledge that this mission could very well be the last they would ever undertake. Captain Valerius felt a surge of pride in his men as he ordered his carefully laid plans for the assault into motion. Each of these men and women had fought and bled with him before. Captain Valerius would have it no other way.

The SWAT team all pounced upon the house at the same time. There were twelve of them, including Captain Valerius. For this mission Captain Valerius had them enter the safe house via four distinct entrances. This would confuse the enemy and make it more difficult for them to coordinate their defenses while trying to find a clear escape route, but it also put the team at a greater risk of being killed as they were divided. Captain Valerius deemed it a risk that was necessary. He would not be branded as the man that let Silas get away.

Captain Valerius burst through the front door with two of his SWAT team members. They had a rough idea of the layout of the building. Captain Valerius had determined that his team would move through the rooms on the far west side while the team entering through an eastern window would clear the eastern rooms on the first floor. The other two teams would clear the second floor. After clearing those two floors, all of them would descend down to the basement together, where it was determined the fiercest resistance would most likely be. Captain Valerius moved through the front foyer and then went through a couple of bedrooms. Groggy men and women were scrambling to grab their weapons to counter the attacking assault team, but the sudden assault did not give them a chance. Captain Valerius and his team quickly executed them. They moved through the kitchen, but it was empty. By now, despite the suppressed weapons the SWAT team was using, the SWAT team was well aware their presence was known in the safe house. They began to proceed much more cautiously.

On the second floor Sergeant Violi led her team of three through the few rooms that were strewn with various weapons and bedding. The few people the SWAT team found were quickly shot several times to ensure that they would not survive. Their bodies would be later identified; Captain Valerius did not want to take a chance that Chancellor Silas could slip away while people were being arrested when it was much quicker to kill them. Sergeant Violi was satisfied with the speed and effectiveness of the assault, but she had expected a much fiercer resistance in the safe house. This concerned her greatly.

When they proceeded into the third room that they were supposed to clear, they found the room almost completely enveloped in darkness. Several figures however crowded the room and most of them were pointing weapons towards Sergeant Violi and her two fellow SWAT team members. Sergeant Violi unleashed a barrage of bullets, as did the two SWAT team members with her. The muzzle flash of the assault rifles in that close space revealed that the figures were mannequins, with real guns tied to their arms. Sergeant Violi flicked on her flashlight attached to her rifle and inspected the mannequins closely, seeing some pocked with bullet holes from her team's itchy trigger fingers. She checked the room closely, moving slowly forward past rows of densely congested mannequins ensuring that each one was indeed a mannequin.

She was almost clear of the room when she heard the harsh thump of two distinct objects hitting the ground. The sound was familiar to her. It was the sound of dead body dropping to the ground. Dread welling up inside her, she whirled around intent on killing whoever was attempting to kill her. The only thing she saw before she died was the point of a knife as it made its way directly into her right eye.

The other team on the second floor moved into the room filled with the mannequins. They saw the mannequins, but were able to recognize them quickly as they already had their flashlights on. They were trying to reconvene with the other trio on that floor, but had been unable to establish contact with them by radio. Unfortunately, they found all too quickly the reason for the silence on the radio. All members of the trio were lying in a pool of their own blood with no sign of whoever had attacked them. They flipped over the body of Sergeant Violi to bring her face up to check her pulse. As they did so, the second trio noticed the final mistake of their lives, the body had been connected with a string to a Claymore mine, and the act of rolling her over had caused the string to set off the Claymore. The trio's death came quickly as their bodies were obliterated, and much of the second floor was destroyed as well.

On the first floor Captain Valerius heard the sound of the Claymore going off, and it filled him with a sense of trepidation. He feared that the information that Chancellor Silas had been in the safe house had been merely to set up a trap, one that he had walked all too quickly into. He desperately tried to contact the two SWAT trios on the second floor. After receiving no answer he made a decision.

He quickly radioed the other trio on the floor and ordered them to meet up in the kitchen to try to fight their way out. Soon all six were in the kitchen and began to move cautiously, towards the front door. Captain Valerius knew his perfect record of completing missions was likely to end that night, but he was not going to throw the lives of his men away so rashly.

Captain Valerius and the five men made it safely through the rooms they had already cleared, all being the same as it had been only a few minutes previously. When they reached the front door, the loud report of a single shotgun round echoed through the house. Two of the SWAT team members fell to the ground, fatally wounded, but not dead yet. They contorted their bodies to attempt to return fire before death overcame them, but they could not see their assailant. As they died, the four remaining members assumed a prone position and looked for a target to present itself. Captain Valerius could see his men sneaking nervous glances at him in an effort to receive guidance and encouragement that they would survive this ambush. Captain Valerius ignored their glances in an effort to locate the position and condition of their enemies, not to mention to hide his mounting fear.

A few moments passed, but it seemed like minutes as the remaining SWAT team members swept their flashlights through every space leading out of that room in an effort to locate their enemies or a safe escape route. Suddenly a grenade came rolling in among them from the direction of the front door, Captain Valerius swiftly kicked it back in the direction it came from, but as he did so a bullet pierced his kicking leg. The grenade only moved eight feet away before it exploded. Shrapnel pierced the heart of the nearest SWAT team member. The rest received only minor injuries. The surviving three members unleashed a barrage of bullets at the front door, but doubted their efforts met with success as they still had not directly seen their enemy. They stopped firing and listened. Another couple of tense moments came when the blast of the shotgun was heard again, but this time from behind them. One assailant was blocking the front door in front of them, while it appeared another was behind them. The SWAT team members turned around to face the new threat. The shotgun was fired in two shots that were so impossibly fast the sound of the two shots almost blended into one. Captain Valerius saw in his peripheral vision the deaths of the last of his teammates even as he focused on killing his adversary. He brought a handgun to bear on the figure dressed in urban combat fatigues and pulled the trigger. The bullet hit the man square in the torso, but the man did not even flinch. His shotgun fired another deafening round and it obliterated Captain Valerius's arm that held the handgun. It now hung uselessly at his side, but Valerius still tried to pull a knife out with his left arm. He attempted to throw it with his weak hand, but it missed the mark and flew wide of the man. The stranger pulled out his own knife, after slinging his shotgun over his shoulder.

"So you want to have a knife fight. Too bad you already threw yours away." The assailant pressed the knife against the throat of Captain Valerius.

"Who are you?" Captain Valerius asked in awe.

"I am the man who killed your entire SWAT team singlehandedly. I am the man responsible for Chancellor Silas living another day. I am the man who is about to kill you, but not before you know this. I am the man who is going to overthrow the government of Maevin." Nemesio then slashed the man's exposed neck with the knife.

"You are the man who killed the entire SWAT team singlehandedly, Nemesio." Stated Chancellor Silas, emerging from an adjoining room, he held a handgun in his hand, but had not used it during the fight. Nemesio had insisted on doing it alone to keep Silas safest. He had managed to get behind the SWAT team by sneaking around the side of the house in the shadows without being detected by the SWAT teams outside and using a window to get behind them while they thought he was still near the front door. "But, it remains to be seen about the rest. We still have not escaped this assault. There are certain to be at least one other SWAT team outside doing perimeter control. If you do manage to get me out of this situation unharmed then I will have much faith that you will be the man to overthrow the government of Maevin. I see however that you have not gone without injury yourself."

"The bullet from his handgun did hit me, but the bulletproof vest will ensure I only have a very painful bruise. It is well for the shot would have pierced my heart had I not worn it. I should be thankful this man did not attempt a head shot. However, this is no time for idle chatter. You are right about additional teams, though you underestimate how badly Larkin wants your death. There are four SWAT teams outside. Give me a moment to prepare our escape. Once I exit this building stay hot on my heels." Nemesio took the radio and ear bud off of Captain Valerius and listened momentarily to the very frantic chatter on the radio. Nemesio then went down into the basement and emerged with an RPG-7 in his hands. He crouched in the shadows of the front door and fired. It hit the vehicle the SWAT team was crouching behind. The radio became even more alive with chatter, none of which was intelligible due to competing voices. Nemesio took advantage of this opportunity and quickly led Chancellor Silas out of the back door. He fired the RPG-7 once again, having already re-loaded on his way through the house. Another car exploded, which disoriented the survivors of another SWAT team that had been taking cover behind it. Nemesio charged straight past them with his assault rifle firing rounds at the survivors. Nemesio and Chancellor Silas quickly disappeared into the night, Chancellor Silas now completely in awe of Nemesio in a way that he had never been of anyone else ever in his life.

December 13, 32 PAW

9:54

"I cannot believe Captain Valerius failed me." Commander Franklin stated dejectedly to Agmund. "He had never failed me before. We were so close to killing Silas. Reports are there was only one man that was seen getting away from the safe house with him. I find it hard to believe, but this one man evidently killed all of Captain Valerius's team, and then proceeded to break through the blockade we had set up. We must find both the traitor Silas and this unknown man."

"I have heard rumors of the Stasi using a new man whom was incredibly effective, but this is unbelievable. I will do my best to locate Silas, but I fear he will be even more cautious and difficult to find after such a close call. For now I think it is best for us to proceed with your original plan, but with me in charge of executing it. I do not want us to make the same mistake twice of letting him get away. We shall draw the noose closer around his neck. Let us narrow down the amount of places he has to hide in, the number of people for him to cowardly hide behind. He will eventually become so desperate that he will make a mistake."

"That all sounds fine and good, but each day he survives is another day this government grows weaker. Time is running short Agmund, we must kill him. Without him, and this unknown killer, the Stasi will die and the government will once again have a firm stranglehold on Maevin. Supreme Commander Larkin desired that none past myself know this, but you are a man of impeccable character, our government is on the brink of disaster. Supreme Commander Larkin desires the death of Silas above all else. With him dead, the threat to our very existence will die. The Muslims are nearly gone, the Christians are growing stronger somehow, but they are not enough of a threat to be a concern. We can easily deal with them if the Stasi are taken care of."

Agmund seemed to soak in all this information and then gravely asked, "Speaking of Christians, do you still want me to pursue this stranger that broke into here or is he no longer a priority?"

"He is a priority, but not a big enough one for me to have you trifle with him. I know an assassin who is very good at what she does. Indeed, Brava may give you a run for your money. She is bolder than any other assassin, has no remorse, and is extremely lethal with a variety of methods. Most females in her line of work use stealth or their feminine charms to get the job done, not her. She is cunning, brave, and has no fear of death or pain. I have used her to fill a few contracts, and have never been disappointed before. I will send her after the stranger. You will lead the rest of the assaults on their known safe houses and bases as you see fit, but keep in mind the priority is to kill Silas. If you accomplish that you will never need for anything else the rest of your life. I promise you that."

"I do not doubt that. I will begin planning immediately."

Chapter X

December 18, 32 PAW

19:49

Brava sat in a run-down restaurant that supposedly sold all kinds of meat, although Brava was certain it was all either dog or horse meat with different seasonings. Not that it mattered to her, she had eaten worse before and it would not stop her from eating this. Her mind barely processed the taste of the food as she slowly chewed waiting for her target to show up, if he even would. It was no telling how long it would take. The target had been rumored to visit *Milica's Carnivore House* frequently, but in the last two days Brava had not seen him once. Brava patiently sipped her bitter coffee after her meal while reading Maevin's only official newspaper. It took her nearly an hour and a half after finishing her meal to take up the entire time until closing time, at 22:00. The hour following would certainly be used to close up and then head dutifully home before the 23:00 curfew. It made her sick how the people of Maevin could so willingly just accept some of the crap the government required of them. But she had to remind herself that not everyone was so pathetic. She had just got done reading a news article in which a group of young teens living together refused to pay taxes until the government began using the tax money to improve the outskirts of the city. They had gotten evicted out of their home. Brava was surprised the government had not done more to send a statement.

As she got to thinking about the negatives of the Maevin government, she thought about how much worse the alternatives would be. Most people she reasoned, particularly herself, were much better off with the current government than say the Stasi, the Muslims, or even worse, the Christians in charge, she found herself thinking. The government may not be the best, but it was the best current option. Besides, since she did freelance contract work for them quite often, they treated her very well. In fact she was above the law in most instances.

At five minutes to 22:00, Brava walked out the door of the dingy diner. It had been another evening wasted eating poor food and watching the various people that came into the diner. She found herself pitying some of them, but despising the majority of them. They were the working class of the city, the ones that made it run and work, working numerous hours but still not being able to afford a higher standard of living. The rest of them were low-lifes, trying to make a life out of crime, even though Larkin had legalized many things that were illegal in the past including gambling, prostitution, abortions, drugs, and loan sharking. They decided those were not good enough for them, or perhaps maybe that they were not good enough, either way Brava decided the fools were pitiful.

As she walked down the sidewalk away from the diner, Brava heard the door of the diner open behind her. She turned around to see if it was anyone following her, but was surprised to see no one emerge from the diner. It must have been someone entering it instead. Brava thought it strange for someone to enter the diner so late. There was no way a food order could be made in that short amount of time. Brava was ready to dismiss it as someone just returning because they forgot an item in the diner, maybe a coat or something, but she could not take the chance that it was possibly the mark that she had just missed.

How to return without tipping off the mark, indeed if it was even the mark in the first place, was the question that now perplexed Brava. Deciding that if it was so easy for her to assume that someone had merely forgotten something, it would not be a stretch to assume whoever had entered the restaurant and the remaining few patrons would assume approximately the same thing if she returned to the restaurant now. Besides, the mark should have no idea who Brava was or that he had a bull's-eye on his forehead that said one hundred thousand marks. She turned around and took the several steps back into the diner.

Walking back to her table along the far wall, Brava got a good look at everyone in the diner. There was no one new in the building as far as she could tell. The person must have stepped into the back, making it likely that it was an employee or someone related to the owner that was coming in to help close. Still she did not like assuming that. It left things uncertain. She went to her table and started poking her head around as if looking for something.

After a minute or so, a pudgy man with a countenance that was almost as drab as the restaurant emerged from the kitchen. From her previous visits, Brava knew it was the man whom owned the restaurant and was its namesake as well, Milica. As he waddled up to Brava, she managed to peer around his wide shoulders into the kitchen. The door was still swinging back and forth and she noted a man in a stark black cowboy outfit. He was openly wearing a silver belt buckle that brazenly displayed a cross, itself a crime worthy of execution. The man also had a couple of guns openly displayed on his hips inside Old West style holsters. Brava made eye contact briefly before the door swung back closed. It was definitely the mark. When the door swung back into a slightly open position before closing for good, Brava could not see anyone. The target had moved out of sight, but to where? Did he suspect anything?

She dismissed the thoughts almost immediately. Chances are he was just friends with the owner and was grabbing some food or helping clean up in another part of the kitchen. There had never been a target that had suspected her until it was far too late. Her attractive, innocent features and lithe body made it nearly impossible for anyone to suspect the truth of what she did for a living.

"Do you need help with anything Miss?" Milica asked, as if justifying her thought. Who had ever heard of calling a killer Miss?

"Oh, I just left behind…," Brava chastised herself for not coming up with a detailed cover story for coming back into the restaurant beforehand even as she came up with the needed details. "A slip of paper with some phone numbers on it. It will be hard to do business without those numbers." She of course had brought no paper with her. Whenever she went on a mission she took an absolute minimal amount of possessions with her to ensure she left behind a bare minimum of evidence. The less evidence the better her chances of getting away with the hit. It was strategies like this that had kept her one step ahead of the enemies she had made with past assignments. Maevin was a complicated place for a mercenary to work, where all factions were hated by the other three factions.

"Oh, what kind of business do you do?" Milica asked another question, which annoyed Brava, restaurant owners tended to be very nosy and talkative at times. Those were traits that she despised in her line of work.

"I work for the government actually." Brava said, taking careful note of any signs of nervousness that Milica betrayed. It was obvious on his face and demeanor as soon as she said government. She could not have been paying any attention at all and noted the nervousness emanating from him. Of course, that may not mean much more than what everyone already knew, Milica would not be too happy if the health department ever did find their way out of the center of the city to the west side of the city where *Milica's Carnivore House* was, not to mention the man in the back who was already committing two capital offenses, possessing firearms and wearing a religious symbol.

"Um…well I don't see it anywhere, and as you can tell we have not cleaned your table yet since you left a couple of minutes ago. Tell you what, I will send one of my waitresses over to clean your table and you are more than welcome to look as she clears the table." Without hearing an answer from Brava, Milica bustled away, obviously anxious to get away from this government employee.

As the young, nervous waitress cleared the table, Brava made a show of looking for a slip of paper. However, during this time, Brava was actually thinking of how to perform the hit. Working under the assumption that her target was a close friend of Milica, he was likely to stay for a while afterwards. Then it was a simple question of whether to wait for the target to leave the diner or to break back in and kill her target, Milica, and perhaps the pretty little waitress who was evidently closing with Milica tonight.

Brava left the restaurant after her fruitless search, mumbling something about possibly forgetting it at the office after all to put on a good show for the bashful waitress. She went outside the door and then waited for twenty minutes in the shadows of an alley across the street from the diner. It was then that the waitress left, the last to leave besides Milica and the target. She then decided to kill them both, Milica had talked to her face-to-face, as did the waitress. Between the two of them, she could possibly be identified. While it was true that the government would likely clear her of any charges the police of Maevin initially arrested her on, she did not want to take the risk in the first place. She prided herself on being able to fill her contracts with a minimal amount of attention. The double homicide would definitely attract more attention, but it was better than leaving Milica to give a description of her. The shy waitress had barely looked up the entire time she was in the restaurant so she decided not to worry about that loose end.

Brava checked her handgun, a .38 caliber snub nosed revolver. It was loaded with hollow point bullets and ready for action, and now that the scene was clear of any witnesses, she was ready as well. She strode across the street quickly and within moments had silently picked the lock of the front door. The cheap door made for a very poor challenge to Brava's very practiced lock-picking skills. Once inside she paused and listened for Milica and the target to be talking. Hearing a conversation would accomplish many things for Brava. It would ensure that the target and Milica had not heard her entrance, allow her to ascertain their location better, and mask some of the noise that Brava made as she made her murderous approach. However, after a minute of waiting, Brava heard nothing. Maybe the pair had left through the back entrance Brava thought, unsure of how to proceed when she was unsure of the condition and location of her quarry. She moved forward cautiously, past the front counter towards the kitchen. It was dark in the dining area, a fact she felt thankful for as it concealed her movements, but it also made her much more nervous as well. With her heart beating fiercely inside her chest, she found her way to the kitchen doors. Standing up tall from her crouching position, she managed to look through the window of the swinging kitchen doors. Inside Milica was washing dishes by himself.

She tried to locate the mysterious cowboy in the kitchen as well, but could not see him. None the less, she felt that he must surely be in there. She grabbed a towel that was on a cart next to the kitchen doors and wrapped it around the barrel of the gun to soften the sound of the gunshot. She pushed the door open a crack, and aimed the shot at Milica's wide back. Taking a deep breath and exhaling it, she squeezed the trigger in a smooth motion. The shot was amazingly quiet, even better than what Brava had hoped for. There was also a satisfying spray of blood on the wall in front of the sink to let Brava know her shot had definitely done the job. Milica slipped to the ground, the thump of his considerable weight falling to the hard concrete was the only noise he made. Brava waited a moment, and lined up a shot for the target, certain that he would rush to the side of his friend at any moment, but no one came to his side.

Suddenly it dawned on Brava the mistake she had made. There was no doubt the target had been in the kitchen and was a friend of Milica's, but she had told Milica that she worked for the government. Undoubtedly Milica had told her target. The target probably bolted out the back of the building a long time ago. She had now killed her only link to her target. She went forward into the kitchen while chastising herself silently for her stupidity and stood over Milica, whom was surprisingly still alive. She was about to question him about her target, but chose to enjoy the moment. The last few moments before her targets died were always an intense and curiously pleasing experience for Brava. She stared into his face, curious as to what was going through his mind and what he felt. She always wondered what death was like; having dealt it out so often herself she felt that it would be strange to not at least ponder about it from time to time.

As she peered into his face though she saw a strange peace in his expression that she had never seen before, indeed he had never looked that happy during the last few days she had seen him. She wondered if his life had really been that awful that death would be a welcome release. She heard the kitchen door swing open at that moment, taking her away from the moment she so strangely enjoyed, watching her victims die. She whirled the gun in the direction of the kitchen doors, desperate to bring her gun to bear on the intruder. The intruder was the mark, Rhys, coming back from the restroom. He had either suspected she was in there or was much quicker than her because she never even saw him draw his weapon. The muzzle was already pointed at her head. As she hurried to bring her gun on to its target she hoped he would hesitate. He did not fire immediately and Brava's fast reflexes were rewarded. She managed to fire her gun before he fired his, but the shot missed wide of him, in her adrenaline enhanced rush she had moved the gun past the target before firing. She had risked it all on one shot and had missed, the intended victim pulled the trigger slowly and surely on his gun and the bullet embedded deep into Brava's brain, ending her brilliant career. In the end she had been done in by the very thing that made it so enjoyable for her, watching her victims die close-up.

Rhys first made certain that the female assassin was dead. There was however no real doubt, his .45 caliber hollow-tip bullet had entered square in the middle of her forehead. He looked at her, feeling pity that such a beautiful, young woman would have lived such a violent, short life. He felt no anger towards this young woman. He knew the true blame rested upon whoever had hired her. However, Rhys found it ironic that he would be the one to have compassion on such a violent, short life. "I guess one pities the life he knows best the pitfalls of." Rhys commented out loud, unsure of what had motivated him to speak such a thought out into the open. Regardless of the statement, he was anxiously on the move to the side of his friend, Milica. Rhys could immediately tell that Milica had been mortally wounded, but on closer inspection found that he was still alive, for a little while longer at least.

"Milica, Milica, can you hear me?" Rhys asked earnestly, but gently. It was strange how death made one seem so humble and quiet Rhys thought.

Milica slowly opened his eyes and saw Rhys, but it was a couple of moments before he recognized him. "Rhys, my good friend, are you okay?"

"I am Milica. Maybe God still has a purpose for me to fulfill. I am too far in to avert my course now whether or not God approves, but unfortunately that course has caused your life to be taken from you."

"It is okay. I will soon be in heaven. I may not agree with the course you have decided to take Rhys, but I am glad anyhow that I died tonight instead of you. Promise me you will make Maevin a better place while spilling the least amount of blood as possible, Rhys." Milica coughed up some blood; Rhys tenderly used a towel to wipe the blood off of his face. When Milica looked up at Rhys again, Rhys nodded his head as a promise to Milica. "I pray that God will find a way to improve your intended course along the way. I know you are dead set on this mission of yours, but

Rhys think of your salvation. I know that Heaven will be glorious my friend and I look forward to it. I am glad I am soon to be in the presence of my Father. My only regret is that I could not persuade you to abandon your path that so blatantly abandons everything He has taught us through His Good Book. You have turned your back on God, Rhys. I pray He does not do the same to you when Judgment Day comes."

"I pray that God uses my actions to further His Kingdom. I hold no hope for myself."

"That is heartbreaking to hear…but the troubles of this world have no hold on me anymore, I will praise God in Heaven, despite the pain he has given us both in our lives." Milica's eyes glazed over. Rhys had seen enough deaths to know that Milica was dead beyond a doubt, as loath as he was to admit it. He wiped his prints from the place and left with a heavy heart and his conversation with Milica still ringing in his ears.

December 19, 32 PAW

22:52

Commander Liam, the Maevin City Council member specializing in Public Relations, walked into a building he was very familiar with, the Maevin City Media Corporation building. This building was responsible for the output of all media for the city. In reality it was just another branch of the government, strictly controlling what ideas were put before the citizens of Maevin. A few pirate stations had tried for the thirty years the Maevin City Media Corporation (MCMC) had been in existence to broadcast anti-government material financed by the various factions that opposed the government. However, these were short-lived and did not have nearly the audience that the MCMC was able to have. Part of Commander Liam's job was to make sure that the MCMC was the only voice heard in the city.

Commander Liam was going to make his voice heard tonight throughout the city via the MCMC. At eleven pm, when a curfew was in effect, yet early enough that most people were still awake, all televisions in the city would automatically tune in to his address, even if they were off. All stations would broadcast the address by Commander Liam. Commander Liam had been ordered by Supreme Commander Larkin to make a public address denouncing Nemesio, informing everyone what he looked like, and formally announcing a five hundred thousand mark reward for his death, or information leading to it. He was informed that the broadcasting room on the seventeenth floor was ready for him as he rode the elevator to that floor. The broadcast would be live to prove that Commander Liam was still alive, an extra measure Larkin had decided to take to ensure that the conspiracy theorists in the city would have no ammunition that he had already been killed by

Nemesio. Commander Liam took it one step further and left his security guards at home.

Commander Liam stepped out into the lights after handing a technician a memory stick that would allow him to read his speech off of the teleprompter. A few last minute details before the eleven pm curfew rolled around were handled, such as make-up, lighting issues, and getting the cameras in position. At precisely eleven pm, Commander Liam spoke in his booming, passion-filled voice, which seemed strange coming from such a small man.

"Citizens of the great city of Maevin, you have undoubtedly all become aware of the threat that Nemesio made against all the Council Members by now. Indeed he has already carried out one of the threats. It has come to my attention that many of you are made nervous, and some even excited, by the prospect of this government failing. As one of the Council Members, you may want to know what I, Commander Liam, have to say about how this threat makes me feel. I feel nothing, for there is no serious threat. He caught Commander Matthew unawares and took us by surprise. He got lucky with that one, but he will not be lucky again. Maevin will use the totality of its resources to ensure that Nemesio is captured and executed for his treason. Those whom still have the fortitude to believe in Supreme Commander Larkin and his benevolent government can help as well. There is a five hundred thousand mark reward being offered to anyone who can prove they took justice into their own hands. The same reward will be offered to anyone who gives information to the Maevin City Police Department that leads to his death or capture. Again I report there is absolutely nothing to fear of Nemesio, this government has survived the civil strife that has divided the city of Maevin since its inception, but I tell you we are so close to victory, do not lose faith in us now. The Stasi are on the run and will soon be eliminated. Help us bring down one of their chief traitors.

"Some of you may be wondering what the culprit looks like. I have an artist's rendering of what he looks like." Commander Liam held up a picture of a man with a bald head and crazed eyes dressed in black tactical clothing. A knife in the right hand of the drawing was covered in blood. The camera zoomed back out after closing in on the drawing to put its focus back on Commander Liam. The men in the room stood transfixed as behind Commander Liam they saw Nemesio, live in the flesh with a knife in his right hand. Before they could react Nemesio brought his right hand out and cut the throat of Commander Liam wide open. He then stood before the cameras, almost as though he was the drawing coming to life. Blood dripped off the keen edge of the knife blade. His eyes held a crazed look as he stared into the cameras. They were still broadcasting a live feed out to every television in Maevin.

"Commander Liam twisted the truth when he spoke about me. There is much to fear, but only if you support the government. I will kill the rest of the Council, and then Supreme Commander Larkin as well. No one can stop me, and I will kill anyone that tries. Commander Liam lied, the government is losing its iron grip on this city, and that is making them desperate. He stated that I would not kill anyone else and he had nothing to fear. I promise this to you all, Larkin and the rest of the Council Members will perish before New Years, with Larkin dying last. For those of you that are excited by the prospect of the government failing, I encourage you to be ready to guide this city into a new era. To those who are frightened by that same prospect, stay out of my way. It will all be over soon enough."

With that Nemesio disappeared out of the lights, a few people rushed forward to check on Commander Liam's lifeless body. Several MCMC guards chased after the direction Nemesio had left the camera. Someone finally ordered the cameras to stop rolling as the guards crossed through the vision of the camera.

Nemesio frantically ran up the three stories to the roof, where he had entered from. On top of the roof he had a glider stashed. He grabbed it as he heard the door to the roof behind him open. Several bullets whizzed past him as he jumped off the building. Soon he was gliding through the crisp, moonlit air, satisfied that another mission had been successful.

December 20, 32 PAW

13:10

Rhys entered Paul's office unannounced. Paul was currently meeting with one of his disciples. Rhys assumed it was the end of the meeting for Paul was closing in prayer. Paul had tried doing the same thing for Rhys, but Rhys had refused each time until Paul finally stopped offering. Paul did not stop praying with Rhys in there and thus he stood near the door uncomfortably waiting for Paul to finish.

"Lord," Paul prayed, "Maevin is a city full of temptations, despair, and heartache. But, there is also hope as well. Let Timothy see that hope and love others even when he knows fully that those You call him to love would kill him in an instant if they knew he was a Christian. Also give him peace that You will protect his family, but even if You choose not to Father, that we will all get to sing and glorify Your Name in Heaven someday. That will be a glorious day, where there is no darkness, no despair, and no fear. Timothy is struggling with all that right now Lord and is living in fear, help him to live in faith alone Lord. Amen."

With that Paul and Timothy looked up and saw Rhys standing there. Timothy nervously walked out of the office after thanking Paul. Rhys got a good look at Timothy, he looked frail and worried, but there was something about him that Rhys liked. Maybe it was the fact that Timothy was struggling so much in his faith that made Rhys sympathetic.

Even more likely was the fact that Rhys had once been like Timothy, before the business of killing people had changed him.

Timothy left and Paul turned his attention to Rhys. "I hear there has been an attempt on your life."

"Your information is correct. I managed to kill the mercenary assassin, but not before the woman killed my friend, Milica."

"I did not know you have friends."

"I have very few friends, now even less." Rhys stated this, but hid his reservoir of emotion behind the impenetrable exterior he could wield at will.

"I am sorry for your loss. Do you know who hired the assassin?" Paul found it hard to be sympathetic about the death of a man he did not know when the man that was a friend of him did not seem to be greatly affected.

"It was Commander Franklin. I understand he knows it was me who broke into the Police Headquarters and took videotape of the torture room where Jasper was killed."

"Well you are too useful to lose. We must cut this off at the source. You must kill Commander Franklin." Paul spoke as though the answer was obvious, and as simple as it was obvious.

Rhys looked surprised. "You would have me stir a hornet's nest by doing so. Can you imagine the firestorm I would bring down upon my own head if I would kill their CRZ Commander? I would not like to imagine it."

"You have already bombed the CRZ headquarters once before. What makes you so doubtful this time?" Paul asked very surprised at Rhys's pessimism. It had always lurked under the surface of everything Rhys said, but it had never caused him to not act before.

"That was different. I pinned it on someone else, but Commander Franklin knows about me this time. If I kill him it is only a matter of time before they come to suspect me. I am now on the CRZ's radar, and it will not be easy to operate as freely as I once did Paul."

"I see your point, but listen to mine. Ordinarily the killing of the Maevin Chief of Police would be a major concern indeed, but not now. You see, since Nemesio's antics live on TV last night for all of Maevin to see, the murder of the CRZ's Commander, especially one so recently appointed will seem of little concern, relatively of course. Nemesio is drawing all the interest and ire of the Maevin government. You heard Commander Liam's address. Nemesio, and of course Silas, have the full attention of the Maevin government and all its resources."

Rhys nodded his head slowly; it was indeed a sound argument. "I see your point. Even if it is apparently a murder, I should have little to fear. Certainly I will have less to fear if Commander Franklin is dead than if he still lives. He seems intent on trying to keep his job by removing the evidence I gathered through murdering me."

"Exactly. Cut off the head of the snake before he sends more assassins after you."

"You mentioned that Nemesio is drawing all the attention of the government, is that allowing Christians to thrive?"

"We are enjoying a period of lessened persecution, that is certainly the case, but I would not say we are thriving. Timothy is a good example of what is typical of us these days. We are witnessing so much death, pain, and turmoil that all seems dark ahead. There is no real hope, only a slim hope that we can survive while the government and Stasi tear each other apart. In their ashes, we may rise, but I fear the condition our hearts and spirits will be in after abiding so long in darkness and fear. We may very well be forced to extreme measures."

Rhys' attention peaked at this comment, although only a close observer would ever be able to notice a change in expression or thought no matter how extreme upon Rhys. "What do you mean by extreme measures?" Rhys asked nonchalantly, he wanted Paul to talk freely on this point.

"Well, if the government and Stasi do indeed kill each other off, then the Christians are poised to take control of our future by taking control of the government. As one of the Christian leaders, I believe I could help make a significant difference in government policy. I have been thinking of the best way to go about things and have concluded that perhaps the Old Testament way of going about things would be good."

"Do you mean an eye for an eye Paul?"

"No, I was thinking more about Joshua's conquest. God promised the land of Canaan to Israel, but the problem was it was occupied by other nations, stronger nations. Maevin is the same way. Currently the government and Stasi are so much stronger than us Christians, Israel in this example. God strengthened Israel and enabled them to defeat these other nations. They failed in the end because their conquest was not complete. They were ordered to destroy all. They didn't and it caused them to fall back into sin. If we do not completely eradicate all unbelievers, then we too may fall back into sin and idolatry just like ancient Israel did."

"Paul, how can that be what you really want for this city? I do not commit these violent acts in the hope that they will continue, but in the grim hope that my acts of violence will be the last acts of violence that need committed. That once I am through with this, that there will be no more need for anyone else to commit the atrocities I have done. There is a light at the end of the tunnel, but you will merely make the tunnel cyclical in your desire to end it once and for all. There is no light at the end of a circular tunnel." Rhys seemed incredibly concerned, while the more Rhys talked the more frustrated Paul became.

"Rhys, it is merely a thought I have had so far. Indeed, merely a wish that I will be in a position to do something in the government us Christians will hopefully form when you are through with your job. I pray we can find a better path, one that will not make us Christians kill."

"Let me know if you think of a better plan, Paul."

"I will. For now, what do you know of this character Nemesio?"

"Nothing, at least not more than anyone else. He is an agent of the Stasi. He is rumored to have caused the murders of many people. He also is rumored to have saved the life of Chancellor Silas himself. No one knows much about him except what he has advertised to the entire city of Maevin. My contact in the Maevin Police told me that the night Chancellor Silas was almost caught; an entire SWAT team was KIA. A couple of other teams were seriously injured and suffered some fatalities as well. None of the Stasi that were raided survived besides Nemesio and Silas it seems. Make no mistake about it; Nemesio is a force to be reckoned with. Why do you ask?"

"There may come a day when I ask you to stop him. If he is true to the Stasi cause, Christians will not be safe once the government falls with that madman killer running around." Paul said.

"Let the government take care of him, there is no way that he will accomplish all he promised. Pride will be his downfall, as it is for many men." Rhys said softly, and then he left Paul's office contemplating the new information he had learned about Paul's plans for the future of Maevin.

Chapter XI

December 22, 32 PAW

2:58

Agmund crept through a fence of a decrepit airport on a clear, cold night. The waxing three quarter moon gave the airport a solemn lighting. Airplanes had become pointless towards the end of the nuclear war. People gravitated towards the few safe zones left on the planet and soon those areas, which had been so rural and desolate in the past, became cities. The surviving, isolated cities became independent or perished. There was no interdependence, trade, or communication between cities, the nuclear radiation that covered the majority of Earth had made that impossible. Some self-proclaimed experts claimed the nuclear fallout would dissipate within a century. Others stated that Earth would never fully be free of nuclear radioactive zones that were above the safe threshold. Either way, it would be a long time before travel between cities and eventually continents became an issue. By then a new generation unused to travelling outside of the walls of their own city will be the ones to decide whether or not to try to contact or visit other cities. Until then the airport would not be useful for its original purpose.

As Agmund carefully picked his way through the airport complex everything appeared to be no different than any other airport on Earth, abandoned and a waste of space. Agmund's sources told him quite differently though. The airport consisted of several large buildings. There were three hangars grouped together at the northern end of the airport. At the eastern end of the airport was the terminal. The southern end housed the air traffic control building. A few maintenance buildings were scattered across the western end. Agmund's target was the air traffic control building. Agmund's information told him that this building was the main hub of the abandoned airport, which the Stasi had quietly turned into one of their bases many years earlier.

Agmund had chose the air traffic control building as his target because it enabled him to have a confined area, the type that was best for close quarter combat where the limited range of his sword would not be a disadvantage. Not only that, but it was deemed the most critical area to neutralize early as it commanded a dominant view of the rest of the airport. Agmund also felt that the traitor Silas would be most likely to stay there if he was at the base at all. No one had heard of his whereabouts since he was nearly caught and killed in a safe house raid. Commander Franklin had informed Agmund just how badly the government, particularly Larkin, wanted Silas dead. Franklin also emphatically insisted that Nemesio needed to die before he killed any more Council Members, and he was fully expecting that Agmund would be the one to be able to bring down that particular threat to the government.

Regardless of whether or not Silas or Nemesio was at this airport, it was one step closer to ending the Stasi threat once and for all. What made this mission so difficult was that this Stasi base was quite different than the previous two that Agmund had already neutralized for a few reasons. First of all, it was not underground. Secondly, Agmund's sources informed him that there were many families living there. Finally, and most importantly from a logistical standpoint, the base was spread out among four buildings. Each building could communicate with the others through the air traffic control building. Anything but a simultaneous assault would put the attacking teams that arrived late in serious jeopardy. Because of this, Agmund had chosen to go with a small attack force of mercenaries; indeed there was only one person to attack each of the buildings. As Agmund approached the building he had assigned himself to assault, his earpiece told him that the three other mercenaries were crossing the fence as well to proceed with their final approach to their target buildings. Each mercenary was a highly effective killing machine with no remorse and a history for bravery and an ability to operate best alone against incredible odds. Each one was a lone wolf, a characteristic Agmund shared with them. For the mission Agmund had in mind, he needed that particular trait.

Agmund soon stood outside the entrance to the air traffic control building. It took only thirty seconds to pick the lock and enter the building. The first floor did not concern Agmund; he wanted to get to the top floor quickly as he felt that would be where the majority of opposition would be. More importantly though, the communication equipment was also housed on that floor that Agmund needed to neutralize before it could be used to communicate an attack to the other sectors of the base. He approached the stairwell that would lead him up. As he approached the bottom step of the staircase, he paused. He had thought he had caught a glimmer of light on the step. He kicked the thick layer of dust on the floor and watched it float up into the air and settle back down. Sure enough, there was a nearly imperceptible beam of light that shone on the dust as it settled in a certain spot. The first step was definitely booby trapped as an alarm, but Agmund wondered how many other steps were. He doubted the Stasi had access to many of these expensive security defenses. Also, the more of these sensors there were, the more likely that their own members would accidently trigger them. This would cause too many false alarms which inevitably would lead to an actual alarm to be treated as another accident. Thus, Agmund felt confident this was the only step that had a motion sensor connected to an alarm.

He took a couple of steps back and then ran forward, leaping clear of the laser and landing softly on the fourth step. However, his sheath with his sword inside of it hit the step heavily as he landed. He pulled out his sword and listened to see if anyone nearby had heard his mistake. As he did so, he heard shuffling of feet above him. He traversed the next dozen steps quickly, bringing himself right below the landing that marked the halfway point to the next floor. The stairs reversed direction and another sixteen steps brought a person to the second floor. Agmund did not climb these next set of steps. He stopped and listened to see if anyone was coming down the stairs. Agmund distinctly heard two men coming straight towards him. The careless, unhurried sound of their walk told them that it was likely they were expecting to meet a fellow Stasi member whom had merely made too much racket trying to not set off the alarm at the first step.

Agmund listened as the shuffling feet came down the stairs from the second story. He crouched against the wall in the shadows, poised to strike as soon as a target presented itself. He did not have to wait long. These guards had never experienced an attack before and had become complacent despite the attacks the other bases had experienced recently. Their weapons were still strapped inside their holsters as Agmund sliced each of their throats deeply when they reached the landing. He grabbed one of the guard's bodies with his left hand and positioned his body to stop the other from falling.   Agmund lowered them softly to the ground, careful not to allow himself to betray his presence again by sloppily allowing sound to echo in that stairwell.   As they were lying on the grounds, they bled to death inside of a minute.   Agmund had little desire to kill any more people than necessary and even less of a desire to raise the alarm to the rest of the base and fail in his mission.

He climbed the stairs quietly up to the second floor, stopping at the second floor landing to see where the men had likely come from.   He found himself looking at four chairs surrounding a nearly bare table.   The table held a deck of cards and some cups of coffee.   Behind the table was a padlocked cabinet full of guns and ammunition.   What interested Agmund was not the cards, nor the weapons, but the fact that there were three steaming cups of coffee on the table.   Agmund paused, unsure of where the third person was.   The options were numerous.   The third guard could have gone upstairs to report the disturbance, could have left his post to go to the restroom, or could be upstairs or on the second floor for an unknown reason.   Agmund assumed the third guard was not reporting his presence as the chairs were pushed in.   Agmund knew the guards he had already killed did not appear to be in a hurry, so he felt confident that the third guard knew nothing of his presence, unless the third person had somehow learned of his presence after the two men had descended the stairs.   Agmund knelt next to the door that entered the second floor.   Anyone coming out of the second floor would not be able to see him because the door swung out. If someone came down the stairs from upstairs however, Agmund would be easily spotted and would have a difficult time closing the distance in time to avoid getting shot and bring his sword within range.

After a few very tense minutes, the door to his immediate right swung outward towards him. It shielded his presence, but also prevented him from ascertaining who his foe was until they stepped forward. A skinny, short figure stepped out into Agmund's view. Agmund stood up and raised his sword to strike his enemy down. He was about to bring the sword down into the back of the person's head when the person turned around. Agmund's opponent was a mere teenage girl. The girl tried getting her pistol out of her holster, but her nervous hands did not enable her to bring the gun out. Agmund struck the girl with the palm of his right hand behind the girl's left ear, knocking her out. He took a deep breath and looked in her youthful face. It went against every fiber of his being to strike a female, but he had no choice when the enemies he fought were so desperate as to often sacrifice their own children's lives to oppose the government. Agmund was one of the few that refused to kill these young people, particularly females, whom were merely following their parents' footsteps, and often their hatred as well. Each time he refused to kill a teenager though, he put himself at risk of being killed before he could incapacitate them without causing them permanent harm. He propped her up against the wall and then acquired the girl's gun before moving up. There were only three more floors to go to the control station.

Ignoring the doors to enter the third and fourth floors, Agmund made his way directly to the control room. He cautiously paused at the top, his eyes barely over the stair railing looking into the room. It took a few minutes for his eyes to adjust to the complete lack of lighting after being on the luminous stairway. The stairs enabled entrance to the center of the room. The reason for the poor lighting soon became obvious as Agmund's eyes dilated. Large windows were in place of the walls on all four sides. Any lights would betray the presence of the Stasi at the base. There were five people on that floor. None of them appeared to be Silas or Nemesio, though the darkness made it impossible to be sure.

Of the five people, one of them did indeed draw Agmund's attention though. Sitting in front of a computer only a few feet in front of Agmund was an elderly, portly man with thinning, white hair. The person had several communication devices in front of him. It was obvious that he was responsible for coordinating any information among the spread out base. The elderly man's back was towards Agmund. He noted the other four people in the room, all facing outward with binoculars. Agmund was surprised that he had not been spotted on his approach to the building. The four sentries continually peered out, obviously confident that they were safely protected from behind by the guards posted near the bottom of the stairs.

Agmund crept forward, making his way among the maze of cubicles that were placed randomly throughout that upper floor. The carpeted floor made it easy for him to approach undetected. He was soon right behind the old man, close enough that Agmund held his breath and stretched his hands outward. His right hand closed like a clamp over the elderly man's mouth. With his left arm he choked the man until he was unconscious. Agmund quickly drew the old man to the ground quietly. Taking the handgun tucked into the man's pants, Agmund took the magazine out and placed it in the trash bin, careful to hide it under pieces of paper. Then he placed the gun behind some of the communication equipment. Agmund planted an explosive on the communication devices and made sure the trigger was synced to it. He then dragged the elderly man to a nearby cubicle and listened for any signs that he had been discovered. Still no one noticed him.

Agmund then made his way towards the windows of the floor that were facing westward. He knew that area to be the widest open, and did not want that mercenary assigned the maintenance buildings to lose the element of surprise. Agmund could not assume that the sentries had no way of contacting the other parts of the base directly without the old man. If that mercenary was spotted the entire mission would be in severe jeopardy. Agmund crept slowly from cubicle to cubicle, planning on sending that sentry into unconsciousness as well. He had made it a couple dozen feet, nearly halfway to his mark, when the sentry's attention perked up visibly, but not due to Agmund. He had spotted the mercenary. He whirled around quickly as Agmund disappeared into a cubicle. "Sound the alarm, we have an intruder on the west side!" the sentry shouted as he ran forward to the middle of the room to where the old man was stationed. His attention had been on finding the old man so he had not noticed Agmund before he made it into the cover of the cubicle. The other sentries took a quick scan of their areas, before turning their attention to the center of the room as well. None of them could see the old man. The sentry coming from the west side only took a few seconds to reach the cubicle in which Agmund was hiding. As he crossed the door of the cubicle, Agmund's sword pierced through his ribs on his left side deep into his chest. Agmund stood up tall and wrenched his sword out of the sentry's side. The man fell dead to the floor. The other sentries wasted no time in emptying a magazine of ammunition from their respective handguns at Agmund now that they were fairly certain that the sentry was dead. The muzzle flashes in the dark, enclosed spot momentarily made the shooters lose their sight of Agmund. While changing magazines, they scanned the room for Agmund but could not see him. The three remaining sentries each moved forward to the spot they had last seen Agmund located at from their different directions, seeking to confirm the kill.

The sentries all arrived at about the same time; they could not see the body of Agmund, just the body of their fellow Stasi colleague. However, the one pointed a trail of thin, but fresh blood leading away, towards the western edge of the building. They quietly followed it, desiring to finish the kill, or find the dead body. Their guns drawn out, they all three walked forward following the blood trail. As they followed it past a cubicle, Agmund quietly stepped out of the cubicle after they had stepped past his hiding spot. The sentries had taken the bait of the blood trail he had planted using the blood of the man he had killed. It was only a matter of a few strokes of his sword to finish off the guards on that floor.

Agmund did not linger over his kills; the gunfire would have warned everyone else in the building that all was not right. He ran over to the staircase and quickly descended. He paused before rounding the corner to the landing leading down to the fourth floor. The landing was crowded with seven men, all with guns drawn. Fortunately for Agmund they all faced downstairs. They had not been able to determine the gunshots had come from above in the twisted acoustics of the building. Nor did they even remotely suspect that the threat had already snuck past them. Agmund leapt down into the middle of them, making it impossible for them to use their guns for anything but clubs for fear of shooting each other instead of Agmund. A few of the men managed to strike his body with the butts of their guns, but the strikes were wild and did not do any real damage. Agmund approached the fight with a much calmer disposition, and with the better weapon for the situation. His sword deftly made killing strokes until only two of them were still alive, although they were not uninjured. Agmund mercifully dispatched the one who was in the most pain. The one left was a smaller man whom Agmund had severed the right arm off of early in the fight. Still, the man had continued to fight on. Agmund sheathed his sword and the man wildly tried to attack. A powerful kick to the chest from Agmund sent the man back against the floor and into a door. Agmund's opponent now sat against the door to the fourth floor clutching the bloody stump that used to be his upper arm. He looked intent on making sure Agmund did not enter that door.

"What is your name?" Agmund asked the young, short man.

"My name is Kori."

"Is Chancellor Silas here?"

"No, fortunately he left an hour ago."

"Is it truly fortunate to postpone the inevitable?" Agmund asked, strangely wanting to talk with this young man.

"Why do you hate us so?" the young man asked wanting to know before he was killed why he had died. Evidently

Agmund was not the only one who desired answers from a complete stranger.

"The Stasi must perish to guarantee a better future for this city. Can you not see that the Stasi and the government's perpetual war is tearing this city apart? I seek to end that war."

"Can you not see the atrocities the government you protect commits? Can you not see that the Stasi desire a better future as well? I can see but I don't think you can. I think you only know how to kill. You do not know how to really live."

"The Stasi would merely be different from the government you say I protect, not better. No, in your quest to destroy the ultimate evil in your eyes, you Stasi have transformed into something just as horrible, if not worse. Now answer me this, who else is left in this building?"

"If you have made it this far, then I imagine you have killed our guards and sentries. If that is indeed true, there are no combatants are left. This building used to be full of families. The government has diminished our population to the point that we only need to use the fourth floor and we still have spare rooms. I beg you to leave the families alone, we have all suffered enough."

"You are an intelligent young man, misguided by Stasi propaganda, but intelligent none the less. So families are on this floor. I have no quarrel with your women and children. Lead them out of this place in exactly fifteen minutes from now. You will have ten minutes to get well away from this place. Do not leave before or after that or more people that you know will be killed. This time it will be by hands I do not control."

"Why do you spare us when you hate us?"

"I have nothing to gain through your deaths. Besides, you are not one of the people I hate Kori. No, those that I hate will not be spared."

"You gained something from the death of these six men I knew?" Kori gestured at the bloodied bodies lying on the floor.

"I was merely protecting my own life. There are lives I have yet to take that I hope will greatly benefit this city. You are lucky, yours is not one of them." Agmund brought out the trigger and set off the explosive to destroy the communication equipment. It was one last step he needed to do before leaving Kori. He could not allow Kori to warn the other buildings that the facility was under attack. As it turned out, Agmund had nothing to worry about. By the time he had exited the building, the other three mercenaries had all reported their missions to be successful. Agmund wondered if any of them had come across families, and what they had done about it. Knowing there was nothing he could do about it now, he made his way into the city to report to Commander Franklin. SWAT teams would arrive in thirty minutes to clean up the mess, and take the credit for the raid. The people needed reassurance that the government could win this war against the Stasi. Larkin insisted the public know nothing of Agmund, at least for now.

December 22, 32 PAW

8:01

Nemesio found Chancellor Silas in the last place one would expect to find him, in the middle of a government park in the middle of the city. Silas had spent the night travelling from place to place after leaving the airport base on a gut instinct. Reports had come in that the Maevin Police had managed to eliminate his assets on the base. The Stasi had only one base left. He was sitting on a bench at the end of a small pond feeding the several ducks in the area in an effort to clear his head and think. The ducks were the result of a few Maevin corporations whom were working hard to restore some of Earth's population of animals that had been devastated just as much as humans by the nuclear war. Nemesio sat down next to Chancellor Silas. Chancellor Silas looked at him, but it took him a few moments to recognize Nemesio sans his tactical clothing and gear. He looked exactly like the rest of the government employees in the park. Nemesio was a master of disguise when he needed to be, although he felt naked without all his weapons on his person.

"Nemesio, I thought we agreed not to see each other."

"I need to ask a favor of you."

"What can I do? The government has nearly eliminated us Stasi. We have only one base left and it is only a matter of time before it is attacked. I have no cards left to play. The government is going to win, even if you manage to pull off your mission." Silas looked as though he had already lost everything dear to him.

"Silas do not give up hope just yet. I may have one card left for us to try, but I cannot abandon my mission to put it in play. The mission I have given myself is going to take the entirety of my efforts and work; as such I need you to contract someone to do this mission for me, for us. I have heard rumors of this man being able to complete any mission, for free."

"Who?" Nemesio noted the glimmer of anticipation in Silas's eyes.

"Rhys." Nemesio said. There was no longer optimism in Silas's eyes, but there was also not any despair, just shock.

"He is the Christian's toy, doing their dirty work for them for absolutely no pay. Why do you want him?"

"Because the card we need to play, the only one left to us, is to make a temporary alliance with the Christians and Muslims. They will add greatly to our strength and are used to guerilla warfare. They have no real bases, so they will be difficult to eliminate. We will help them take the fight to the government who is hurting as well from our recent attacks. This will bewilder the government and give me more time to finish my mission. Once we are in power, we can use that power to quash the Christians and Muslims once and for all."

Nemesio watched as Silas's face slowly recovered from his initial shock. Silas finally spoke after a long pause. "It is the only chance we have left Nemesio. I see no other options on the board. Yes, it can work. I can see it now. We must use these two pawns to protect the king from getting checkmated. During that time, you, the ever deadly queen, we will be obscured from view momentarily and be allowed to complete your mission. There is only one question I have, Nemesio. Do we have enough strength to defeat both the Christians and Muslims once the government is defeated or will we lose that battle? I do not want to trade one unwinnable war for another. As unbelievable as it is for me to even think, I would almost rather have the government in power than the Christians and Muslims again."

"We are not strong enough, yet. The Christians and Muslims have largely been shielded from this war as the Stasi and the government has traded blows. This alliance will bring them into the civil war and weaken them in the process. They are highly motivated and have much to gain. They will fight to the bitter end, at least some of them. Others take the so called 'high road' and do not participate in any kind of warfare. Those will not be an issue once we are in power."

"Do you believe the Christians and Muslims will want to join with the Stasi? We have not exactly been friendly to each other since The Atomic War."

"They will if they have any wisdom at all. If the Stasi are extinguished, then there will be no greater threat to the government than the Christians and the Muslims. It will only be a matter of time before the government recovers in that case and makes all religious zealots extinct."

"Yes, yes it could possibly work. Your plan is indeed sound, and will possibly allow us to win this war after all."

"You do not sound so enthused."

"I am confused on one point still, what is this mission you need him to do?"

"I need him to infiltrate a top-secret prison. I have recently recovered evidence pointing to the existence of a top-secret prison twenty miles north of the city. Evidently it was built in an area about half the size of Maevin that was discovered to be radiation free. Larkin does not kill all religious zealots. He has found that some of them do not fear death. These he takes to this facility. There are many Muslims and Christians there, among some others. These others are primarily political opponents and Stasi members. Basically anyone Larkin wants to die a slow, painful death." Nemesio reported the facts of the prison as though he was relating what he had for lunch that day.

"Why did I know nothing of this prison until now? Do you have any idea of how many of my men and women could be there, perhaps even my daughter!" Chancellor Silas was extremely upset; Nemesio had never seen him so angry. Luckily as it was during working hours, the park was quite near deserted. No one paid them any attention. Even if it had been crowded, Nemesio doubted anyone would have done anything. An angry person in Maevin was not a new phenomenon, even among the elite of the city.

"Your daughter?" Nemesio asked in surprise, trying hard to remain cool to encourage Silas to settle down as well. He had no clue Chancellor Silas had any children.

Chancellor Silas regained his usually cool demeanor, although it took much greater effort than usual. Once he was calmed down he seemed even more downcast than the beginning of the conversation before Nemesio had given him a renewed hope. "Yes, my daughter was captured by government forces when she was 17. She was going to take over the Stasi for me when I was killed or captured, or back when I had more hope, she was going to take the reins of the government when I passed away. She is the only child I have ever had. That was eight years ago that she was captured. I have searched for her feverishly ever since, but have found no trace of her. To imagine, she may have been rotting in this prison for years." Silas seemed to have been able to control his anger, but his sorrow was quickly coming through at the thought of his own daughter undergoing so much suffering.

"I am sorry to hear that." Nemesio said, his own eyes beginning to water. "I will mention that any Stasi members are to come to you directly. If she is there, you will get to see her soon. I will make no mention that one of them is your daughter just that you desire all Stasi."

"You have no idea how much that would mean to me. Or maybe you do. Have you ever had a child, Nemesio?" Chancellor Silas asked as he caught Nemesio's face betraying the inner sorrow he felt.

"I had four children what seems like a lifetime ago." Nemesio said distantly, as if his mind was no longer in the present. A single tear fell down his cheek. His eyes came back into focus as he looked into Chancellor Silas's troubled face.

"You do understand my pain." Silas said, knowing then that Nemesio's four children had all been killed.

Nemesio became uncomfortable and sought to change the subject. "Anyhow, have Rhys bring a prisoner to the facility in a Radiation proof vehicle under the disguise of a Maevin officer. He needs to gain access to the Central Command Room. It controls the entire facility electronically. If he can take control of that room, he can take control of the entire prison. Have him release all the Christians, Muslims, and Stasi so we have additional strength to finish this civil war against the government. By releasing the Christians and Muslims back to their people, we take a step in showing the Christians and Muslims just how serious we are about banding together against the government."

"What makes you think Rhys will willingly work with the Muslims? Will they not kill each other all over again as they have for centuries as soon as they get the chance?"

"No one knows if he is actually a Christian from the best I can tell. However, he will recognize the value of having every possible person to resist the final attacks of the government available. The man may not be a Christian, but he is definitely interested in the best interest of the Christians."

"This is too true. Nemesio, you have impressed me once again. I always knew you are a gifted killer, but you have proved to be an extremely gifted strategist as well. You have discovered a card left to play when I saw only despair. This card will hopefully prove to be a very strong play as well. Good luck with your quest to kill the Council. Stay alive, I will need you once Maevin is ours."

"You stay alive as well my friend. I will come visit you once it is all done. But I warn you, do not betray the Christians and Muslims until the government is extinct."

Silas laughed. "I have stayed alive this long, I hope it has not all been so Larkin could kill me right before I get to hear the news that he has died by your hand."

"Now that would indeed be unfortunate for you." Nemesio stood up and left the park.

December 22, 32 PAW

10:42

"Agmund, you are a miracle worker, and you only used three other people to get the job done too! Now the Stasi have only one major facility left. It will only be a matter of time before we find it and you neutralize it. You are incredible. Is there anything I can do for you as a reward?" Commander Franklin gushed in gratitude towards Agmund.

"To tell you the truth Commander Franklin, there is still one loose end that is bothering me."

"Silas? Do not worry about him. He is a coward on the run as he always has been. The difference this time is he is running out of places to hide. We will have him killed shortly. And if your recent success is any indication then it will likely come by your blade."

"No, Commander Franklin that is not the loose end that worries me. That loose end that concerns me is the one we know so little about. That loose end is actually two people, Rhys and Nemesio. The only thing we know about both of these men is whom they take missions for and that they are really good at accomplishing those missions. To be frank, that makes me very nervous."

"I see. What do you want me to do about that situation?"

"I want you to contract Rhys to kill Nemesio."

"What? How do you think that will solve anything?" Commander Franklin was completely flabbergasted.

"It will allow us to know more about both men. We will learn more about Rhys to see how he responds to your offer. We will then learn more about Nemesio through Rhys. Hopefully one of these threats will be eliminated and we will only have one left to deal with. Or through some miracle they both manage to kill each other then our only problems left are ones that we are well informed and positioned to handle."

"I just attempted to kill Rhys. He must know I put the contract out on his head. What makes you think that Rhys will even hear a proposal by me?"

"Rhys will do anything to help the Christians, even though most Christians consider him an evil man. Make it seem like this will help the Christians."

Commander Franklin thought for a few moments before a menacing smile broke out on his face. "I think I can handle that."

"Good. I knew you could. I will come back to you when I know where the final base is."

Chapter XII

December 25, 32 PAW

21:02

Commander Franklin paced his office nervously. Kelly, his secretary, notified him through his earpiece that his visitor was ready. He told her to wait a couple of minutes before sending him in. During the first minute Commander Franklin made sure that his weapons were all where he wanted them in case his visitor became uncooperative. He also checked in with a dozen of his top CRZ soldiers waiting in readiness hidden in other rooms on that floor to make sure they could hear him and were prepared. He then sat down behind his desk and wiped the sweat off of his forehead just seconds before his visitor treaded into his office. He stood there watching Commander Franklin warily as the door clicked ominously shut behind him.

"Rhys, I am glad you have come to hear my offer of how we can work together to make both the government and the Christians happy. I hope we can put our past misunderstandings behind us." Commander Franklin tried looking hard at Rhys's dark, foreboding eyes as he spoke but found his glance wandering to Rhys's guns displayed blatantly at his hips cowboy style. The guns themselves however did not look anything like an old six shooter. Commander Franklin knew these particular 1911 models were one of the newest and deadliest models on the market.

"I came to hear the specifics of how your plan could help the Christians." Rhys's voice was as cold as his glare.

"How does your own area of the city sound?" Commander Franklin had hoped this statement would soften up Rhys's demeanor. It had no effect.

"You mean our own prison area of the city?"

"No, it would not be a prison, Rhys. It would be your own area that you could reside in if you desired. You Christians could worship there freely as long as you lived and stayed in that area. There would of course be security measures to ensure that there were no unneeded interactions between you Christians and the rest of us."

"I would need better details, but I imagine this generous Christmas gift would not come without a price."

"Christmas?" Commander Franklin thought hard. Oh, he remembered now. He had only been seven years old when he had last heard of Christmas. That was how old he was right before The Atomic War. His family had been deeply religious. They had celebrated the birth of the man they called their Savior that day, Jesus. They exchanged gifts and sang happy birthday to Jesus as if he was actually present with them. No non-Christian in Maevin celebrated the date of the claimed birthday of a claimed Savior, even though many of the older residents remember fondly the Christmases of their youth. Too many deaths could be attributed to the so-called Christian nations' defense of their faith. Commander Franklin had been fortunate enough to survive The Atomic War. His family had not been so lucky. "Oh, yes. Christmas. That must be today. Well, to answer your question. The reason I brought you here today was because I want you to perform for me a small favor."

"If it was small you would have taken care of it yourself Commander Franklin." Rhys said with his glowering eyes. Commander Franklin became nervous under that stare and began watching Rhys's guns as distrustfully as Rhys was treating Commander Franklin's offer.

"True. Maybe it is a large favor. However, I believe it is a favor you would be happy to perform. I want you to kill Nemesio." Rhys seemed to relax greatly at the news of the assignment. Commander Franklin took a deep breath and began to relax as well.

"I do greatly desire that the Stasi are extinguished. However I have a better idea of whom I can kill."

"Yes, I see. You want to kill Silas instead."

"That is true, but I had someone else in mind first."

"Who?" Commander Franklin was thoroughly confused now.

Rhys made no vocal reply. His actions spoke loud enough however. He drew his gun before Commander

Franklin could even bring one of his hands onto the handle of the guns he had hidden beneath his desk. Rhys fired his gun once. The bullet struck Commander Franklin in the right shoulder, completely disintegrating his joint with the hollow point round. Commander Franklin frantically radioed a Code Black, meaning Rhys was to be killed immediately and that his own life was in danger. Rhys however seemed to have been prepared for this. He knocked over a top-heavy bookshelf of over five hundred books that Commander Franklin finally had Kelly unpack for him and put on the shelves. The heavily laden bookshelf fell over the entrance of the door after an adrenaline enhanced effort. The weight of the bookshelf was too much for the CRZ soldiers to overcome. Their futile pushing did not make the door open. They frantically called for more reinforcements, and explosives.

Rhys turned back to face Commander Franklin now that he knew the two of them would not be interrupted for a while. Commander Franklin was now standing, a 9 mm pistol in his left hand leveled at Rhys. Rhys had been forced to holster his gun in order to push the bookshelf over, he was defenseless. Commander Franklin fired the trigger multiple times as Rhys dove forward to use Commander Franklin's heavy desk to shield him from the bullets. It was a risky move, but it was the only cover available to him. As Rhys dove, Commander Franklin felt certain that he had at least managed to hit Rhys a few times out of the eight shots he had fired. Commander Franklin knew he still had seven bullets left in the gun, but hoped Rhys was already dead. He waited for signs to hear that Rhys was still alive. He heard absolutely nothing.

Commander Franklin circled slowly and quietly around the desk, taking a very wide route. He held his gun up; ready to fire at anything that moved or even remotely looked like Rhys. Commander Franklin made it to where he could finally see the front of the desk, but Rhys was not there. It was then that he saw Rhys's cowboy hat and a gun poke over the edge of the far side of the desk. Before Commander Franklin could shoot, a bullet hit him high on the shoulder, just grazing it. The pain of the bullet was enough to make Commander Franklin drop his gun. Rhys was in front of him holding a gun to his face in an instant before Commander Franklin could recover his gun. Commander Franklin noted that Rhys was bleeding from a couple of slight bullet wounds on his arms. There was one bullet however that had nearly been fatal. A bullet had hit just above the right collar bone of Rhys and tore through the shoulder muscle. Commander Franklin knew it was a very painful wound, but unfortunately not one that greatly affected the mobility of the right arm.

"Why did you decide that I had to die Rhys?"

"I first decided not to kill Nemesio, at least not until he has destroyed the government for me. As for the decision to kill you, your actions made that decision easy enough. You need to die because you tortured and killed Jasper among many other Christians. The second reason is because you contracted Brava, whom killed my friend in trying to kill me. Third, well, that reason you do not get to know."

"Why not?"

"I can't give away all my secrets just yet, but you can die knowing that your death will benefit me greatly. Your death is just a small part of ensuring that Larkin will die."

"Do you think that Silas will treat you Christians any better?"

"Do not worry, Silas will die too. Now is the time for you to die. I will allow you the same chance you gave Jasper though, a chance to fight for your life."

"How do you know about that? How do you know I gave him that chance?"

Rhys just gave him a small smile and put his gun back in his holster as Commander Franklin stood up. Commander Franklin lashed out with a left leg high kick. Rhys backed up, but it still nearly caught him on the jaw. Commander Franklin did not let up, he came forward letting kick after kick fly, knowing that if Rhys got inside his outer guard that he would have the upper hand due to Commander Franklin's gravely injured right shoulder and slightly injured left shoulder. Rhys however managed to duck below one of Franklin's many high kicks and swept Commander Franklin's legs out from under him. Commander Franklin fell hard to the ground. Rhys placed his left knee directly on Commander Franklin's bullet wound on his shoulder and began raining fist blows down upon his face. Soon, Commander Franklin's was unable to fight back anymore. Soon, Rhys was nearly out of breath and his hands hurt. He stood over Franklin's body and looked down upon him with contempt.

"Commander Franklin, I decline your offer." Rhys pulled out his gun and shot Commander Franklin square in the forehead once. He holstered the gun and cast a quick look at the door. A lot of noise was coming from the other side and it looked like the door was about ready to give way. Rhys moved to the wall of Commander Franklin's office and pulled out a small bag from behind a couch set against the wall. Inside were a grenade, rope, and a rappelling device. Rhys pulled the pin of the grenade and chucked it at the far corner of Commander Franklin's office. Commander Franklin had a corner office with windows all along those two walls where the grenade now rested. The explosion caused glass and metal to fly out into the city streets far below. There was also a large crater where the corner once was. By this time Rhys was already clipped into his delay device. He threw the rope around one of the remaining steel frames for the window and tied a quick trucker's hitch. Within a few moments he was down on the city streets. Instead of taking off though into the dusk, he ran into the underground parking garage of the CRZ headquarters. The guards had left to go to the top floor to help Commander Franklin. Within moments Rhys found what he had come for. He took the keys and started up the nuclear radiation sealed truck and took off into the night, no one being the wiser that Rhys had accomplished more than killing Commander Franklin.

Rhys soon made it to the edge of the city's stone walls. He stopped right in front of the wall. He climbed out of the vehicle and pushed aside a door that had been disguised to look like the wall. Behind it was a tunnel that led outside the city. Rhys turned around to re-enter the nuclear radiation sealed truck when a figure dressed in black stepped out of the darkness nearby. He approached Rhys confidently. Soon the two men were only twenty feet away from each other, the stranger standing between Rhys and the truck.

"I still do not know if I can trust you Rhys."

"I know, but you have little other choice. You risk much to give your people a better future. I applaud your bravery."

"That is high praise indeed Rhys for you to applaud my bravery after what you have just done. I see you have not escaped without injury though."

"Fortunately the bullets caused no real damage. I even lost less blood than I had anticipated. Let us go, before we attract any attention."

Both men piled into the truck. Rhys drove into the tunnel and then stopped. He got out and closed the camouflaged door, thankful that he had discovered this secret of Maevin long ago. Once through the tunnel he sped north. Halfway there he stopped to dressed his wounds and change into a CRZ uniform in the back of the vehicle. In the pocket of his long jacket he pulled out official paperwork denoting the prisoner to be dropped off. Rhys had managed to get his hands on an actual document; however he had not gotten his hands on the actual prisoner to be transported. The other occupant changed into prison garb and allowed Rhys to handcuff him. Everything was coming into place nicely, now the most difficult part of Rhys's mission was ahead, just another ten miles north. During those last ten miles Rhys and his passenger went through the details of their mission one more time, the passenger was quite vocal about his nervousness in placing so much faith in Rhys. Rhys did little to reassure him, he knew that the man had much to be nervous about for he was risking so much.

Chapter XIII

December 25, 32 PAW

22:33

Rhys and his volunteer prisoner were soon in sight of the prison complex Aamina. The surrounding area was truly a wasteland due to high radioactive levels. There was no growth, and very few signs that there used to be any kind of habitation outside the walls of Maevin. It was here that his mission to bring the Stasi, the Christians, and the Muslims together against the government had brought him. Rhys had killed the Commander of the CRZ, and every CRZ employee knew it by now. It was fortunate for Rhys that where he travelled now would have no indication of what he had just accomplished, or so he hoped.

Out of the desolation ahead rose a city roughly half the size of Maevin, but it was even more secured. It appeared that the architect and building crew had drawn heavily from the designs of ancient castles in creating this facility. There was only one entrance, from the north. Rhys drove around the city, now a smooth road that had obviously been repaved recently. There were guard stations approximately every four hundred yards. His progress as he drove around the city was being closely monitored he knew. Aamina had obviously been built to not only keep prisoners in, but everyone and everything else out as well, though Rhys doubted that they had to worry about such matters in a radioactive desert. While Rhys drove around the outside of the city, his prisoner climbed through the back window into the prisoner area in the back of the enclosed truck. Rhys latched the transparent window behind him.

Rhys soon came to the gate. The gate was lowered down to allow him to cross over a ravine. The ravine ran about forty yards wide, and just as deep. It stretched a full hundred yards long. Its uniformity suggested it was man-made. Rhys marveled at the excessive security of a facility surrounded by nuclear radioactivity. Rhys waited patiently for the gate to drop down and then drove the truck forward. Rhys's passenger in the back became even more nervous even as Rhys allowed himself to become calmer. He always became calmest during a mission, a peculiar trait that had saved his life many times over.

There was a guard station in the middle of the road. Rhys stopped there. All but one of the guards kept their position. The youngest man, probably only in his early twenties with sandy blond hair and vibrant green eyes approached.

"You are a new driver. My name is Hegs. I will go with you to put the prisoner in his cell. What is your name?"

"My name is Rhys. It's a pleasure to meet you Hegs."

"Who is the poor soul you bring with you?"

"His name is Vamir." Rhys said, handing him the papers, thankful that the guard did not seem to have a photo to verify the fact that it was indeed the prisoner named Vamir. Rhys tried to get Hegs to talk about something else before he could prove Rhys wrong about the photo ID. "This place is really something. They didn't tell me it would be this huge or that the security measures would be so impressive."

"Well, that's the government for you, working their butts off to cover their own butts. It's about the only times politicians are properly motivated to actually do anything."

"Too true. Say, could I get a tour of the facility after we drop off the prisoner?"

"Of course, but it's not much of a tour, the facility was built with function in mind more than appealing aesthetics. If you see just one tenth of the city, then you will have seen it all. It's built in ten parts, all of them identical to each other. All of them can run independent of each other which was very useful when this complex was started twenty years ago. Back then only one of the sectors of the city was used. Now, all ten of the sections house prisoners."

"Well, after we take care of this prisoner then we will see a tenth of the city." Rhys stated.

Hegs got in the truck and looked around the interior. "Did they send you by yourself?"

"Yup, just me and the prisoner. They are getting stretched thin in the city. Everyday brings us closer to the end of the battle between the Stasi and the government, but everyday also means the death of more people on each side. We are getting thin, but they keep telling us the Stasi are getting stretched even thinner, in fact it is believed they are only down to one major facility that they control, we just don't know where yet. Makes me wonder how they know it is the last one if they don't even know where the last one is."

"Yeah, more politicians just saying the way they see things when everyday we actually see the results of their decisions. That's the building there." Hegs said, pointing to a small one story structure. The majority of the surrounding buildings looked like housing or buildings that enabled Aamina to be entirely self-sufficient, hard to do in such a desolate wasteland, but ponds, greenhouses, and productions facilities all made it work. There was no large building that looked like it was a prison in the area though, just one large building in the center of the prison facility.

Rhys pointed to the building he had stopped in front of under Hegs' directions. "Is that where they hold the prisoners, you could only fit a handful of men in there."

"Actually it is where we hold the prisoners, a tenth of the ones at this facility."

"How many prisoners are there at this facility?" Rhys asked.

"You are bringing the eight thousandth two hundred and fifty-seventh prisoner to this facility to date."

"Are you telling me that there are over eight hundred prisoners in that small building? It's got to be only a thousand square feet."

'It is only a thousand square feet, but it has ten floors below the surface. It seems like the guy who built this thing liked the number ten a whole lot. Regardless of that though, the guy did create a very excellent prison. We have never had a problem with any prisoners escaping, they are all held below ground. Not only that, but they don't last long. Something about never breathing fresh air, seeing the sunlight, or seeing other prisoners helps make that possible. It truly is a slow, miserable existence. Death is much better, but we make sure that suicide is impossible. That's the way Larkin wants it. Heck, we used to have the prisoners wear clothes, but they kept hanging themselves with their clothes. Now they stay in their cells naked and there is nothing they can use to kill themselves anymore. Larkin wanted a prison in which a prison sentence would be worse than death and he truly succeeded."

"That is truly incredible." Rhys stated quietly. He did not like the obvious pleasure Hegs took in his job, but kept it to himself for now.

"You hear that back there Vamir. You are going to wish you were dead before long. Then you will die in this place, but long after you lose your mind." Hegs jeered back at the prisoner in the back. Neither Rhys nor the prisoner said anything. Rhys stopped the vehicle and got out. He then pulled the prisoner out of the back of the enclosed truck. Rhys and Hegs pushed the prisoner forward through the unlocked door. With no one but workers and guards allowed topside, there was no reason to lock the door. Four prison guards greeted them as they entered the building.

"Who is this?" the prison guard captain asked.

"Vamir." Hegs answered.

"No, you misunderstood me Hegs, I know who the prisoner is. I received the report this morning. Who is this guy?" the captain pointed at Rhys.

"I am Rhys." Rhys said calmly. Rhys offered the paperwork forward. "I need you to sign this."

The captain took the paper and pen and signed it quickly. "I have not seen you before. How long have you been running prisoners?"

"This is my first one. Got to start sometime right?" The men chuckled at Rhys's joke even though Rhys did not crack a smile.

"I was told about this one," the captain said to Hegs. Rhys got very nervous at this statement. The captain did not seem like a very friendly man to strangers. "I was told to give him more than just our usual indoctrination."

"I'm sure you will enjoy that. You hear that, Vamir, you're already famous here." Everyone laughed at this, Rhys still did not. He was relieved that he was not the one receiving the special treatment, but he feared what would happen to the prisoner. He watched the prisoner get led away, hands cuffed behind him and a bag over his head, completely helpless. He had not handpicked him so he could be tortured. There was nothing he could do about it at the moment though. He had a mission to accomplish now. Rhys would just have to accomplish it in a hurry. The prisoner had known what he was risking when he agreed to help Rhys. The prisoner was now depending upon Rhys. Rhys was determined not to let him down.

Hegs turned around and exited the building. Rhys followed him out, but not before casting one last look in the direction of the room that the prisoner had entered.

"Hegs, this all looks pretty cool, but you are right after a few minutes it is dreadfully dull to the eyes. Is there any chance I could get a tour of that building though?" Rhys pointed to the large building in the middle.

"Of course, Rhys. That is the central command building. It coordinates activities between all ten of the sections of the facility and houses the only communication to Maevin herself via an underground cable."

Rhys drove on the prison's roads to the central facility. It was a ten story building, a fact he took in with no surprise by now. As they entered the building's exterior elevator

Rhys watched Hegs hit the button for the tenth floor. "Now," Hegs stated, "the first nine floors are a bore, they are just administrative offices, but the tenth floor is a gem. It houses all the communication and controls for the entire facility. Virtually everything is controlled electronically in this facility, right down to the prisoner's toilets. There is a team constantly up there, monitoring every inch of this facility. The only spot that is not watched are the various housing areas for the employees."

"This place is a true wonder." Rhys stated. "If the architecture wasn't so dreary I would think about asking to switch my assignment out here." The elevator door soon slid open and he walked into a place with more electronics and technology in it than any one building in Maevin had. Along one full wall that measured one hundred fifty feet in length were monitors that showed various views of the city and its buildings. The other walls had communication equipment, primarily for those within the floor to each other. Another section had controls, for the various things that the city needed done. There were probably fifty people on that floor, all of them assisting in the function of the city, namely to make the prisoners' experience in Aamina the worst possible while making the employees' experience the best possible. Rhys noted the exits on that floor. There were only three. One was right behind him, the other two to his left and right.

Rhys took in as much information about the floor as he could, and then sprung into action. He pulled out two Government Issue Glock .38 caliber pistols. He began shooting, his first hollow point bullet entering right behind the left ear of Hegs as he stood directly in front of Rhys. Everyone screamed, a few tried attacking Rhys, others tried fleeing. Rhys shot the ones that tried attacking and fleeing. Most of the bullet wounds were non-fatal. A few people tried to send out a communication or hit the alarm in the central column of the floor. None of them made it there as Rhys's bullets tore through their tender flesh. After almost a dozen people were shot, the remaining thirty odd people froze in their tracks. Rhys calmly walked to the central column where the alarm was.

"This facility is now under my control." Rhys's voiced boomed with authority. "You will all do what I say otherwise you will die." As an added emphasis Rhys loaded two fresh magazines into his pistols. "First, let me have communication with this entire facility. If you do not cooperate with my every command I will begin executing more of you."

A young woman spoke up timidly, "That would be my station, sir."

"Good, that is one woman who has saved a life today."

Rhys walked over to the woman's station, still keeping an eye on everyone else. She placed a microphone on to a desk in front of her. Still holding on to his handguns and keeping an eye on everyone else, Rhys talked into the microphone. Speakers throughout the city broadcasted his message. "My name is Rhys. I am now in control of the central command building. I have two demands. First, bring the prisoners Vamir, Zahir, and Rachel unharmed to me. All three of them are to enter the exterior elevator of this building alone. Secondly, everyone else abandons their stations and surrenders to me in front of the building. To signal your cooperation put all your weapons in a pile at the base of this building. If either of these conditions is not met then I will release all the prisoners, whom I am certain would love to get revenge on you. If you do what I say, then no one else needs to be harmed."

Rhys stepped away from the microphone and began barking orders. "Now, lock down the front gate and keep it locked. Lock the guards out from controlling it. Lock down this floor, no one gets in or out. Send that elevator to the bottom, but keep it closed until I say otherwise. Everyone attend to your stations, except for those who can communicate to Maevin. If anyone goes near that station they will die. If that was your station, attend to the injured. Report all activity to me."

The next twenty minutes were a blur as Rhys tried to keep up with all the action. The guards outside the building tried in vain to come up with a plan to send a message back to Maevin before surrendering. Similarly no luck was made in the vain attempts to enter the elevator or breach the tenth floor of the central building. Finally, some of the prison guards began to give up, putting their weapons down in a pile next to the building. The prisoners were retrieved and ordered into the elevator. Rhys ordered the elevator to the top floor. He kept an eye on the people of the floor, anxious to see if his prisoners were unharmed.

The three prisoners entered the room and looked around in wonder. Both Zahir and Rachel seemed to be very malnourished and worse for the wear. Vamir had obviously been beaten, but did not appear to be much concerned with that. He was the only one that seemed to know what was occurring. He absolutely beamed with happiness as he spoke. "Rhys, you did manage to do it after all! I have doubted you for over a month now that you would deliver on your promises, but you have pulled through! Ah, praise Allah. When you came to me saying that you had orders to kill me, but you did not desire to do so, that you a Christian wished to save my life after Paul had ordered you to kill me, I did not trust you. I had no other option though than to listen to you. This entire time it seemed like I had no option. Then I spent the last month in hiding, allowing none to see me, not even my fellow believers. You were the only one that came to visit me, to remind me that you had not forgotten about me or your promise. At times I was hopeful, but most of the time I was full of despair. I did not think any man capable of giving me what you had promised. Praise Allah that you have been able to pull this miracle off. You have given me control of this prison facility to keep as a haven for all Muslims to be safe from the government, the Stasi, and the Christians. Maybe one day we Muslims and Christians will be at peace with each other. For now though you have delivered the impossible to us Muslims, a new Mecca!"

"Yes Farooq, I had doubted I would be able to accomplish the mission as well. I had doubted that Paul would even accept my evidence of your death. But, there is still much work to be done, for both of us to accomplish. You have your task here of making this a safe haven for all Muslims. There are still many Muslims in the city of Maevin to transport here. There is a small fleet of trucks located here similar to the one I brought you here in that will be able to help you serve that purpose. Christians from here will need to be brought back into the city of Maevin. The guards and other employees of this facility will accept that you Muslims are in charge of Aamina now or they will become prisoners themselves. I imagine they will fear that much more than they will fear you in charge Farooq. I too have the hope that one day we Christians and Muslims will be at peace with each other, but for now I know it is best that we have our own cities. At least I know that we will be able to part as friends Farooq. That alone is a start."

"It is indeed my friend. May God bless your paths."

Rhys seemed to flinch at Farooq's genuine wish of well-being. He recovered quickly though before Farooq could apologize for somehow offending him. "You have much to attend to Farooq. May Allah be praised in this city." Farooq shook hands with Rhys. Rhys walked over to the microphone on the desk of the young lady and made an announcement. "Employees of Aamina, I am relinquishing control to my friend Farooq. He is the leader of the Islamic Movement. This facility will no longer be a place of fear, pain, and despair. This place will now be a haven for all Muslims. The employees of this facility have a choice. Obey Farooq's commands or be thrown into the prison cells below. No one will be forced to be a Muslim, but you will be forced to obey Muslims. He will release all the prisoners if you do not obey his commands. Anyone mistreating any prisoners of any religion or none at all will be executed. If you accept his governance of this facility you will live your life much as you had before here. It is under these conditions I relinquish control of this facility to Farooq."

Farooq stepped forward and began making commands in the control room. Soon a list of all the prisoners and their offense was in his hands. He looked over the list quickly, marking any Muslims that he knew personally. These men that he knew would be the first released and help him govern the city. Others from the city would be next to help him. After he had full control of the facility Christians and political opponents of Larkin would be sent back to the city of Maevin after they had a chance to recover their strength. It was a monumental task, but Farooq eagerly accepted it.

He worked furiously fast as though he was trying to make up for a month of inactivity within mere moments.

Rhys now attended to one of the other two prisoners that he had requested. "Zahir, come forward." Zahir was a well-built man, but prison life had made him frail. His eyes still had a keen brightness to him though that shone despite his circumstances. "Zahir do you know me?"

Zahir looked intently upon Rhys's face. "No. I do not believe we have ever met before."

Rhys breathed a sigh of relief. "My name is Rhys. We have not actually met, but we have a mutual friend. He once told me about you. He said you were the man that had led him to accept Christ. Then a few months after he accepted, you disappeared. He looked for you for a very long time. He never did find you. It seems he felt guilty about it and told me to relieve his guilt."

"What was this man's name?" Zahir asked, clearly curious as to whom Rhys spoke of.

"Ah, so you have led more than just one man to Christ. This man used to work with you before you tried to quit Larkin's Personal Security Guard. His name was Gideon."

Zahir's eyes seemed to simultaneously register sorrow and happiness. "Gideon, he was a great friend of mine. I noticed you used the past tense to refer to him. How did he die?"

Rhys became sorrowful as he spoke, a rare crack through the solid exterior wall he had built around his heart. "For months he debated trying to quit Larkin's Personal Security Guard, but feared what would happen to his family. He cared little what happened to himself, but his family was a different story. After what had happened to you, he just could not bring himself to attempt it. A little over two years ago Larkin found out that Gideon was a Christian and executed his family in front of his eyes. His eldest son and wife were nailed to a cross in front of him and beaten to death. Gideon died with his family."

Zahir's eyes shed a tear. "That is awful...words of sorrow cannot do justice to what happened to Gideon. At least we can rejoice in the fact that they are all united in Heaven now."

Rhys moved on to business. He felt as though he needed to remove himself from the emotions welling up inside. He once again wielded his impenetrable barrier of indifference. "Zahir, I have asked you to come to me for a two-fold purpose. One, as a personal favor to Gideon I wanted to rescue you personally from your imprisonment. Secondly, I need your help. As I understand you were once a Muslim before becoming a Christian."

"That is correct Rhys."

"Well, I need you to help Farooq here. You will be the Christian representative that will ensure that Christians are given just as much of a priority as Muslims. As a man who is formerly a Muslim I believe you are well suited to establishing good relations with them. Also, your former military expertise will come in handy when running missions in and out of the city. You will come with me and I will show you the hidden tunnel you will use to transport Muslims into Aamina, and Christians into Maevin. Once back in Maevin, the truck I brought here will be all for you."

"Is Farooq aware of this plan?" Zahir asked.

"Yes. He is quite aware of it. In fact when I informed him about you he seemed to be quite excited. Despite my personal efforts, Farooq still harbors some ill will towards Christianity. With you here he can concentrate more fully on what he actually wants to focus on, reestablishing a Mecca of sorts for his fellow Muslim brethren. You will help with security and taking care of the Christians in this facility. This will alleviate much of the load off of Farooq. During the course of this, you may even show him a better example of what a Christian really is than myself. Just tonight I have spilled much blood. I understand that you quit because you could no longer pull the trigger even to save your own life on the missions Larkin gave you. Well, you are a much better example of the forgiveness, tenderness, mercy, and love for all life that all Christians should be. You may just convince Farooq that Christians and Muslims can live in peace in the future, and that it will be in his lifetime rather than much later."

"Rhys, I may have spilled less blood than you, but I do not believe myself any better than you. You have risked much for no personal gain for yourself. That is truly commendable. You know little of the sins I have committed even during my imprisonment. There were days during the last four years that I wished that God would never had breathed life into me. Of course, it was always in those darkest moments He shined the brightest. I had nothing else to do but to review Scripture I had memorized, pray, and worship Him. The more I did those things, the less this place became a prison for my spirit and mind."

"Zahir, I have turned my back completely on God, in circumstances arguably little better than your own. God gave me a chance to start a new life of helping others who lost loved ones due to the government. I took that path for a short while, but was too often reminded of how badly the government needed to be defeated. Instead of waiting for God to choose His timing to stop this government, I decided to make my own path and completely abandon God. I chose to set on a path of murder and retribution instead of helping those God put in my path. Along the way I have destroyed some innocent lives. I have done the very thing that caused me to take this path in the first place. In the end, those that remain will have a better life, but I will still have nothing. Nothing is too good for someone whom has abandoned God."

"Rhys, I know little about you and your situation, but we always have a choice. God will forgive whatever you have done if you repent."

"Zahir, I cannot ask for forgiveness for something I have no regrets about doing. I will not turn my steps off this path that I have embarked on. I am too close to the ultimate payoff. Now, if you will please go over the prison lists with Farooq and get on the same page with him before we head back to Maevin. I still have one more person to talk with."

"As you wish Rhys. Just remember, God will accept you back in His arms."

Rhys ignored Zahir's parting comment and walked towards the last prisoner Rhys had requested. Zahir shook his head and said a silent prayer for Rhys before introducing himself to Farooq. The two soon were deeply engrossed in conversation about the most imminent concerns, the smooth release of prisoners and finding shelter for them all while keeping the prison employees under control.

Rhys walked up to Rachel, a petite girl with large, expressive gray eyes. There was a certain amount of beauty lying below the tough exterior. "Rachel, your father informed me you might be here. It took much effort, but I was able to discover that you were here before I even arrived. Eight years is a long time, but you look like you handled it well enough."

"My father sent you? So he is still alive. Is Larkin still alive or did my father manage to kill him?"

"Both men are still alive. The city of Maevin itself has nearly been destroyed because of their actions though. Their rivalry has resulted in the deaths of almost everyone who has attempted to stand in the way of their goal of killing each other. They are running out of people to shield themselves from the other person. The end of this twenty year civil war is coming near. Silas and I both want you to be there for it."

"How is it that you, a Christian, are working for my father? My father hates all Christians, as do I." The women's stare almost made Rhys frightened, even though the gaze came from a woman whom weighed only ninety pounds in her malnourished state.

"The Stasi have needed reinforcements for a long time. I am merely the first of them. An alliance between Christians, Muslims, and the Stasi against the government is allowing us to match the government in strength. What happens when the government is no more is anyone's guess. All I know is that it is the only chance for a better future for all three groups."

"Well, much has happened in Maevin. On the way back maybe you can explain it all to me."

"I will. I will explain to both you and Zahir what has happened. We head back in an hour. Let us look into getting you a shower, clothes, and a good meal."

"Rhys, even though you have saved me, I still hate your kind." Rhys felt pity for the girl. She had so much hatred in her, even to the one who had saver her life.

"I am used to being hated Rachel. Come; let's get ready for the trip back to Maevin."

Chapter XIV

December 26, 32 PAW

7:00

Commander Prilezio leafed through the numerous memos that were on his desk when he arrived to work at 7 am in his office that was just behind his mansion, attached by a covered walkway. His job was to oversee all security measures of the city of Maevin, and lately his job had become even more hectic than normal. One memo had a memory device attached to it. Commander Prilezio put the memory device in his computer. A video came up on his computer. A figure stepped into the frame. Commander Prilezio's eyes went wide as he realized the man in the video matched the description of Nemesio. He looked at the memorandum and his eyes managed to widen even further when he read the frank message signed by Nemesio, "Repent of your crimes against this city or die." He frantically pushed the panic button under his desk. He jumped out of his seat and brandished a 9 mm pistol as he heard a voice. It took him a moment to realize that it came from his computer; Nemesio in the video was talking to him.

"Commander Prilezio, you have committed many atrocities against the citizens of this city including but not limited to torture, rape, kidnapping, extortion, bribery, embezzling, and murder. Never the less, if you repent of your sins and accept God into your heart I will spare your life. To demonstrate your compliance, please open all the windows in your office. If you do not do so, I will kill you. You have thirty seconds to decide." In the video, Nemesio started a timer; it counted back from thirty seconds towards zero. Commander Prilezio began pacing the room. He expected security forces to arrive at his office at about the exact time his thirty seconds would be up. He began wondering where Nemesio would attack from. He kept looking out the closed windows, trying to get a heading on where the attack might come from. He kept one eye on the computer screen however, keeping an eye on the countdown.

"Accept God, ha! I would like to see Nemesio try to get in here and kill me!" He exclaimed boldly, but feeling far from bold as the countdown reached zero.

From the four corners of the room came a soft hiss. Prilezio saw the air filling with gas. The gas began to choke him. He fell on to his hands and knees and began crawling towards the windows desperate to open them. Right in front of him Nemesio dropped to the floor, a gun already in hand with a silencer attached. He had been hiding in the rafters of the ceiling all the time, using the video and memo to distract Commander Prilezio. He was wearing a gas mask. The mask distorted Nemesio's voice, but his words rang crystal clear to Prilezio. "I told you to open the windows Commander Prilezio. Now you are a dead man."

Prilezio was shocked by the sudden appearance of Nemesio, but remained indignant to the end. Prilezio's voice came out in gasps and was extremely raspy. Nemesio had to kneel close to him to hear his anger-filled words. "You may kill me, but you will surely die. Before your video was even finished I alerted my men to come here. They will be here soon to kill you."

"Commander Prilezio, you have expected them to show already, but I will let you in on a little secret. When I broke into your office this morning, I planted that video and memo, but I also tampered with your panic device and gun. Your gun is loaded with blank bullets and your panic button is equally as useless. So, answer me this, why did you not accept my offer?"

"I would rather die than allow some belief in an unreal god to rule my life." Commander Prilezio growled.

"Consider your wish granted." Nemesio calmly said as he pulled the trigger in two quick successions. The bullets pierced each one of Commander Prilezio's knees, guaranteeing he would stay in the toxic fumes until he died. Nemesio kept the memory device there and left the office. He wanted the evidence to be found. Commander Prilezio had relied so much on his own strength and security of his massive estate, full of excess while the majority of the city starved and crowded into apartments way too small for their needs. Nemesio had little trouble leaving without drawing attention from the guards to himself even though the sun had begun to peek above the skyline of the city. It promised to be a beautiful day.

December 26, 32 PAW

12:44

Nemesio approached Chancellor Silas in the last Stasi base. Silas was awaiting word of Rhys's mission. As soon as he saw Nemesio appear before him in the room Silas had converted into his office, he asked about his daughter. "Did Rhys find my daughter?"

Nemesio was surprised that his first question was about his daughter. Silas did not even know whether or not Rhys had been able to make it to the Aamina prison complex at all. The hope that his daughter was still alive was evident on Silas's face.

"Yes he did. His mission was successful. Many Christians have begun to be freed to help our efforts. However Rhys has betrayed us. Rhys is holding your daughter ransom and is calling it insurance for your continued compliance. He says if you ever fall back on the deal you made with him and mistreat any Christians he will cut her into pieces and send them to you." Nemesio said with sorrow in his voice. It was hard news to pass on to a father. Nemesio knew this all too well.

"What?! How can this Christian do such a thing and still call himself a Christian? The rest of his kind allows themselves to be walked all over, ridiculed, and killed. They call it turning the other cheek, forgiveness, and mercy. Where is this man's compassion? I want him killed in as barbaric and painful way as you can possibly devise and my daughter safely with me. Nemesio, find and kill Rhys. If you can bring him to me alive so I can do it so much the better. Either way, the most important thing is to not allow him to hurt a hair on my daughter's head!" Silas was emotionally distraught, but also entrenched in a rage of fury. Nemesio walked away calmly, thankful Silas did not blame him for suggesting using Rhys in the first place. His concern was not Rhys or Silas's daughter. His targets were still the Council Members and Larkin. He would need to succeed in those missions quickly to appease Silas though.

December 26, 32 PAW

16:56

Agmund made his way through the CRZ Headquarters to the upper floor. Agmund noted that the men in the office were particularly grim this morning. This had happened randomly throughout Agmund's time working for the CRZ. He had learned it typically meant another of their soldiers had died the previous night. As Agmund came to the top floor however, he noted that things were even more amiss than usual. The top floor was crawling with investigators. The door to Commander Franklin's office was blown open, with men standing guard outside. Signs and tape showed that the room was under investigation. Agmund came to the open doorway and looked inside. Anyone looking at him would have noted his shocked expression.

A tall man with a bald head, but a thick red beard came out of the room. He had fiery, green eyes that instantly engaged a person. Agmund recognized him easily. His face was plastered all over the center of the city. It was Supreme Commander Larkin. Larkin was the first to speak. "Good you are here, I was hoping to speak with you. Agmund, do you know what happened here?"

"No, Supreme Commander Larkin. I came here expecting to meet Commander Franklin. Is he dead?"

"Yes, he is dead. Do you have any guess as to who killed him?"

Agmund thought for a moment. His face again registered shock. "Don't tell me it was Rhys."

"It was Rhys. He used this bookcase here to block the door while he and Commander Franklin had a firefight. Rhys won it, although we have found traces of blood other than that of Commander Franklin's to suggest Commander

Franklin did manage to injure the man before he died. What is most interesting though," Larkin's tone of voice turned threatening. "Is that it appears he had help from an insider. Rhys somehow got his hands on rappelling equipment and a grenade from somewhere inside this office. We are confident that he did not bring it in with him. Now, it was your idea for Commander Franklin to meet with Rhys and give him the assignment to kill Nemesio. Is that not true?"

"That is true. I was hopeful that we could eliminate one of our enemies and set them against each other. I encouraged Commander Franklin to keep many men nearby at his disposal. I did not imagine Rhys would be able to escape from the top floor of this building. It is true; he must have had some inside help to get him out of there. Killing Commander Franklin was not the hard part, it was getting out of the building safely that was. Do we have any leads on who it could be?"

"Well, I at first suspected you since it was your idea, but you have shown absolutely no leanings towards helping Christians. Indeed pretty much everyone knew about this meeting between the two in the building. After a very thorough investigation, we have discovered six Christians that work in this building." Supreme Commander Larkin nodded at a guard at the entrance. Agmund doubted that this investigation Larkin spoke of was indeed thorough.

The murder of Commander Franklin had only happened the previous night.

It was then that six CRZ personnel filed into the room in shackles. They all appeared to have been abused. Agmund noted that one of them was Kelly, Commander Franklin's secretary. All but one he recognized as soldiers for the CRZ, including one that was Franklin's bodyguard. They all were forced to kneel with their faces toward Agmund. Larkin stood right behind the prisoners staring at Agmund's reaction. There really was none that Larkin could see.

"Agmund, I want you to execute these prisoners for me. They have been found guilty of treason and for religious zealotry. Cut each of their heads off and I will no longer suspect you at all."

"Larkin I have no problem with cutting their heads off, but I think it would be best to find out more information from them first. Who knows, there could be more Christians in this building, indeed maybe even in this room. Those vermin all need to die. Let's not be hasty in our executions."

"You are a wise man. Commander Franklin did well to recruit you to our cause. But, I am already ahead of you. Kelly was the only one that we knew was a Christian. She was the one that informed us of the five others. Those five have been interrogated as well. Now, let us get on with it. You kill these men and women and you will no longer work for Commander Franklin, but you will take missions from me personally. You do not kill them then I will assume that you are the one in league with Rhys and the rest of those Christian scum."

Agmund looked at Larkin who seemed eager to see how Agmund was reacting. "Very well, Supreme Commander Larkin. You are indeed ahead of me." Agmund ambled over to the prisoner on the far left. He took one swing for each prisoner and cut the heads off of each one. Larkin's eyes never wavered off of Agmund. The prisoners each begged for their lives when their turn came, but Agmund did not waver at all. Finally, only Kelly still remained. Agmund was about to kill her when Supreme Commander Larkin spoke up again.

"Agmund, I have changed my mind. I do not want her head cut off. I want her to suffer more. Make it a slow death for her. It is likely she was the one that planted the bag as she is in Commander Franklin's office the most." Larkin allowed himself a slight smile of pride in his devious scheme to push Agmund even further.

"As you wish Supreme Commander Larkin." Agmund said with no emotion. After ten minutes of bloody work, Kelly finally died. The entire time Larkin stood there with a smile on his face as Agmund went about his dour business without any hesitation or emotion. He took no obvious pleasure in his work, but did it well never the less. Everyone else in the room had left. They could not handle the sight, much less the sounds and smell of what Agmund was doing to Kelly. When Agmund was done, Larkin applauded him.

"You are truly a piece of work Agmund. I have no doubts anymore about your capabilities and your opinions towards Christians. Now, do you want to hear what your first mission is?"

Agmund was wiping his sword off on his cloak. He still betrayed no emotion. "Yes, it will be my pleasure to serve you as you best see fit."

"Good. I want this Rhys to die by your sword. Bring his decapitated head to me when you are done."

"Supreme Commander Larkin, would I not be put to better use helping to finish the fight against the Stasi?"

"I have others searching for their last base. I am certain that is where Silas is, preparing his defenses along with Nemesio. When we discover the location, I will contact you and you will lead the attack against it. Keep this cell phone on you at all times." One of Larkin's associates handed Agmund a phone, which he reluctantly took. "The full resources that I have at my disposal will be at your disposal then." Larkin stuck his hand out. "To a great partnership."

"To a great partnership." Agmund said and stuck out his blood stained hand. The two men's handshakes were strong as iron, their expressions just as hard.

December 27, 32 PAW

17:45

Paul was sitting at his office desk poring over files of information from every corner of the city with reports on the current numbers of Christians in secret congregations. Paul had released the ban he had enacted on meeting in groups. The government at the time he had enacted the ban had been too effective in finding and destroying these congregations. At the expense of some fellowship, Paul had decided that the ultimate survival of Christianity was more essential. Now that the government had its hands full just battling the remaining Stasi, Christians had been able to meet and bring new members into their fold more than ever. It was beginning to look promising for Christians.

Paul looked up as his door was opened. Rhys calmly entered. Paul was about to greet him when another man followed Rhys in. Paul had never seen this man before. He was tall and carried himself as though he was some kind of dignitary. His lean face suggested that he had not enjoyed too many full meals of late. His hair and clothing however showcased a well groomed appearance. He sat down as Rhys did. Paul and the man Paul did not know waited for Rhys to make the introductions.

"Greetings Paul, this man's name is Zahir. I recently freed him from prison. He is one of the strongest Christian men I know. I brought him here to meet you and see how you could best use him."

"It's a pleasure to meet you Zahir. If you don't mind my asking, why were you sent to prison?"

Zahir looked at Rhys briefly. They had both discussed earlier that they did not desire for Paul to know what prison he was a part of, nor the amount of Christians that would be quietly streaming back into the city in the coming weeks. Paul still believed Farooq to be dead and had no idea that he was actually trying to start an Islamic city out of the former prison Aamina. Paul had made it too clear he wanted all Muslims dead to trust him with the reality of what Farooq was trying to accomplish. Zahir spoke confidently and clearly, despite the question possibly leading to more questions that he would be forced to either not answer or lie about. Zahir was determined not to lie, so he would choose not to answer if he was forced to. "I was put in prison because I was a Christian. I know what you are thinking, Paul. Christians are executed, not put in prison, in this city. Larkin decided that he wanted to punish some with a fate worse than death. The prison Larkin had constructed made that sadistic idea a reality. God however had a different plan than the government did for my life. I am free now, and desire to follow His will for my life more than ever. Rhys has told me much about you, how you are the unofficial leader of all the Christians in this city. Indeed, he tells me had it not been for you the Christians in this city would have died out a long time ago."

"Hard times make for even harder leaders and the hardest decisions imaginable. It was kind of Rhys to speak so highly of me. I guess I am the leader of the Christians. Soon, I pray, we will be able to be official leaders in a new government. Indeed I am already making some plans on how to handle the aftermath of this civil war if this government and the Stasi are defeated enough for the Christians to be put into power."

"You believe that the Stasi and the government will weaken each other enough. Rhys too seems hopeful that that will happen. That is for the best. Not many Christians are warriors, though. Those that are forced to take that road risk falling into hatred and fear, not to mention being plagued by guilt. The Stasi and the government must be made very weak indeed if we are to take control of the government and help the people of this city recover and enjoy life once again." Zahir stated, enjoying picking the mind of one who had so much power to shape Maevin's future.

"They will weaken each other almost to the point of extinction. Once they are that weak, Rhys and all the mercenaries that we can afford will finish the job for us. Mercenaries may not be too fond of us, but our money spends just as well as anyone else's. With them out of the way, we will be able to worship freely once again." Paul stated.

"What about the Muslims, Paul? What do you desire to do about them?" Zahir asked.

"They too shall be taken care of by the mercenaries, the few that are left of them. We cannot afford to have another civil war. Once this city is freed from the tyranny of the government and the oppression of the Stasi we will not allow it to slip back into civil strife!" Paul exclaimed passionately.

"What do you mean by taken care of by the mercenaries, Paul?" Zahir asked another probing question, even though everyone in the room knew the answer already. He wanted to know as much about Paul and his plans before he stated his opinions, if he chose to share them at all.

"We have not stopped fighting our war against Islam. It has merely died down in the past thirty years as other factions have been a greater threat to our survival. We will finish the war once and for all in this city, and it will be in our favor. Only then will our victory and control of this city be ours."

"Paul, you wish to execute all Muslims the same way the government executed Christians. How can that not be the ultimate hypocrisy?" Zahir now was getting very passionate as well in this discussion. As a former Muslim, he still had many friends that he knew were Muslim, at least he had four years ago before becoming incarcerated.

"Zahir, I told you earlier, hard times make for hard leaders whom must make the decisions no other leader would be forced to make in peaceful times. Christian leaders are not exempt from that. In the past decade I have made some decisions that still haunt me, but look at how far we have come during those ten years."

"Paul, we have not come anywhere. Most Christians in this city fall into two categories, war mongrels and frightened souls too scared to do anything." Zahir stated. "I did not rot in prison for four years only to become one of those two. I emerged from prison to see what I could do to make a difference without inciting violence and free Christians of fear by making them secure in the knowledge that God will protect them if it His will. Although I am in great debt to Rhys," Rhys gave a slight nod of his head in response, the only sign he had shown he was listening during the conversation. "I do not support his ways. He is killing those whom may still have a chance to repent of their ways. Your namesake Paul wrote nearly half the New Testament after a life of murdering Christians. I pray that Rhys will repent of his ways before it consumes him entirely. There is no doubt that he is being effective, but he is putting his very soul in jeopardy of eternal damnation while sending souls to hell before they have a chance to be redeemed by the power and blood of our Lord and Savior Jesus Christ. That cannot be the Christian example of this city, nor can the example be that we need to kill all Muslims and nonbelievers in this city. That is why we have suffered so much persecution in the first place, and I say we have deserved that fate many times over."

Rhys for the first time spoke up. He had pretended to be uninterested in the conversation, but now it was apparent he had followed every word. "Zahir, you are right. My soul is in serious jeopardy of hell. You know only a fraction of the sins I have committed. However, I took upon myself the great burden of seeing this city freed from those who want to vanquish Christianity to nothing. I will see that through. I still have plenty of enemies out there. When they are gone I will not allow myself to shape this city's future, it will be in the hands of God and those whom He appoints. As for you Paul, I hope you too will not shape this city's future. You have shared in some of the sins I have committed as well. Your soul too is in serious jeopardy."

Paul retorted, "My soul is secure, Rhys. I will not have a killer judge my actions! For all the sins I have committed I have done great things for the Christians of this city. For a decade now I have worked harder than anyone else to put Christians in a position to survive and maybe eventually thrive. We are so close now. I deserve to be part of those whom are in power once the government falls."

Rhys stared at Paul steadily. It began to make Paul nervous. "Careful Paul of your pride, it is clouding your judgment and your ability to discern God's will."

"So says the man whom has single-handedly put it upon himself to vanquish Christianity's foes! You say you put it upon yourself, as if you are better than God! Once the hard part is over you will step aside and allow our Lord to work! You are the hypocrite!" Paul said, his voice rising.

Zahir spoke up as things began to escalate between the two men. "We all have to be careful of our pride. You both are men of great power, and that means you must be diligent about checking your pride. As Rhys alluded to there is still much work to do before we can even make the decisions we are discussing. Allow me to say a quick prayer for us all." Paul and Zahir bowed their heads, Rhys merely did not object. "Lord, we come to You because this city is hurting and needs You more than ever. I pray that before all is over, that there will be a multitude of souls that do come to You, and the people of this city are not robbed of that opportunity before they get a chance to know You, Father. You are great and merciful. May You show us Your will for the mercy we must show our enemies, all the while advancing Your Kingdom. Lord thank You so much for the small blessings You give us each day. Despite the obstacles, we are now more numerous than we have been for many years. However, I wonder if we lack the quality that we once had. Things are beginning to look up, and as things begin to look up I pray we continually look up to You. Too often, like the world before the Atomic War destroyed it, we allowed our riches to make us content. In our contentedness we no longer sought you. Thank you for the challenges of everyday life. You get us through everything that we face and for that we are immensely grateful. It's in Your name we pray, amen."

"Amen." Paul said. Rhys stood up and left. Zahir issued a quick goodbye to Paul and then quickly left the room to catch up with Rhys. They were soon walking through the abandoned tunnels under the city side-by-side.

Zahir spoke first. "Rhys, I do pray that you will abandon your plans. It is one thing to let the government and Stasi tear each other apart, but you are actively causing it. Your actions do not point well towards Christianity, nor do they glorify God. What makes you think you have the right to decide who needs to die and who gets to live?"

Rhys took a deep breath and stopped walking. He turned and looked Zahir directly in the eye. "You speak the truth Zahir, and better yet you speak it in love. But, it is too late in the game for me to change tactics now. What I have set in motion cannot be stopped, except by my own death. I prayed for two years before I embarked on this mission that God will show me what to do with the life that was torn away from me. During those two years He allowed so much suffering in this city. I could no longer sit idly by and just deal with the aftermath of our evil government. You know what it is like to pray for four years and hear only the answer wait. Well, imagine what it is like to turn your face fully towards His, only to see so much suffering. As God had turned His back on all those that have suffered so much, I have now turned my back on Him. I made these plans myself. I am acting by myself. I wished to act within His will, but he seems to have utterly abandoned me, although sometimes I wonder if he has really abandoned me. I should have died so many times on my warpath. He fully has the power to stop me, yet He has not done so. Some days I wonder if He really has guided my steps along this bloody path the entire time."

"I do not know what to tell you Rhys, I only know that there is a deep shadow of sorrow and pain that you carry on your shoulders. You cannot carry the fate of this city on your shoulders as well. For God two years is nothing. He has had a plan all along, and I don't think it was for you to march the bloody trail that you have embarked upon."

"I appreciate your concern Zahir, but what is done is done. I suffer this fate knowing that in doing so I provide hope for all Christians. I must succeed in what I started; otherwise all the horrible sins I have already committed will be for naught."

"It is not too late to pray to God to show you His will." Zahir said quietly and kindly to Rhys.

"Pray for me, He has not heard my plaintive cries for years." Rhys said with desperation and emotion breaking through his normally stoic exterior. The two continued their walk, Rhys remembering the multitude of violence he had committed while Zahir silently prayed.

Chapter XV

December 28, 32 PAW

14:10

Supreme Commander Larkin walked into his large office, from his rooms adjacent to it. His office was a formidable place in the center of the city that was entirely underground. It had been designed to include every amenity imaginable. The office was actually several rooms that included a full bathroom, fitness room, bedroom, living room, kitchen, and of course his actual office which had its own entrance. Very few got to even enter his office, less got to see that there was more to it than just an office. Larkin took very few chances and many precautions, such as making the entire office complex a nuclear shelter as well. He was determined to remain in power as long as possible. Up until a few months ago that idea had seemed guaranteed, now it was being threatened due to the audacity of the Stasi and the Christians, Rhys and Nemesio in particular. Supreme Commander Larkin wanted nothing more than to have the heads of both of those men in his possession, being severed by his new favorite weapon, Agmund.

Supreme Commander Larkin allotted himself a couple of minutes to prepare his thoughts before sending an instant message to his secretary Nasirra that he was ready for her to send in Commander Elaine and Commander Sylvano. They entered in through the electro-magnetically locking doors, of which Supreme Commander Larkin insisted there be three of them, the last one being one that he controlled personally. As usual he got what he wanted. Those that did not please him normally were killed. Commander Elaine was the Council member whom dealt primarily with education. She was a silver-haired woman with a beak-like nose and equally sharp, aggressive eyes of hazel. Commander Sylvano was the Council member in charge of Commerce. Under his corrupt system businesses that paid the highest percentage of their profits for his "advice" would thrive. Part of that money the government would receive. The rest Commander Sylvano took for himself to spend on his young wife and himself. Commander Sylvano and Commander Elaine almost appeared to be twins. They had both been with Supreme Commander Larkin since he started his rule of Maevin thirty years ago. They were the last two original members of the Council. The only two Nemesio had yet to kill.

Commander Elaine spoke first. Supreme Commander Larkin could tell she was very distraught just by that fact alone. She always let him speak first; as she should in his opinion. The look on her face and the constant uneasiness of movement further provided proof that she was indeed very disturbed by the recent turn of events brought upon by Nemesio. One look at Commander Sylvano told Larkin that he was even more upset than she was. "Supreme Commander Larkin, you must know why we are here. You promised us that Nemesio's head would be in your possession before another Council member died after he killed Commander Matthew. Now both Commander Liam and Commander Prilezio have been killed as well by his hand. Not only that, but Commander Franklin was killed as well. I understand that it was by someone else named Rhys, but the point is we are weak and cannot even protect our own. Those last two men were not paper-pushers, but genuine warriors. Are you expecting us two old farts to be able to survive his threat when those men died?"

Supreme Commander Larkin looked hard into both their faces before answering. "No, I don't."

Both Commander Sylvano and Commander Elaine looked even more disturbed and surprised by Supreme Commander Larkin's response. Sylvano was the first to find his tongue. "Does that mean you are not even going to try?"

"No, I won't try to save you particularly. No, my aim is far loftier than that. I am going to try to save the entire city." Supreme Commander Larkin took some satisfaction in seeing their interest peek significantly. "You see, Commanders, I have made every effort in my power to try to ascertain the location of this Nemesio character and the last location of the Stasi base. All my efforts have failed. Now, I know in order to enjoy my position as I currently do for much longer I need to kill Nemesio, Chancellor Silas, and destroy the last remaining Stasi base. I intend to accomplish that now through an entirely different means. We do not know where Nemesio is, but we do know where he is going to be." Supreme Commander Larkin paused at this moment, making the other two nearly fraught with impatience.

"Where will he be?" Both uttered frantically at approximately the same time.

"That is actually the easy part, my friends." Supreme Commander Larkin continued. "He is going to be exactly where you are, we just do not know when."

Neither Council member looked particularly pleased about this. Commander Elaine was the first to speak her dissatisfaction however. "You expect us to be bait? You are just going to watch him kill us and then you are going to kill him aren't you?"

"Of course not, my dear friends. I will make every effort to make sure that you survive. You will be wearing full body Kevlar vests, the thinnest kind available that is still bullet proof so he does not notice and go for a head shot. Every report indicates that Nemesio does not use armor-piercing rounds. In order to make further guarantees that he shoots you in the vest and not in the head, we will have to make him shoot on the run or from very far away. My men will take care of that. You will of course have to pretend you are dead, and it will hurt, a lot. But, in the end you will still have your life and we will still have a city still firmly in our power. Once he is led to believe that you are both dead he will obviously report his success to the traitor Silas, who is more than likely at the last remaining Stasi base, organizing his final desperate stand against our righteous rule. This risk you take is the only chance you have that you will survive this threat. Any other option leads to sure death. Nemesio has proved he is far too capable and cunning for us to be able to defeat him through anything but setting a trap for him."

Both took a couple of minutes to think it through silently. Then nodding heads at about the same time, Commander Sylvano spoke. "Yes, I suppose it is. Nothing else has worked thus far. This is our only chance, and even if it fails Supreme Commander Larkin, you will be able to still carry out the plan to kill Nemesio, Silas, and the rest of the Stasi scum in fell swoop. Our deaths will not be in vain."

"Who else knows of this plan?" Commander Elaine spoke harshly. She was not quite ready to commit fully to the possibility of being a patriotic martyr without knowing the answers to a few more questions.

"None yet, but my own hand-picked members of my security force will need to be informed. They will be informed at the last possible moment. I understand your concern for your safety and the sanctity of this government remaining in power Commander Elaine, but trust me; I am taking every precaution I possibly can to ensure your safety."

"Not even Agmund knows about this?" Commander Sylvano asked with a certain reverence passing out of his lips as he uttered the name of Agmund.

"He will discover it at the last possible moment. He is one of my hand-chosen men. I want him there to destroy the last Stasi base and separate Silas's and Nemesio's heads from their shoulders. Then my friends, we will live the rest of our lives out happily and in power."

"Thank you Supreme Commander Larkin." Both Commander Elaine and Commander Sylvano said in unison.

"Now let me tell you the specifics of my plans for you two." Supreme Commander Larkin said leaning in towards them both, eager to embark on the mission that could potentially end the most serious threats he had to the security of his government.

December 30, 32 PAW

2:19

Captain Woelfel crouched behind a fountain in the middle of the park. Three hundred yards away sat Commander Elaine and Commander Sylvano on a bench, appearing to be deeply engrossed in a conversation. A contingent of twenty soldiers from Larkin's personal force surrounded them. The best of Larkin's personal force lay in hiding, including Agmund who was now next to Captain Woelfel. There were forty men laying in wait to follow Nemesio after he killed the twenty soldiers guarding the two Commanders. The twenty men were told to protect Commander Elaine and Sylvano at all costs, but Larkin and Captain Woelfel did not suspect that they would survive Nemesio's assault. Now, it was just a waiting game to see if he showed. Once he did show then the forty would attempt to follow him back to the Stasi base where they would call in additional reinforcements and assault the final base. Larkin seemed confident if that was accomplished Agmund would find a way to kill both Silas and Nemesio.

"Captain Woelfel, do you think that Nemesio will show?" Agmund asked in a detached, careless manner.

"Without a doubt, he will show and kill those twenty guards plus the two Council Members. When they are dead he will hopefully assume his mission is done and let down his guard. Then we will tail him to the base. That is when you are going to work your magic."

"Wait, I thought the mission was to keep the two Council Members alive?"

"No, Supreme Commander Larkin does not want us to run the risk of ruining the mission by saving their lives. We are not to stop Nemesio in an effort to save the lives of the Council Members."

"So the Council Members and those twenty men agreed to sacrifice their lives so we have a chance to kill Nemesio and Silas?"

"Not exactly." Captain Woelfel said with a quiet laugh.

Agmund seemed to absorb that information with a slight nod. Then he shifted his weight around uncomfortably. "I am tired of laying in wait here. I am going to check the perimeter again for signs that Nemesio has arrived."

"Suit yourself, Agmund. Larkin made it clear you are free to do your own thing."

"Good, Larkin already knows how I work best." Agmund took off quickly and quietly towards the nearest wall; soon he was lost in the darkness of the moonless night.

Nemesio once again stalked his prey, the Maevin City Council members. He had followed the last two original members to the park. It would be a great opportunity for him to pick off both at the same time. Then all that would remain would be for him to kill Larkin. Once that was done then certainly Silas would demand that he attempt to kill Rhys and rescue Silas's daughter, but that did not necessarily coincide with Nemesio's plan. He knew it would be even riskier to try to knock off both of his targets at once. It meant twice the security personnel to deal with and he knew they would be on their toes as they were the last two remaining ones he had threatened to kill on the Council. He cared little that the Council Members were so rapidly replaced by Supreme Commander Larkin. The point was that the residents of Maevin would discover that the status quo did not have to remain in place any longer, that the citizens of Maevin could make a difference. Nemesio had heard rumors of civil unrest with the government already, but hoped this blow and the final one against Supreme Commander Larkin would remove the fear that Larkin held over the city. Too many people knew loved ones that had died under Larkin's barbaric rule. Some of these had been directly executed like Nemesio's family. Others had been a side result of his apparent lack of care for the poor outside the center of the city.

Nemesio knew the city park quite well, having been there frequently to visit with Silas. The first difficulty was making it over the walls of the park into the park itself. There were four entrances, but only one remained open this late at night. Nemesio would certainly not be allowed in carrying all his weapons, even if they did not recognize the face that had five hundred thousand marks attached to it. The wall was a twelve foot concrete wall topped with barbed wire and razor sharp spikes. It was meant to keep out those that the rich of the city did not wish to be bothered with. The sun disappeared behind the exterior walls of the city, bringing deep darkness to Maevin. Nemesio approached the outer wall of the park, having donned his tactical outfit just a block away in an alley out of his earlier disguise. Nemesio ran forward and leaped high into the air, one foot kicking off the wall on the way up to give himself an extra boost. He grabbed the top of the wall, trying to grasp the wall where the spikes were not located. The outer edge of his left hand was cut by one of the spikes, but Nemesio managed to hang on to the wall. He raised himself up ignoring the pain and hoping the pooling blood would not cause him to slip and fall. Once standing at the top, only his toes delicately placed between the spikes that were a mere six inches apart with the rest of his feet hanging back over the edge, he launched himself into a front flip. The front flip carried him neatly over the three foot tall barbed wire in front of him. He landed softly with a roll on the ground on the other side of the wall. He listened carefully to see if anyone had been made aware of his acrobatic entry into the city park. Nothing stirred, not even one of the many animals that had been placed in the city park by well meaning preservationists. Nemesio took the moment to inspect the wound on his hand. It bled a lot, but by moving his hand around he could tell none of the muscles or ligaments had been damaged. He wrapped his hand quickly and then began his hunt for his prey.

Nemesio nearly crossed the entire park before he found his marks. They were sitting on a bench at the feet of a statue of Supreme Commander Larkin. Twenty bodyguards formed a perimeter around the two Council members.

Nemesio could tell, even from nearly a hundred yards away, that these men were on edge. Nemesio took the rifle off his shoulders that he had brought. He took a prone position in a large stand of oak and maple trees. The trees were approximately thirty years old. A sign near them stated they were planted by Larkin as a promise that he would bring back what was nearly lost forever back to life. Nemesio felt thankful for once towards Larkin; these dense set of trees now provided him with the perfect cover to fire from.

He looked through the night vision scope of his M4A1 and took aim. He considered killing both the Council members first, but no, he wanted to perform those kills close up. Besides, they were not the ones who would be firing bullets back at him once the lead began to fly. Nemesio estimated he could fire three shots before they narrowed his position down. He chose to take out the two that were looking in his direction first, followed by a shot at the guard closest to cover. He fired the three shots rapidly, each one was a headshot. The three crumpled to the ground. Nemesio however did not see it, he was already moving stealthily away from where bullets were being fired in vain at his shooting position.

Now there were only seventeen guards left, five of them had already moved into a semicircle in front of Commander Sylvano and Commander Elaine. Both Council Members were crouched behind the now upturned park bench. Nemesio relaxed, they were not fleeing yet. It gave him more time to take out the remaining guards. He picked out three easy targets, young men whom probably had little practical experience in warfare as their bodies were exposed in the open. These three all fell to the ground as Nemesio shot three more shots. Nemesio moved position once again, this time standing behind the biggest oak tree of the bunch. The guards were beginning to settle into better cover, presenting smaller targets. Nemesio swapped ammunition magazines; opting for one of the two he had loaded with armor-piercing rounds. He switched the gun over to its three round burst fire mode. Two pulls of the trigger later, he had only a dozen guards left, of which five were still in a semi-circle out in the open.

Bullets whizzed past Nemesio as he moved positions. This time they were being fired throughout the entire grove, they had caught on to him moving positions. Nemesio switched his gun to fully automatic and lay down a hail of bullets aiming for the five guards in a semi-circle. Four of them fell to the ground, three of them no longer moved. Nemesio stayed where he was as hot lead flew all around him, but not at the position he had fired from. They had caught on to his original tactic. He had wisely decided to change it.

After thirty seconds of waiting, Nemesio noted the bullets being sent in his vicinity had begun to decrease. Then it suddenly stopped. A full minute later, the firing started again. Nemesio switched the gun's toggle to single shot and watched as three men sprinted to the aid of the two that had been injured, but not killed by him in the semi-circle. He waited until they had reached those men and then pulled the trigger three times in a calm, efficient manner. The three men that had bravely risked their lives fell to the ground, dead. Nemesio changed positions quickly, keeping count in his head that now only six guards remained. Two of those were injured, one was still able to stand, and the other was probably close to dead.

Nemesio climbed a tree this time; it was the tallest silver maple tree in the bunch. The tree's frequent branches made the climb quick and easy. The bullets fired by his enemies passed by harmlessly at the foot of the trees. Once at the top of the tree, Nemesio was quickly able to determine the positions of his enemies. He shot the four that were still behind the cover of anything they could find, including one who had chosen to lay prone behind the body of one of his fellow guards that Nemesio had already shot. The remaining two were able to determine Nemesio's position by his muzzle flashes, but in their intense fear they missed. Nemesio calmly lined up his shots and killed the final two guards. He noted Commander Sylvano and Commander Elaine attempt to run hurriedly away, but their elderly bodies made their progress slow and painful for them. Nemesio climbed down the tree agilely and took off towards the two at a dead sprint. The half moon shone through a short break in the clouds as he crossed the park. He wanted to kill the two Council Members and disappear as quickly as he could into the city.

Captain Woelfel barked into his radio. "All men stand down. There is nothing we can do to save the Council Members' lives. We will follow Nemesio as planned. Remember he cannot know we are tailing him. Only one person keeps an eye on him at a time when we are out of this park. Delta, Omega, and Tango teams will follow via vehicles. This is our opportunity men; let's make the most of it. Notify me if you see Agmund, no one has seen him for nearly half an hour. We will want his help before this night is over."

Commander Sylvano and Commander Elaine stopped trying to run. They saw Nemesio right behind them. He saw them give up their futile flight and slowly swaggered up to his terrified victims. He slung his rifle over his shoulder and pulled out a .50 caliber Desert Eagle. He brought the sights down on to Commander Elaine's head. "Ladies first." Nemesio said with a cocky smirk.

"Answer me this first, Nemesio. Is there nothing you want from us before you kill us? We have many resources. You are a man of great talents. We could do much together. Is there nothing you could gain from us?"

"Commander Elaine, your death will be sufficient enough gain for me." Nemesio pulled the trigger, the bullet making a large mess of what was once Commander Elaine's head.

Commander Sylvano's eyes went wide. He went into shock at the grisly sight of seeing his long-time friend being shot in front of his eyes. "NO! Nemesio, I will do anything, just please don't shoot me."

"There is nothing you can do, for you are a dead man, Commander Sylvano." Nemesio pulled the trigger again. The result was more of the same. Nemesio took a deep breath and then exhaled. "Now time for the finale." He said with his sigh of relief. He took off into the night heading for the Stasi base to report his success to Chancellor Silas. Nemesio did not see or hear a single one of the forty men as they mobilized behind him.

Chapter XVI

December 28, 32 PAW

2:53

Nemesio walked quickly through the maze of city streets once on the outskirts of Maevin. Maevin's interior had the luxury of straight, multi-lane roads that traffic engineers had planned out to maximize effectiveness. However, they had left out personality in those sterile roads. What the outskirts of Maevin lacked in cleanliness and efficiency, it made up in character. The small roads were one of Nemesio's favorites for losing whoever may be tailing him. He had known shortly after he left the park that he was being tailed. The men behind him had slipped up along the way and he had spotted them, but they had made no move to stop him as he pretended that he was still oblivious to their presence. Nemesio's mind ran with the possibilities of losing so many men on his tail.

The shuffling of a foot echoed in the dark alley behind Nemesio. He did not turn around, but kept walking. Turning around would have tipped off his tail that he had been made. Nemesio instead walked forward at the same pace, not varying at all. Ahead a little ways he knew of an even smaller alley that had many twists and turns. It was directly connected to the alley Nemesio was on and only three hundred yards ahead. His heart raced and adrenaline began to pump throughout his veins readying him to either fly away from the danger or stay and combat it. It took him a mere two minutes to reach the spot. The turn onto the smaller alley was right after a turn on the alley he was currently on. It was perfect for turning the prey into the predator. Nemesio turned into that small alley and melted into the shadows, his back pressed up against the coarse brick behind him.

After thirty seconds Nemesio heard the tell tale sign of someone walking up the alley. The alley had a peculiar habit of amplifying noise forward towards Nemesio's position while dampening it going the other direction, one of the reasons Nemesio had out of habit turned down in it the first place. After a few more seconds Nemesio heard the breathing of his foe. The man paused at the intersections of the alleys and looked down the smaller one. Nemesio already had a suppressed 9 mm pistol in hand, leveled at the man's face. Nemesio noted the man. He was a man of average height and build. His clothes were plain enough, but very neat. He held an AK-74 in his hands, a tactical knife, and a Glock pistol in a holster at his waist. He wore a Kevlar vest. He looked like any of the mercenaries or guerillas that roamed the city at night. Indeed he could have even been one of the Stasi, but the last detail Nemesio soaked in before the man disappeared up the larger of the two alleys was his boots. The boots were obviously Government Issue. It was the one consistent piece of equipment for all the different security and law enforcement agents of Maevin. A few seconds later Nemesio watched as several men issued past him. They were all dressed somewhat similarly, but not the same. Their weapons varied greatly throughout the group, but one thing remained consistent, their boots. Nemesio knew of only one unit who would not wear any kind of government identification with them on a mission, Supreme Commander Larkin's own private force. The stream of soldiers did not cease for nearly a minute, but each passed by Nemesio's position. He wondered if he could get away without being discovered so easily.

Nemesio did not have long to ponder it though, after a dozen men had already crossed his path without spotting him, a man turned a flashlight up the dark alley. It illuminated Nemesio vividly. Nemesio wasted no time in shooting the man as he was about to cry out. He shot another one that was in his view and then bolted up the small alley. Its twists and turns soon hid him from sight, but not before a couple of men had fired shots at him. From the sound of the footsteps and shouts behind him, several men were already hot on Nemesio's heels. He ran even faster, hoping that there were not many more than the dozen men he had already seen pass by his position before he had been found, but from the commotion emanating from behind him and his knowledge of Supreme Commander Larkin he counted on there being many more than that dozen. Supreme Commander Larkin already knew Nemesio had killed a dozen SWAT team members single-handedly and evaded a few other SWAT teams in rescuing Chancellor Silas. No, this time it would be much more difficult.

Nemesio's mind raced with what to do as he sprinted through the twisted alley. Nemesio never caught sight of his pursuers, but heard their frantic shouts and running feet. Nemesio knew he could not outrun nor have a shootout with so many pursuers. Plans came to his keen mind rapidly, but each one ended with him dying. As he ran he pulled the pin of a grenade and let it fall behind him. A few seconds later an explosion came to his ears and the sounds of pain-induced screams. The move gave him a little more time, but he had only so many grenades and now they would be looking for Nemesio to drop more. He knew their pursuit however would become a little more cautious which would slow them down, but Nemesio knew this would only delay the inevitable. Still, he could not think of anything more than to delay the inevitable. The Stasi base, and the nearest help, was still a full mile away.

Up ahead the small alley emptied into a small road, but this was much straighter. Nemesio knew that it would afford him little cover compared to the alley he had nearly reached the end of. The back doors of building flew by

Nemesio as he pushed his body forward, ignoring the growing pain in his limbs and lungs at the extended run. Up ahead, just a hundred feet from the end of the alley was a warehouse with the back door ripped open. He ducked into the building, knowing as he did so that he may have just trapped himself inside. There was no doubt in his mind at least a few of Larkin's soldiers behind him would check the building. Still if he could find a good enough hiding spot with exit routes, he may be able to lose his pursuers. He ran through the back storage rooms and into the main warehouse area. Old storage racks and miscellaneous junk had accumulated in the building. But, that is not what caught Nemesio's attention; it was the muzzles of several rifles pointed at him.

The rifles however were not held in the hands of Larkin's soldiers. They were held by a ragtag group of youth, both males and females. The oldest of the young group stepped forward and spoke first. "What are you doing in my building stranger?"

"Let me pass quickly or we will all perish! Government soldiers are chasing me and seeking to kill me. Soon they will find their way in here in their pursuit of me." Nemesio was desperate to not bring these young people into a fight that was not their own.

A young girl spoke before the leader of the young group could speak, "Wait, are you Nemesio, slayer of the Council?"

"Yes, I am Nemesio." Nemesio said quickly, not sure if he had just sealed his doom or given himself hope with that answer. He did not have to debate the point long in his mind though, murmurs of awe passed through the group. The leader however did not forget Nemesio's words.

"How many are pursuing you, Nemesio?"

"My best estimate puts it at anywhere from thirty to forty."

The leader of the ragtag youth shouted orders to the group. "Take cover, we will kill all those government sadists! Long live Nemesio!" Nemesio felt a twinge of horror touch him as he looked around at the approximately twenty youth taking up firing positions throughout the warehouse. They stood no chance against the incoming forces. Nemesio ran to the side of the young leader to warn him of their impending deaths, but it was too late. Larkin's soldiers had arrived. The first few were taken by surprise by the force they faced and were killed, but then more of Larkin's soldiers began to pour in, and they were not caught by surprise. They cautiously and expertly approached. Their training served them well as they worked together to advance into strategic positions of fire. Nemesio looked in horror as the teenagers all around him received mortal wounds. Only a handful of the youth remained alive before long, along with Nemesio who was shooting furiously in a desperate attempt to save the lives of the young people left.

Larkin's soldiers began dwindling as well as Nemesio fired his assault rifle quickly along with the surviving teens. The armor-piercing rounds he had remaining were quickly used up however and he had to slow his rate of fire down to take the more precise headshots. Nemesio noted that no new government soldiers arrived though. He chucked the last of his grenades and watched as the smoke cleared, showing only eight of Larkin's soldiers left. Looking at his own side, only two remained with him, the young girl whom had spoken up and the hard-nosed leader. The rest lay dead in their own blood, a poor match for government trained soldiers with superior numbers, tactics, and weapons.

Nemesio killed two more government soldiers while each of the youth gained one more kill. Nemesio had now run out of ammunition entirely for his assault rifle and pulled out his Desert Eagle handgun. He looked over at the young girl and noticed her smiling at him. She had hope now that they would win and she would not lose her life after all. More importantly, she would have helped Nemesio live to keep fighting another day. Nemesio smiled back at her, but his smile soon turned to an open-mouthed scream of horror. A bullet had pierced through her head, as she was still smiling. Her limp body lay on the ground while she was still smiling up at Nemesio. The young leader let out a roar of anger as he noted her death and stood up, putting himself in the line of fire. He fired several rounds from his AK-47's magazine at the remaining four soldiers. Five shots nearly instantly pierced his torso as he stood. Yet he continued firing. He killed two more of Larkin's soldiers before collapsing to the ground. Nemesio fired two shots each at the remaining two government soldiers. They crumpled to the ground. Nemesio scanned the warehouse quickly for any more sign of hostiles, but could see none. He raced to the side of the young leader, desperate to thank the young man before he died. Nemesio was too late however, the young man had died, his eyes cast over to the young girl whose death had caused him to act so boldly, and so foolishly. Nemesio knew in his heart that the young man had loved that young girl whom had first identified him as Nemesio. As he looked around at the youth that had saved his life Nemesio wept, although he had never even learned any of their names.

December 28, 32 PAW

4:07

Chancellor Silas waited with eager anticipation deep inside his temporary office located in the last Stasi stronghold. Reports had come to his attention that Nemesio was in the base and on his way to report a great success to Chancellor Silas. He wondered what it could be. Nemesio had sworn to kill the last two remaining Council members and Supreme Commander Larkin as well, but killing just one of the two remaining Council members would not be worth reporting as a great success. Chancellor Silas hoped that somehow Supreme Commander Larkin had been killed, but doubted this would happen. He believed he knew Nemesio well enough to know that even if an opportunity to kill Larkin would have presented itself, Nemesio would have chosen to do it as he had promised and waited to kill all the Council members before killing Larkin. Still, Silas could not help himself from dreaming that his sworn enemy Larkin was now dead, a dream that had kept him going for the last twenty years.

Nemesio was soon in the temporary office of Silas. No one else was in the office. The walls were bare concrete, with one exception. A painting of a pre-nuclear war United States city was behind the simple metal desk that Silas was standing behind, whom was too excited to sit. He wasted no time in speaking to Nemesio, "So, I hear you have won a great victory Nemesio. What victory is it that you have won?"

"The five members of the Council that I swore to kill are now dead. There are only a few people left to kill." Nemesio was normally quite full of emotion when he spoke of his quest. Now that it was nearly over he was strangely without emotion in his report.

"That is excellent news; you must have killed them both in just the last couple of hours! You continually surprise me. However, excuse my confusion, but I thought you only had one person left to kill, my most hated enemy Larkin."

"Do not be concerned Chancellor Silas for I will kill Larkin. There is one person that must die before him though. Hopefully, he will be the last but I doubt it."

"Who is that Nemesio?"

"You, Chancellor Silas, that person is you."

Chancellor Silas pulled a gun out of his holster. His confusion over the statement had caused him to hesitate though. By then Nemesio had pulled out his 9 mm suppressed handgun and shot three times. The shots all struck Silas in the stomach. Nemesio listened for any sounds of alarm outside, but it seemed as though no one had heard the suppressed fire of his pistol. Nemesio walked forward and crouched down next to the head of Silas. Chancellor Silas was obviously in pain, but his face showed something more, an intense fear of Nemesio.

"Why, Nemesio, why are you killing me?"

"My real name is not Nemesio, Silas. You left me to die a long time ago. Now, I am returning the favor."

Silas spoke, but it visibly brought him pain, just as each breath did as well. "But why go through the whole charade of being Nemesio? Why did you not just kill me outright?"

"I needed you for the time being, just as I needed my guise as Nemesio. You see, for a time I did genuinely work with you. We both wanted the same things, the end of the government's control of Maevin and the death of Larkin. Where we differed was that I did not want the Stasi to rule in their stead. I did not want you, Silas, to rule in his stead. This city deserves a better life than either group can possibly offer. It deserves a much better future. You need to die now, because you allowed the rivalry between you and Larkin to nearly ruin the entire city, although you succeeded in completely ruining many lives in your greed and selfishness. In trying to defeat the government, you became everything you claimed to loath about them. You had no respect of individual's rights, committed innumerable atrocities, and ruined just as many lives all for the sake of driving the government from power. I needed you to succeed in your goal of stopping the government, but I also needed the Stasi in the end to fail. The Stasi will indeed fail now that they lost you, the glue that held it together. I will send government forces to destroy this place. The Stasi will die tonight, but I will ensure Larkin will not be around to enjoy it. Larkin will be dead before he can learn that the Stasi threat to his government is no more. In the removal of the two leaders both organizations will fall into ruin and chaos. A power vacuum will be in place, and the first free elections will be held in Maevin's short and bloody history. My hope is that the citizens of Maevin will finally get to choose their future. Hopefully they will choose to make Maevin a beacon of light and hope, a sign that mankind will recover from the atrocities of its past."

"What about my daughter?" Silas's breathing had become even raspier. Blood pooled on to the floor. Nemesio knew it would not be much longer before Silas died from the four gunshot wounds. He debated about ending it quickly with a fifth bullet, but decided to answer the question first instead.

"She will find out the truth about her mother. She will discover that you raped her mother. When you found out that she was pregnant, you hunted her down and imprisoned her. You wanted the child, and indeed you loved Rachel, but you despised her mother. You killed her mother on Rachel's second birthday. She will no longer be a threat to this city's future security in her attempts to live up to your legacy, and she will be free to face the truth in her own manner."

"How do you know that?" Chancellor Silas did not even refute it, he was too near death to lie now, even as accustomed as he was to that particular vice.

"This journal I discovered in one of your offices told me the truth, and it will be the proof your daughter will certainly require to believe it. I will give this journal to Rhys and he will give it to her at his own discretion."

"Are you and Rhys in league together?"

Nemesio smiled. "Something like that." Nemesio pulled the trigger and placed a fifth bullet in Silas's head.

He left the base undisturbed, the Stasi forces by now well accustomed to allowing him to do as he wished, still unaware of their leader's death. The Stasi had finally come to an end.

Chapter XVII

December 28, 32 PAW

7:22

Nasirra, Supreme Commander Larkin's secretary, looked up and saw Agmund walk into the underground complex that housed Larkin's base of command. He was dressed in his usual gleaming white with his well-cared for sword hanging from his waist. She had orders from Supreme Commander Larkin to let Agmund pass into his office if he showed up. Larkin was greatly distraught that his plan to find the Stasi base and end the war had failed. He had yet to hear of Silas's death. Agmund walked up to her mahogany desk.

"I desire to see Supreme Commander Larkin. I have important news of which he must hear immediately." Agmund said in a hurried tone.

"Actually he is expecting you. His office is through those doors." Nasirra motioned to the wall; it appeared to have no door at all. Agmund gave her a confused look, but then he saw the door was camouflaged into the décor of the wall. It began to open, revealing another door opening behind it. He entered through the first two doors and waited for the third to open as the other two closed behind him. Once he was closed in, Nasirra messaged Larkin that Agmund had arrived and was waiting for him to admit him into his office. Agmund nervously waited inside, until Larkin opened the door five minutes later. He had never before been in Supreme Commander Larkin's office, but had been informed by Larkin where it was located. He expected a small office when he stepped through the last door, and was taken aback in admiration at the intricate wood work and impressive magnitude and quality of the office. It was also a lot bigger than he imagined. Despite the deadly seriousness of his errand, Agmund could not help but admire the office. Seated behind an intricately constructed black walnut desk sat Supreme Commander Larkin. His face betrayed the pride he felt in his office as Agmund allowed his eyes to admire it. His bald head gleamed in the soft light, the light also glistening off his red beard. He motioned with a calloused, strong hand for Agmund to take a seat before him.

"Agmund, I understand you have some important news for me."

"Yes, I do Supreme Commander Larkin. Nemesio still lives, but I was able to learn the location of the Stasi base. I sent forces there to destroy the base and kill everyone left behind. They should be arriving at the location now." Agmund stared at Supreme Commander Larkin, whom seemed upset, not joyous at the news that Agmund had given him.

"Why are you not there yourself?" Supreme Commander Larkin demanded.

"Because I accomplished my business there already. Now I have business to attend to here."

"I find that hard to believe. Your business is to make sure Nemesio and Silas are dead. You have no business here until that business is accomplished!" Larkin exclaimed vehemently.

"I disagree Larkin." Larkin's face contorted into rage as Agmund did not address him using his usual self-given title of Supreme Commander. "Once you know of what my business here is, you may disagree." A silence that was filled with energy remained in the room until Agmund revealed the true purpose of his visit. "My business here is to kill you." Agmund said calmly enough, although his eyes betrayed the rage inside.

The two men glowered at each other, each one looking for the other to make a move. Finally Larkin asked, "Why Agmund do you want to do that?"

"You still do not know who I am do you? The facial reconstruction surgery was well worth it then. This wig and colored contact lenses helps significantly as well. Well let me tell you why I want to kill you, other than the obvious fact that you are a poison to this city that needs to be exterminated. Two years ago you ordered my family killed in front of me for being a Christian. You left me to die. I was dead for a few minutes before a stranger resuscitated me. This stranger, a Christian man named Milica, then nursed me back to health. I have finally come to get my revenge and free this city from your villainy."

"What is your name?" Larkin asked, although he was not interested in the answer. Agmund opened his mouth to speak but Larkin brought the gun out of the holster under his desk and shot Agmund square in the chest. Agmund fell to the ground, his white cloak being covered in his own blood. He had dropped his guard during his conversation with Larkin.

Larkin came around his desk and knelt down on Agmund's gunshot wound with his left knee. He placed the muzzle of the handgun on Agmund's forehead. His left hand covered the hilt of Agmund's sword ensuring that Agmund would not be able to use it. "I actually don't care what your name is. Whoever you are I am going to finish the job I should have two years ago!"

"Good luck." Agmund said with a painful smile. Larkin felt a pain in his lower back. Agmund had stabbed him with a knife that was hidden in the folds of his cloak. Larkin had made the mistake of assuming that Agmund only carried a sword as a weapon. Larkin instinctively arched his back, which caused the gun to rise above Agmund's forehead. Agmund stabbed Larkin with the knife again; a long, curved blade with an eagle hilt. This time the blade went through the heart. Larkin twitched in agony and the gun slid out of his grasp. He looked down at the knife in his heart before he died and uttered one, questioning word. "Gideon?"

Nasirra looked up as the doors opened leading out of Larkin's office. Her eyes became wide as she saw Agmund emerge covered in blood. He was also holding a gun in his hand, the muzzle of which was pointed at her. She screamed as he pulled the trigger. A dart from the gun struck her in the middle of the forehead, tranquilizing her. Agmund tranquilized a few more guards at the entrance of the building, but then made his way west. A mile ahead was the place where he desired to go next. He needed to change his disguise along the way to enter that place though. He guided himself towards where he had earlier stashed the needed disguise.

December 28, 32 PAW

8:12

Rhys stumbled through the underground complex that Paul used helped by a Christian on each side of him. They half carried, half dragged him into the office of Paul. Paul stood up in shock, but then cleared his desk and motioned for them to lay him down. "Get the doctor!" Paul said to the two young men that had brought him in. A crowd of people waited outside Paul's closed door, all anxious to see how badly hurt Rhys was. They had come to know he was responsible for a great many murders that helped the Christians. Some revered him, others only feared him.

Paul exposed Rhys's upper body to see the wound. "Well, Rhys the good news is that the bullet missed your heart. The bad news is it has not stopped bleeding yet."

Rhys's voice spoke surprisingly strong and clear in Paul's office given his condition. "Paul, I have good news and bad news for you as well. Nemesio completed his mission. The Council Members are dead. Larkin is dead as well. Not only that, but Silas is dead as well."

"That is all good news Rhys! That is actually the best news anyone has ever brought me. What is the bad news?" Paul asked.

"Paul how will you know when to step down as leader of the Christians?"

"We have had this conversation before Rhys. I believe I answered your question with a question of my own. How will you know when to stop the violence?"

"Yes, we did already have this conversation. I answered your question by saying I will know it is time to step down when there are people with less blood on their hands capable of shaping the course of events of this city towards a better future."

"Well, Rhys, has that time come yet for you to stop the violence?"

"That depends Paul. You promised to use the same measurement. Are you going to step down from your position of leadership?"

"Of course not Rhys! I have sacrificed too much for this city not to reap the benefits now. This city, my people, need me now more than ever. There is still so much I can accomplish. I am the only one who can unify this city and lead the Christians."

"No, Paul, you are not. There are many others, but one in particular that I know will do a much better job than you could possibly ever do. I will hold you accountable to your promise since you refuse to do so." With that Rhys pulled the trigger of the gun that Paul had not seen in Rhys's right hand. The bullet entered the bottom of Paul's head, went through his mouth, and exited the top of his head. He was dead before he knew what had happened. Christians immediately entered Paul's office at the sound of the gunshot and wept at the horrid sight. Rhys heard and saw none of it however; he had passed into unconsciousness almost immediately after shooting Paul.

December 29, 33 PAW

16:02

Zahir stood next to Rhys's bed where he had stayed and prayed for the last thirty-two hours. Zahir was in the middle of a prayer when Rhys came to consciousness for the first time since he had fell into unconsciousness on Paul's desk. Zahir continued his prayer, unaware of Rhys coming to. "Zahir, you can stop praying now." Rhys said softly, with a slight smile on his face, although both the words and the smile caused him pain.

"Rhys! You are awake!" Zahir stood there beaming.

"Yes, I am my friend. I doubt it will be for much longer though. You need to know the whole truth about me before I die. First, though, tell me how are things in the city?"

"Things in the city are well. Free elections, the first in Maevin's history will take place the first of the year. The people of this city cannot wait to have a say in their government and hopefully enjoy a new era of posterity for all. Of course, the factions are as present as ever. The Christians have decided to enter me as their choice for mayor. The Muslims in the city care little. They all know that they are being taken to their New Mecca, Aamina, soon. There are some that benefitted or were part of the last government seeking to try to establish a status quo, but they do not have the votes of the masses. Some of the former Stasi are trying to run for government to carry on the dream that Silas had, but they are divided. Early speculation is pointing towards me winning. Unbelievable as it is to me, the Christians in this city believe I am the best option. They have turned up to support me in numbers that exceeded even what Paul had estimated. They are jumping at the opportunity to be able to worship freely. Even those that are not Christians, but live in the outskirts of the city, believe I will treat them fairly for the first time in thirty years and listen to their needs."

"Good, I wanted you to be the one that took over the reins of the city. God has appointed you to be the leader of this city to shape the events of Maevin towards a better future. My work then was not all for nothing."

"Rhys, why did you kill Paul?" Zahir asked suddenly, it was the question that every Christian had been asking for the last day and a half.

Rhys took a deep breath and then just began to cry. Zahir cried as well in seeing Rhys in so much agony. After several minutes of crying Rhys composed himself.

"Let me start at the beginning Zahir. First, I must apologize for lying to you. My name is not Rhys, it is Gideon. Yes, the same Gideon you once knew. What I told you about my family was indeed true. In a sense, Gideon died as well. A Christian named Milica saved my life as I was left to die by the Stasi who had killed the CRZ soldiers before they could finish me, but they were too late to save my family. After two years of searching for God's will, I turned my back on an opportunity I fully believe He wanted me to pursue. The opportunity was to run a support group within the underground Christian community for those that had lost loved ones. I initially did it, but it only made me more furious at God for allowing such tragedies to happen to His people. It was then that I had facial reconstruction surgery so no one could identify me as Gideon. I vowed to not rest until I had taken revenge on Larkin.

"Not only that though, but I wanted to make sure that what had happened to me and all those I had helped in the support group would not happen again to anyone. I wanted to cleanse this city of Christianity's enemies and make it so that Maevin would be a place where God could be worshiped freely and openly. I spent months planning it. I knew I would need to destroy the Stasi and the government. In order to have the power to do that, I needed to know things that could only be known by being in a position of power with both them. Then for the Christians I could work to make sure that balance was kept and the Christians survived the climax of this terrible civil war.

"To accomplish this I took three different identities. I became Rhys, Nemesio, and Agmund. Agmund worked for the government, Nemesio for the Stasi, and Rhys for the Christians. As these three men I committed more atrocious acts than I care to recall all so I could set the Stasi and the government against each other and completely weaken them. I also used them to give the nation of Islam a New Mecca. My training, the same training we had, as one of Larkin's personal bodyguards helped immensely. I disguised myself using wigs, different colored contacts, fake facial hair, my clothing, styles of talking, attitude, and weapons. No one suspected me of being less than true to my respective factions until it was too late.

"To answer your first question: Paul had to die. He had grown arrogant and was going to destroy Maevin with a second civil war, this time a repeat of what had caused Maevin to be founded in the first place. He wanted to kill everyone who was not a Christian. I could not allow him to cause another religious war that would have no end. You see, Zahir, he had to die otherwise my work would have been for nothing. For the future of many, I needed to cut Paul's future short.

"In the end I completed my goal, and I am not sorry that I did it even though I believe I may have condemned myself to hell by doing so. I turned my back on God the entire time. Now on my death bed, I am confessing this all to you Zahir, the man who brought me to Christ in the first place. I fear that not even you my friend, can bring me back to Him now. I have committed so many sins. While I regret that they had to happen, I would choose to commit them all again. For that reason, I cannot ask for God's forgiveness."

The entire time Zahir sat on a chair, looking intently at Gideon while tears streamed down his face. It was several minutes before Zahir spoke. "Gideon I cannot bring you back to God. But, I can see that you are wracked with guilt over the pain you caused others. You may not regret the results, but I think you could ask God to forgive you for your actions even though they may have resulted in what you desired all along. Ask for God's forgiveness Gideon, and forgive yourself as well."

"I cannot ask for God's forgiveness for my sins knowing full well I would do it all over again if I was given the chance. No, I cannot even forgive myself."

"You may be able to with time, Gideon."

"I do not think I have that luxury Zahir."

"Gideon, the doctor says you will mend well. You have no need for such pessimism. As for me, I need some time to think. You have been through an awful ordeal Gideon. I cannot imagine all that has happened to you. I will go and pray and ask God to guide my thoughts on all that you have told me. When I come back we will talk more."

"As you wish Zahir. Just promise me one thing before you leave my side. Promise me that you will guide this city well. Maevin needs to become a New Jerusalem, just as I hope Aamina will be a new Mecca. If it is anything less my actions will have been futile."

"I will do my best Gideon." Zahir smiled at Gideon and walked out of the door. He wanted to walk, pray, and think. When he came back to Gideon's room two hours later, Gideon was dead. The doctor informed him Gideon should have survived. Zahir knew in his heart that Gideon invited death in as the only release from his agony over the actions he had committed. It was the only option available to deal with his actions since he refused to fully repent. Zahir wept for Gideon.

But, he did not have the luxury to weep for very long. Zahir had a promise to keep to Gideon to serve the city of Maevin. Free elections would begin soon and Zahir knew Gideon would not want him to waste time mourning Gideon's death, which he himself had wished for ever since his family was so violently taken from him. Zahir prayed over Gideon's body for God to have mercy on a man that had so violently done so much good for the city, even as it forced him to wrestle with his own conscience. As he said amen, Zahir felt a weight fall on his shoulders. He knew it was the weight of his promise to Gideon to make the most of the work Gideon had left behind for better men to continue on. Zahir left that room resolved to allow God to work through him in a way that would allow him to stay true to his promise.

About the Author

Matthew D. Brubaker is a recent college graduate from Trine University (formerly known as Tri-State University) where he majored in a Business Associate degree in Golf Management while also playing a few years of collegiate golf. Throughout his life, Matt has always been an avid reader, but it was not until college that he discovered his passion for writing fictional stories and for making a spiritual difference in those around him. Since graduating from college, he has worked at a YMCA camp where he enjoys serving others. During his spare time he loves to read, write, and pursue various other hobbies that he enjoys. This book is the first one he has written, though he has several other novel ideas he hopes to complete in the future.

If you enjoyed the book, join Matthew D. Brubaker's fan page on Facebook.

LaVergne, TN USA
06 December 2009
166086LV00001BA/1/P